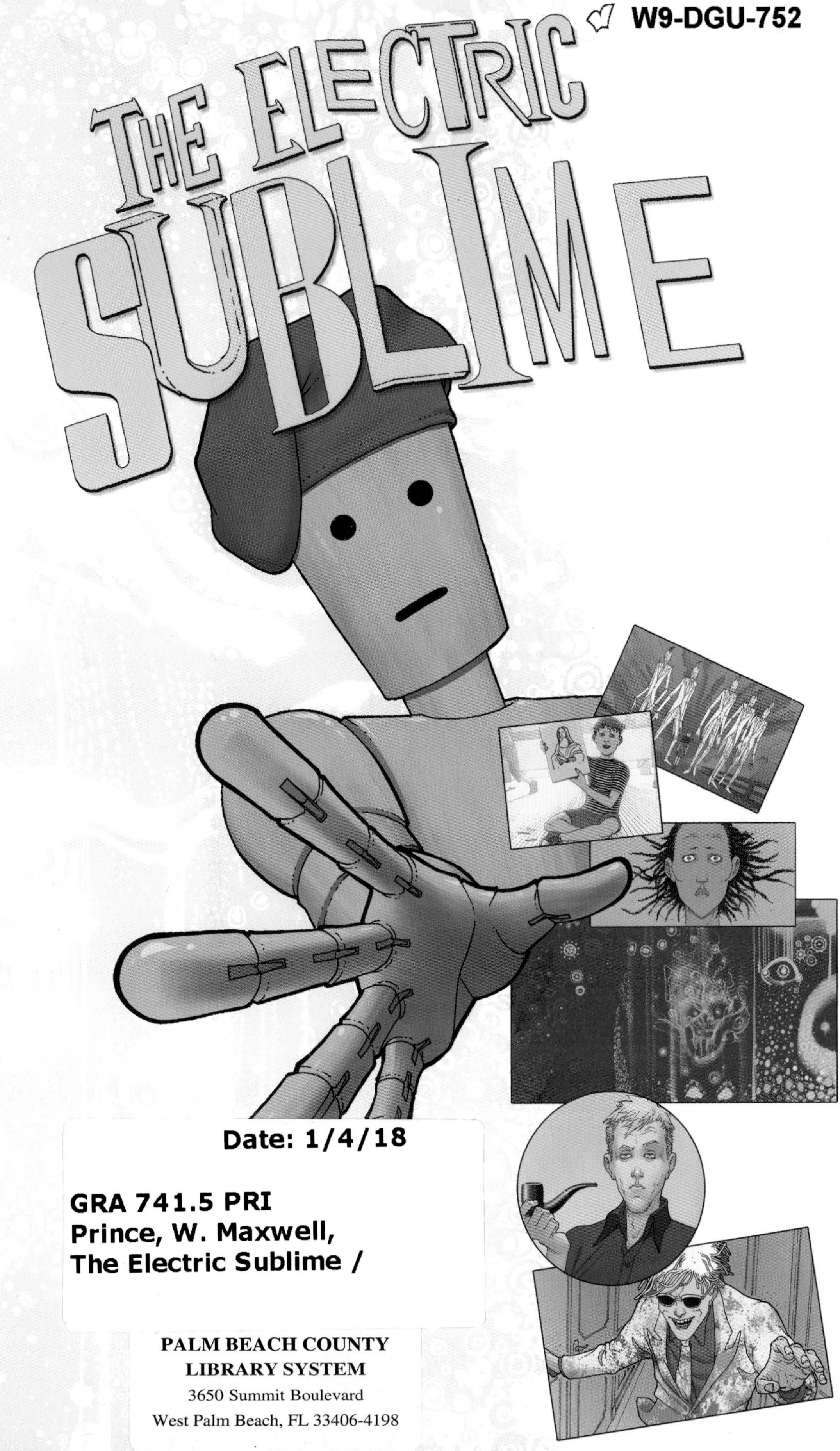
THE ELECTRIC
SUBLIME

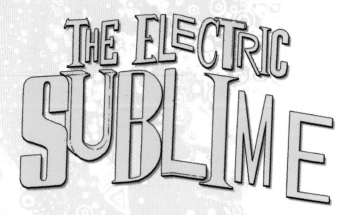

Become our fan on Facebook **facebook.com/idwpublishing**
Follow us on Twitter **@idwpublishing**
Subscribe to us on YouTube **youtube.com/idwpublishing**
See what's new on Tumblr **tumblr.idwpublishing.com**
Check us out on Instagram **instagram.com/idwpublishing**

IDW
www.IDWPUBLISHING.com

Ted Adams, CEO & Publisher
Greg Goldstein, President & COO
Robbie Robbins, EVP/Sr. Graphic Artist
Chris Ryall, Chief Creative Officer
David Hedgecock, Editor-in-Chief
Laurie Windrow, Sr. VP of Sales & Marketing
Matthew Ruzicka, CPA, Chief Financial Officer
Lorelei Bunjes, VP of Digital Services
Jerry Bennington, VP of New Product Development

ISBN: 978-1-63140-866-3   20 19 18 17   1 2 3 4

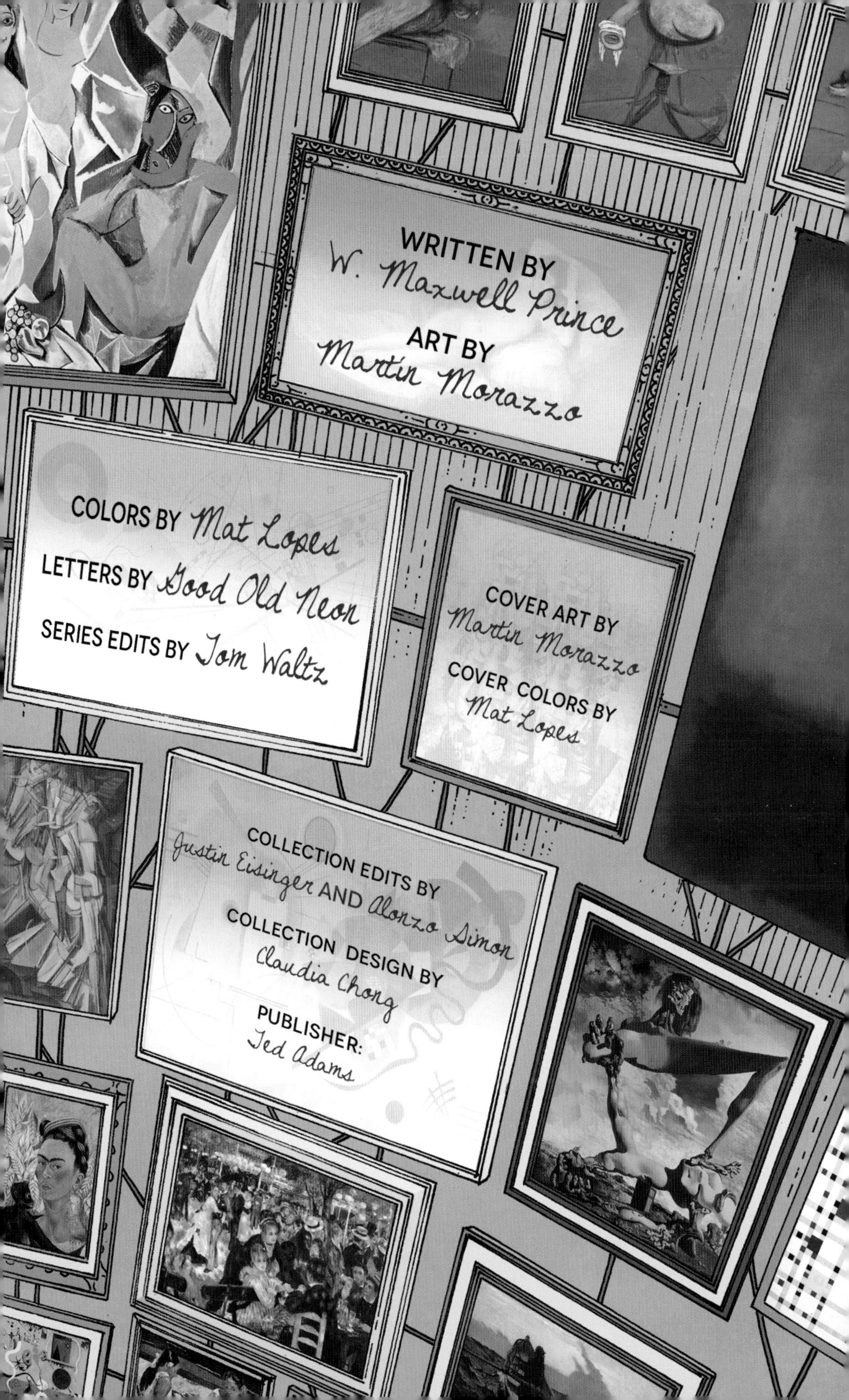
WRITTEN BY
W. Maxwell Prince
ART BY
Martín Morazzo
COLORS BY Mat Lopes
LETTERS BY Good Old Neon
SERIES EDITS BY Tom Waltz
COVER ART BY
Martín Morazzo
COVER COLORS BY
Mat Lopes
COLLECTION EDITS BY
Justin Eisinger AND Alonzo Simon
COLLECTION DESIGN BY
Claudia Chong
PUBLISHER:
Ted Adams

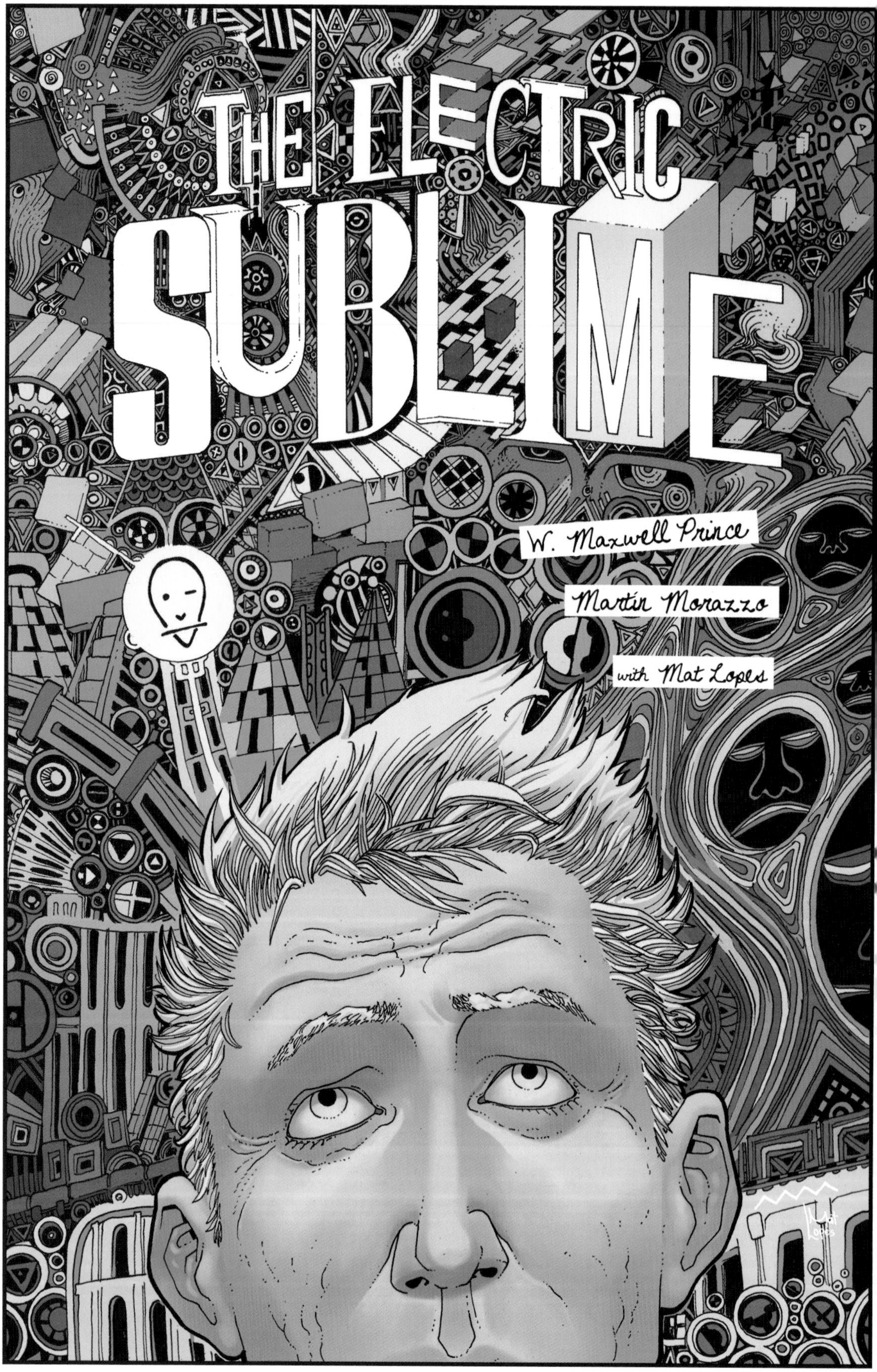
THE ELECTRIC
SUBLIME
W. Maxwell Prince
Martín Morazzo
with Mat Lopes

COVER ART BY *Martín Morazzo* COLORS BY *Mat Lopes*

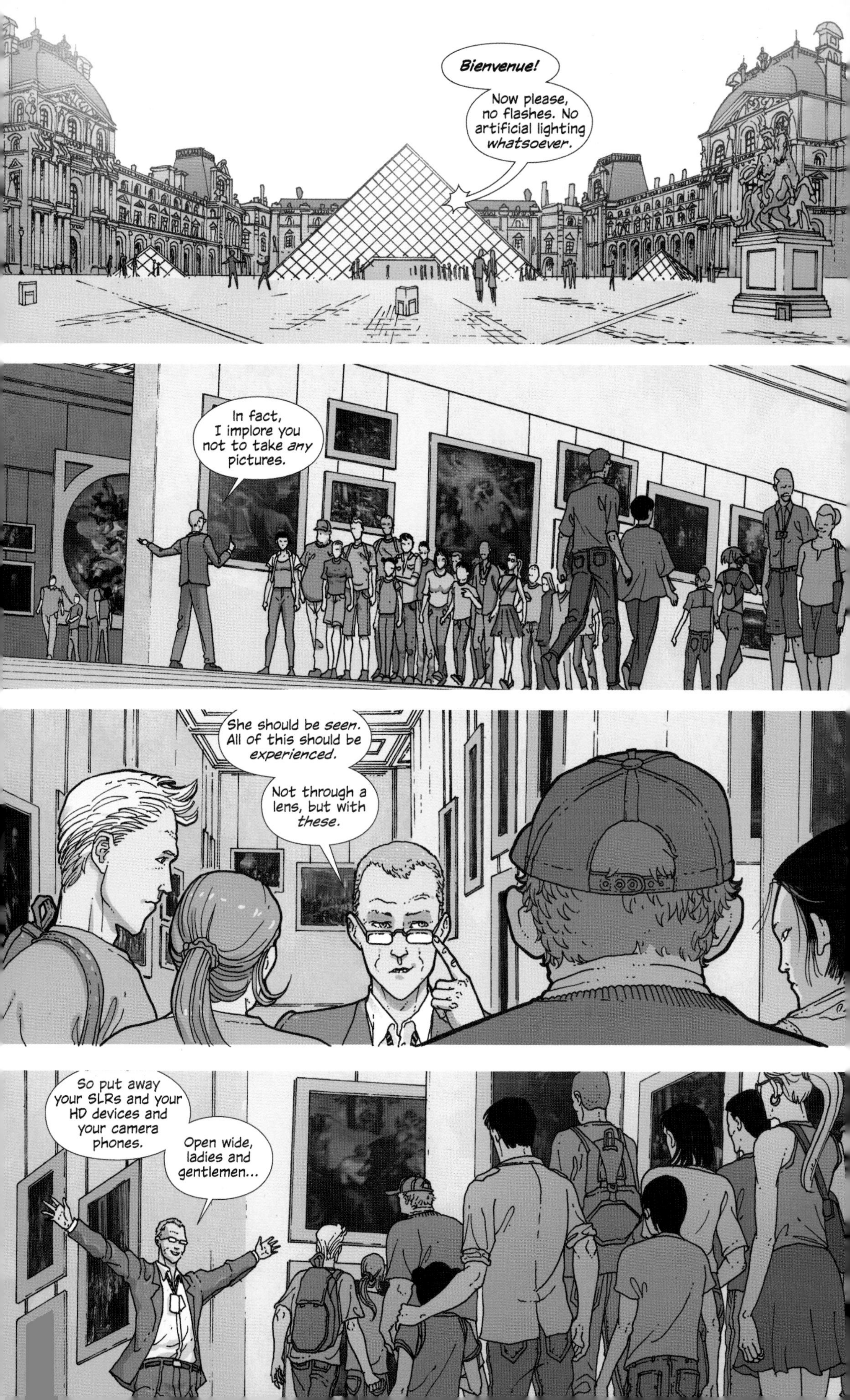
Bienvenue!
Now please, no flashes. No artificial lighting whatsoever.
In fact, I implore you not to take any pictures.
She should be seen. All of this should be experienced.
Not through a lens, but with these.
So put away your SLRs and your HD devices and your camera phones.
Open wide, ladies and gentlemen...

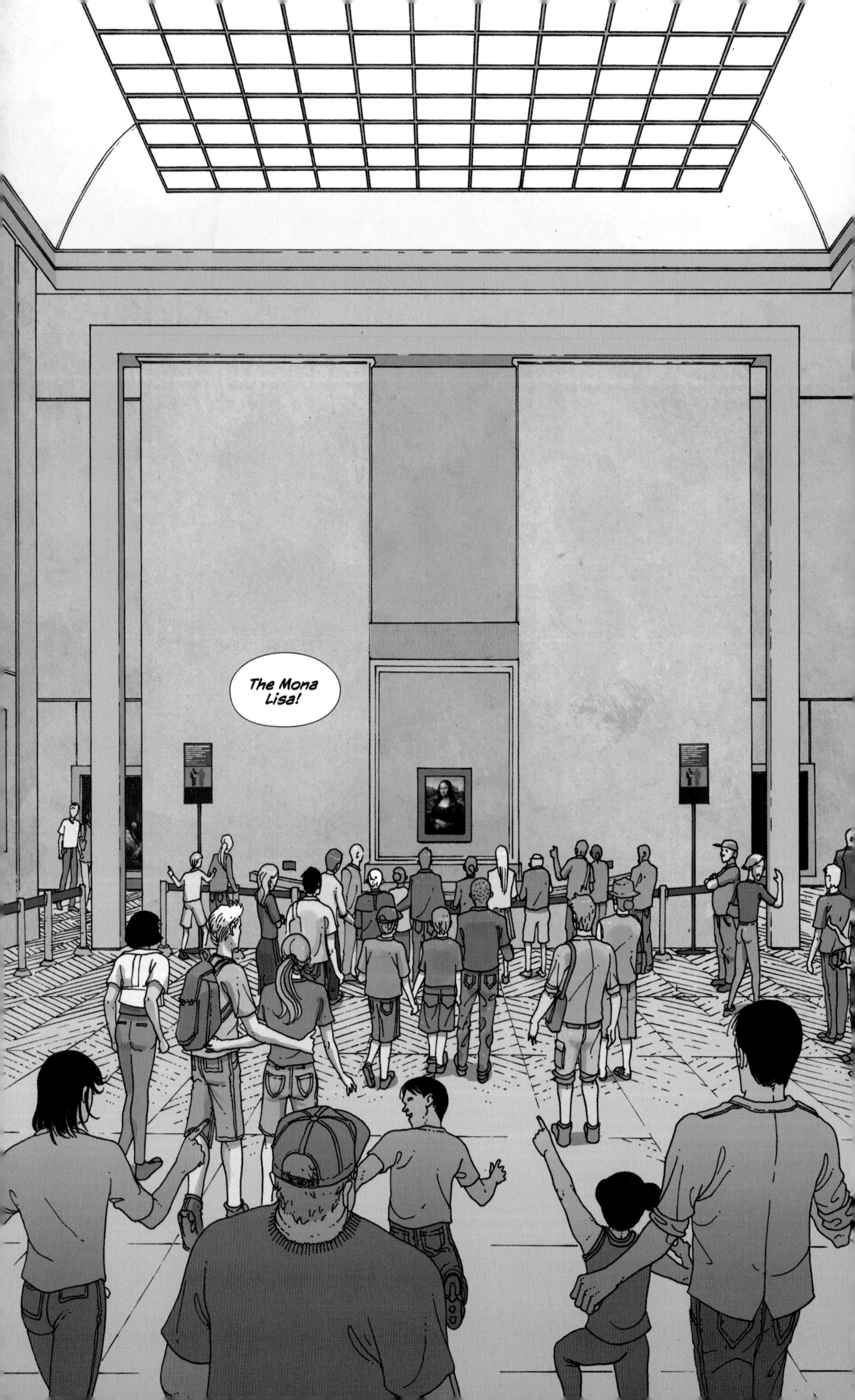
The Mona Lisa!

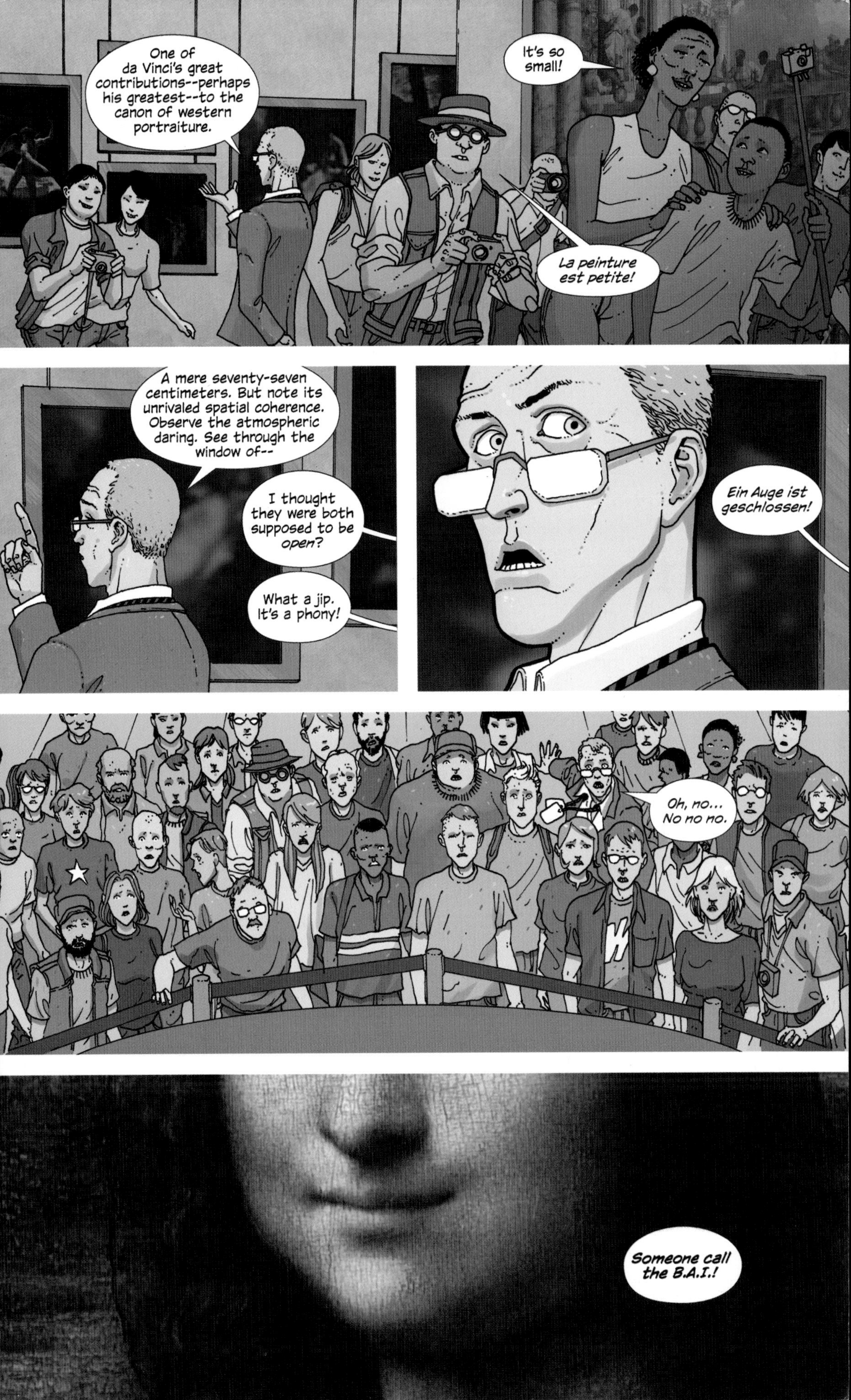
One of da Vinci's great contributions--perhaps his greatest--to the canon of western portraiture.
It's so small!
La peinture est petite!
A mere seventy-seven centimeters. But note its unrivaled spatial coherence. Observe the atmospheric daring. See through the window of--
I thought they were both supposed to be *open*?
What a jip. It's a phony!
Ein Auge ist geschlossen!
Oh, no... No no no.
Someone call the B.A.I.!

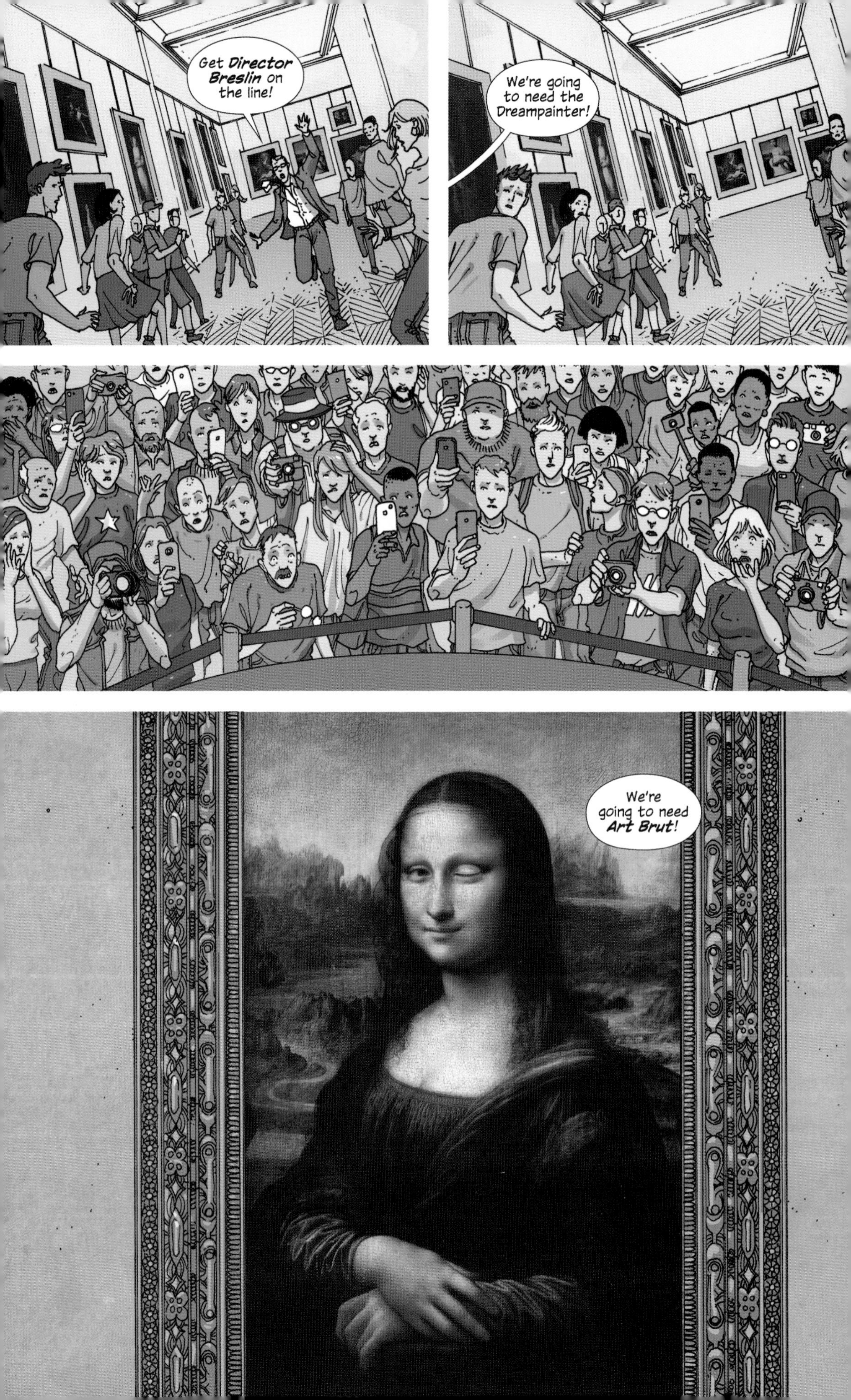
Get **Director Breslin** on the line!
We're going to need the Dreampainter!
We're going to need **Art Brut**!

THE WINKING WOMAN

***

Chapter 1

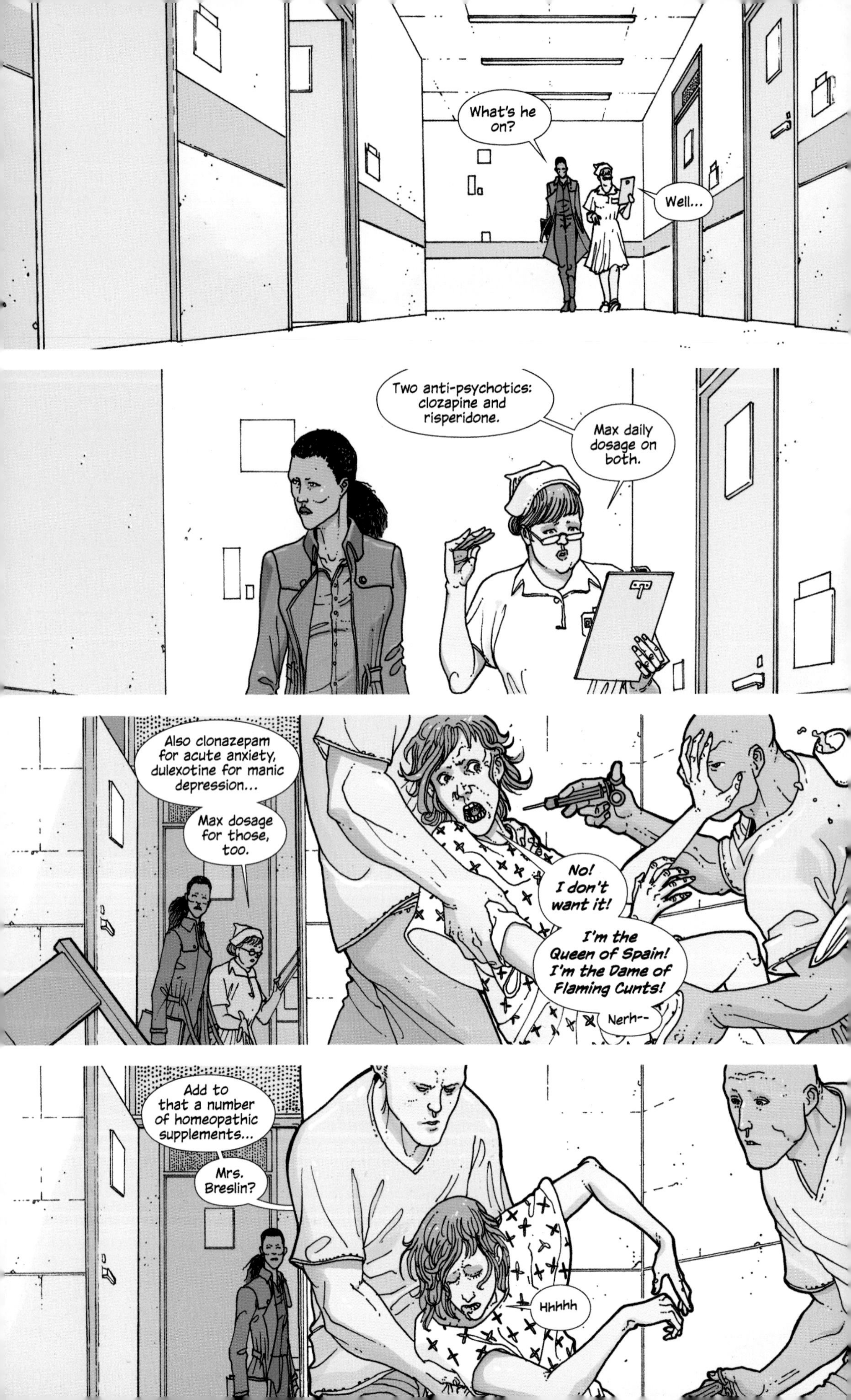
What's he on?
Well...
Two anti-psychotics: clozapine and risperidone.
Max daily dosage on both.
Also clonazepam for acute anxiety, dulexotine for manic depression...
Max dosage for those, too.
No! I don't want it!
I'm the Queen of Spain! I'm the Dame of Flaming Cunts!
Nerh--
Add to that a number of homeopathic supplements...
Mrs. Breslin?
Hhhhh

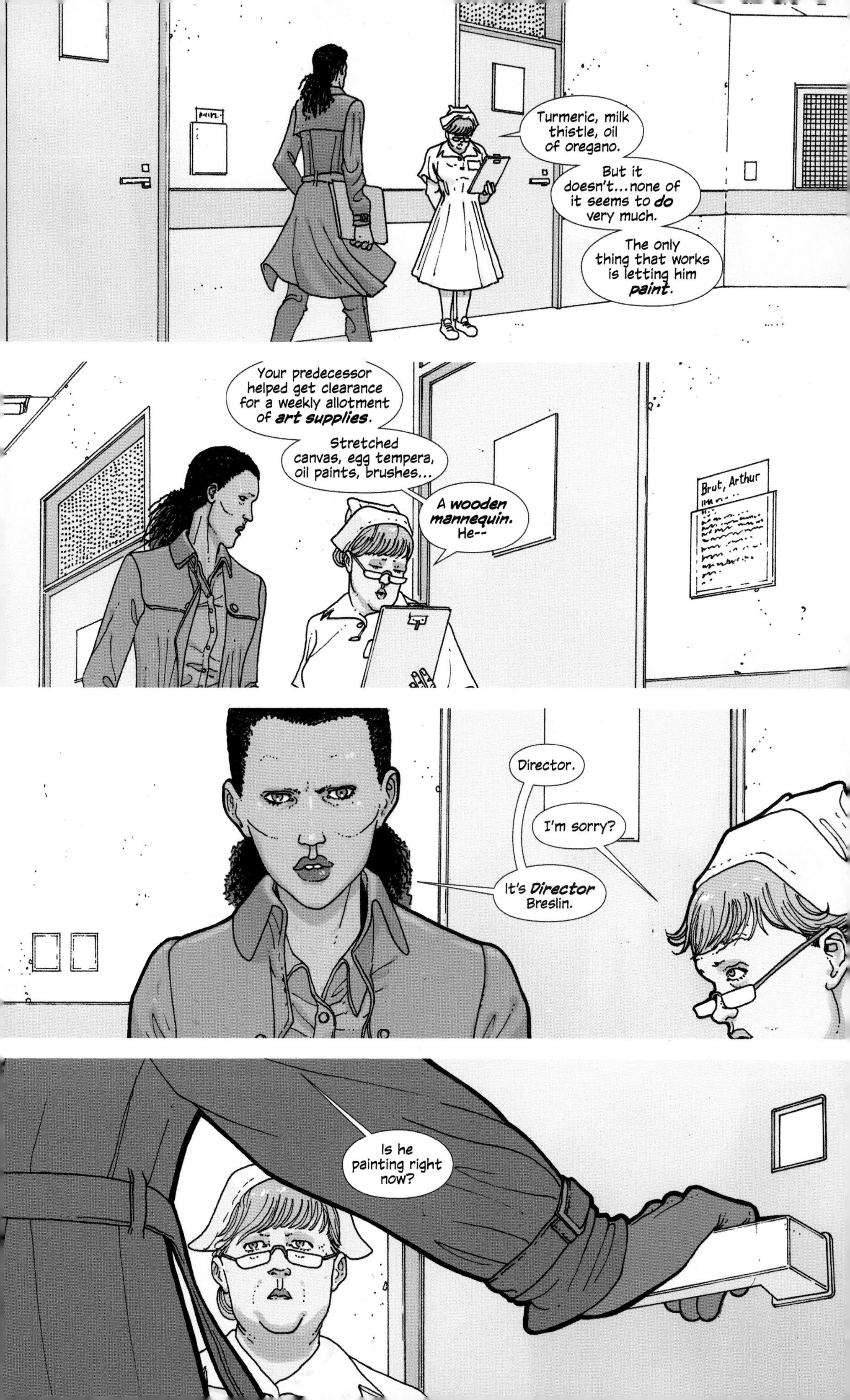
Turmeric, milk thistle, oil of oregano.
But it doesn't...none of it seems to **do** very much.
The only thing that works is letting him **paint**.
Your predecessor helped get clearance for a weekly allotment of **art supplies**.
Stretched canvas, egg tempera, oil paints, brushes...
A **wooden mannequin.** He--
Brut, Arthur
Director.
I'm sorry?
It's **Director** Breslin.
Is he painting right now?

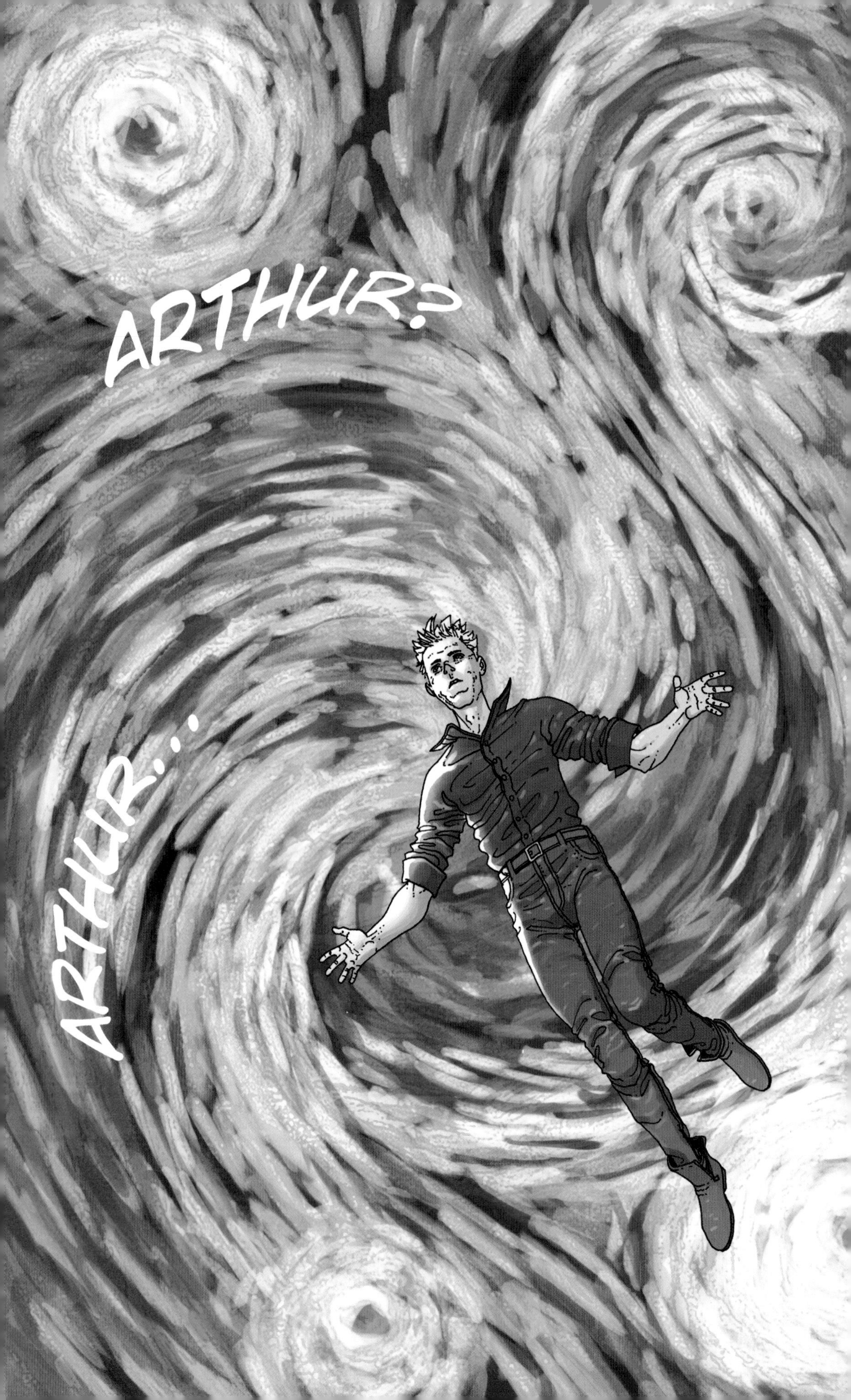
ARTHUR?
ARTHUR...

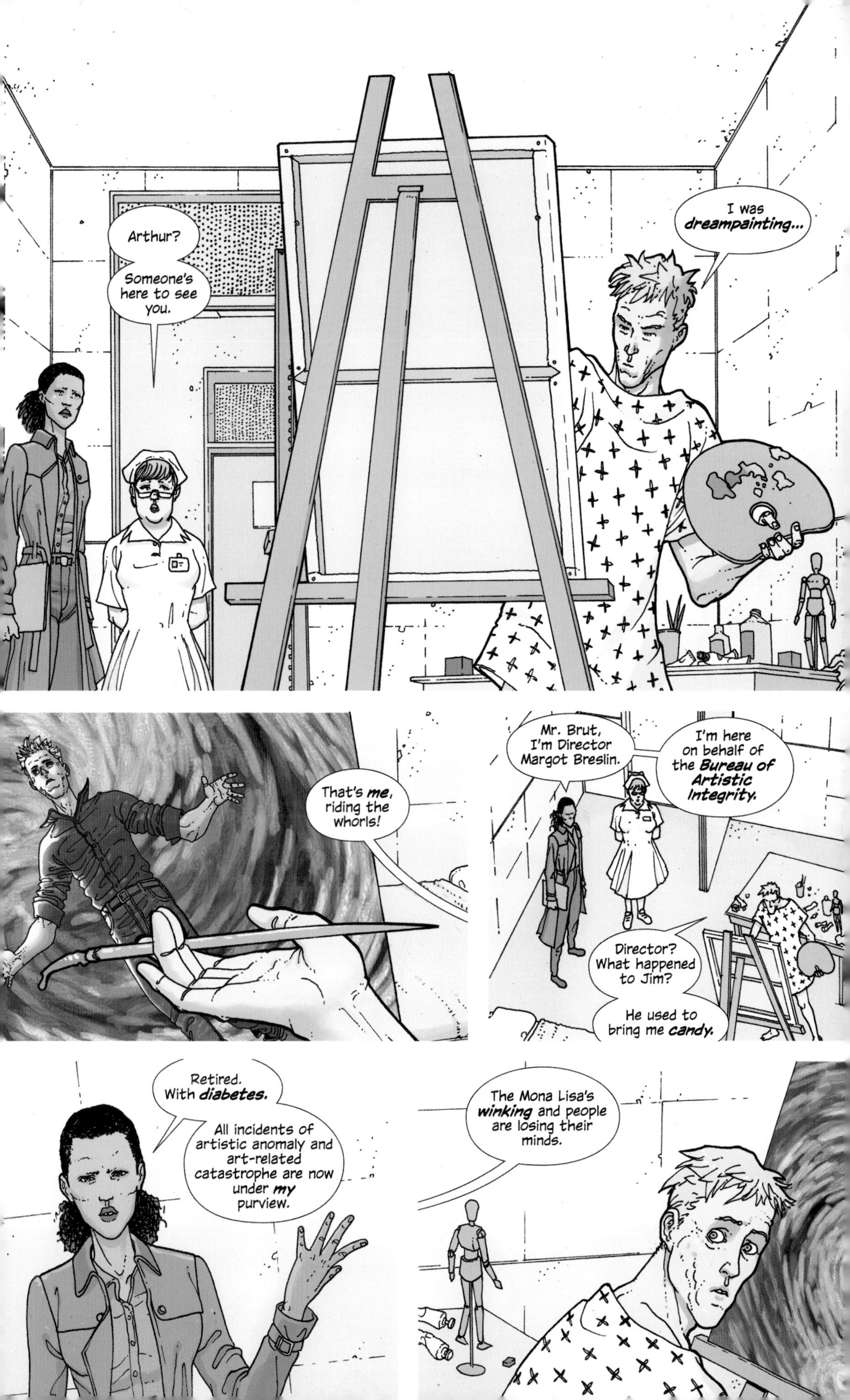
Arthur?
Someone's here to see you.
I was *dreampainting...*
That's *me*, riding the whorls!
Mr. Brut, I'm Director Margot Breslin.
I'm here on behalf of the *Bureau of Artistic Integrity.*
Director? What happened to Jim?
He used to bring me *candy.*
Retired. With *diabetes.*
All incidents of artistic anomaly and art-related catastrophe are now under *my* purview.
The Mona Lisa's *winking* and people are losing their minds.

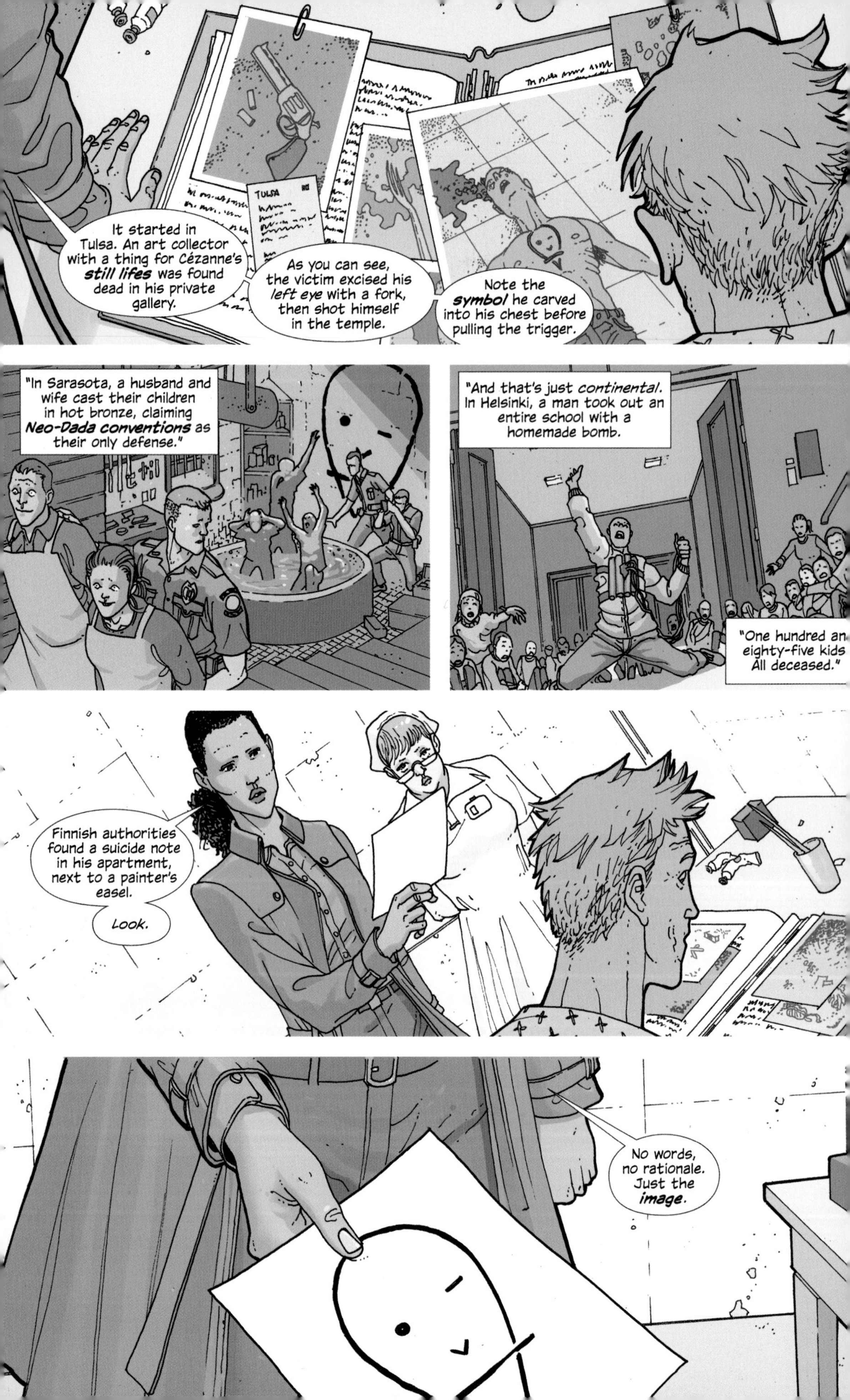
It started in Tulsa. An art collector with a thing for Cézanne's still lifes was found dead in his private gallery.
As you can see, the victim excised his left eye with a fork, then shot himself in the temple.
Note the symbol he carved into his chest before pulling the trigger.
TULSA
"In Sarasota, a husband and wife cast their children in hot bronze, claiming Neo-Dada conventions as their only defense."
"And that's just continental. In Helsinki, a man took out an entire school with a homemade bomb.
"One hundred an eighty-five kids All deceased."
Finnish authorities found a suicide note in his apartment, next to a painter's easel.
Look.
No words, no rationale. Just the image.

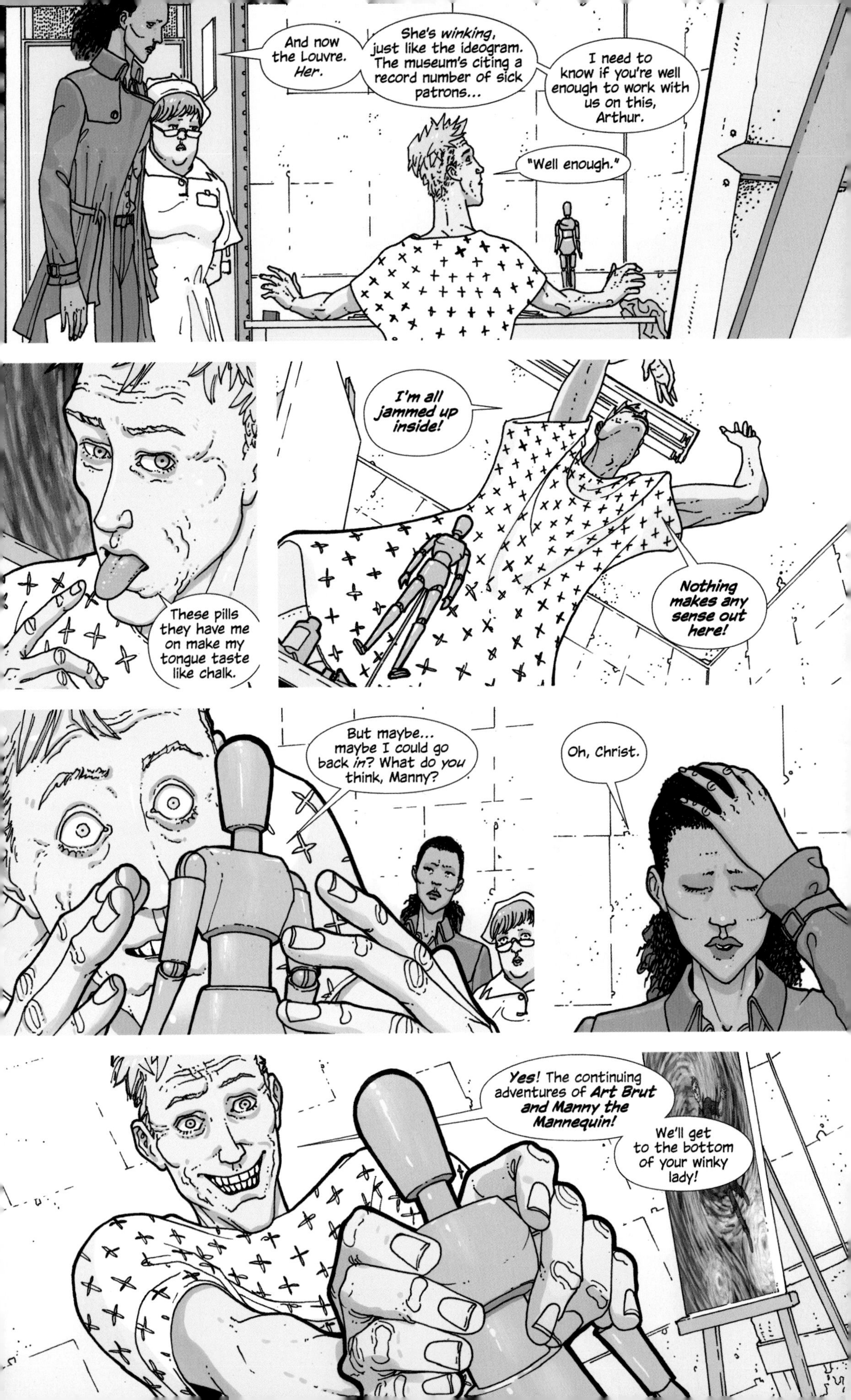
And now the Louvre. *Her.*
She's *winking*, just like the ideogram. The museum's citing a record number of sick patrons...
I need to know if you're well enough to work with us on this, Arthur.
"Well enough."
These pills they have me on make my tongue taste like chalk.
I'm all jammed up inside!
Nothing makes any sense out here!
But maybe... maybe I could go back *in*? What do *you* think, Manny?
Oh, Christ.
Yes! The continuing adventures of ***Art Brut and Manny the Mannequin!***
We'll get to the bottom of your winky lady!

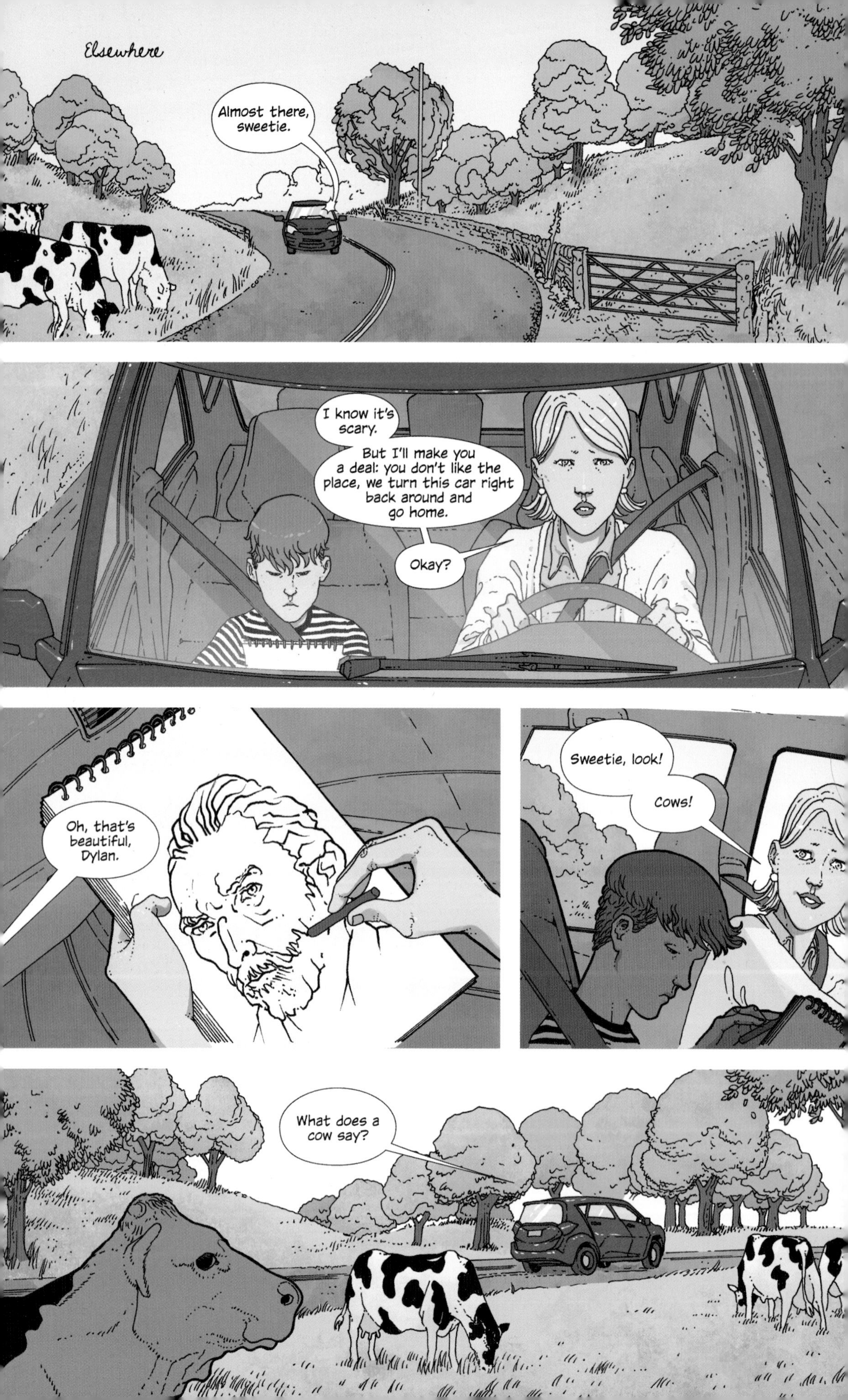
Elsewhere
Almost there, sweetie.
I know it's scary.
But I'll make you a deal: you don't like the place, we turn this car right back around and go home.
Okay?
Oh, that's beautiful, Dylan.
Sweetie, look!
Cows!
What does a cow say?

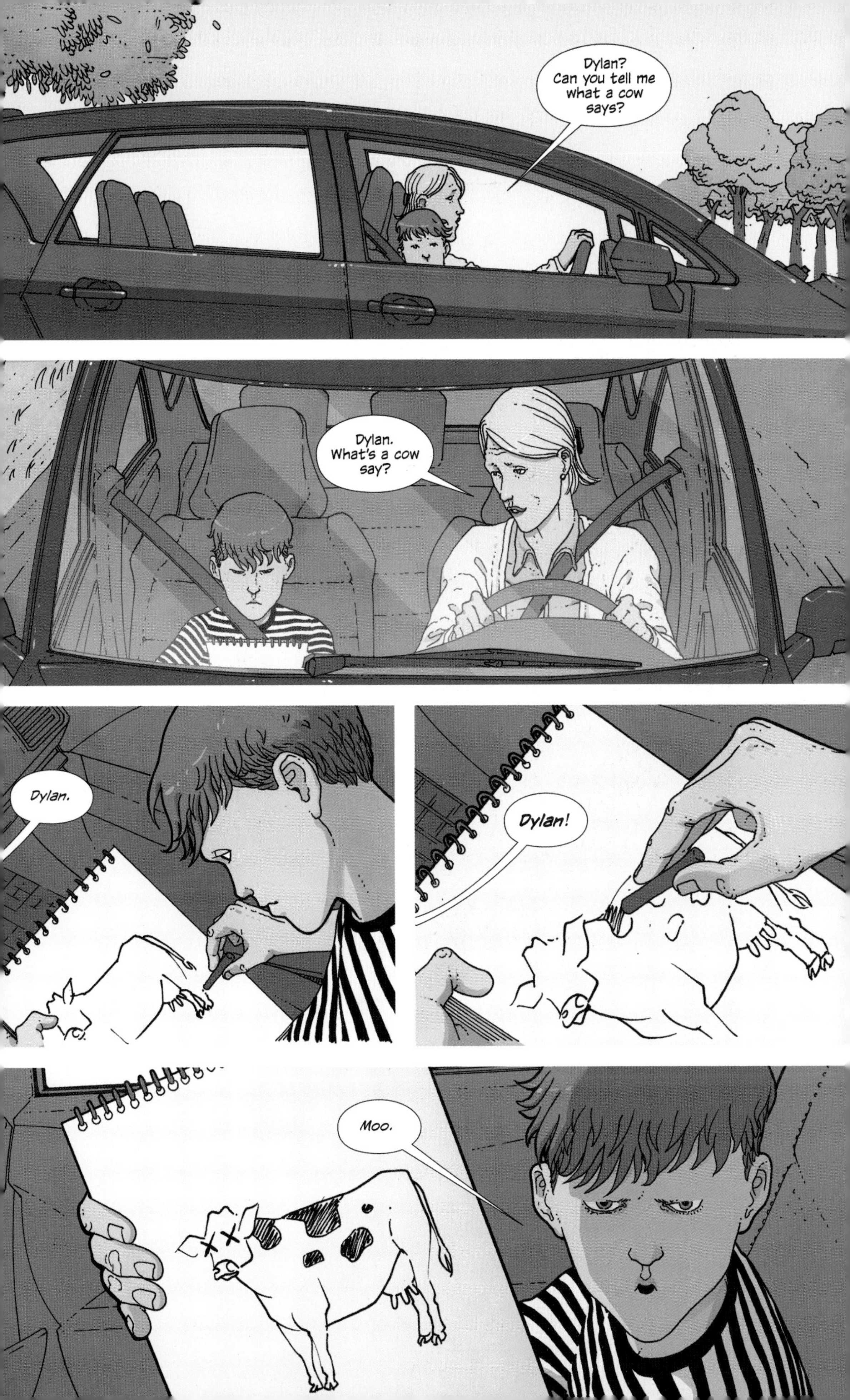
Dylan? Can you tell me what a cow says?
Dylan. What's a cow say?
Dylan.
Dylan!
Moo.

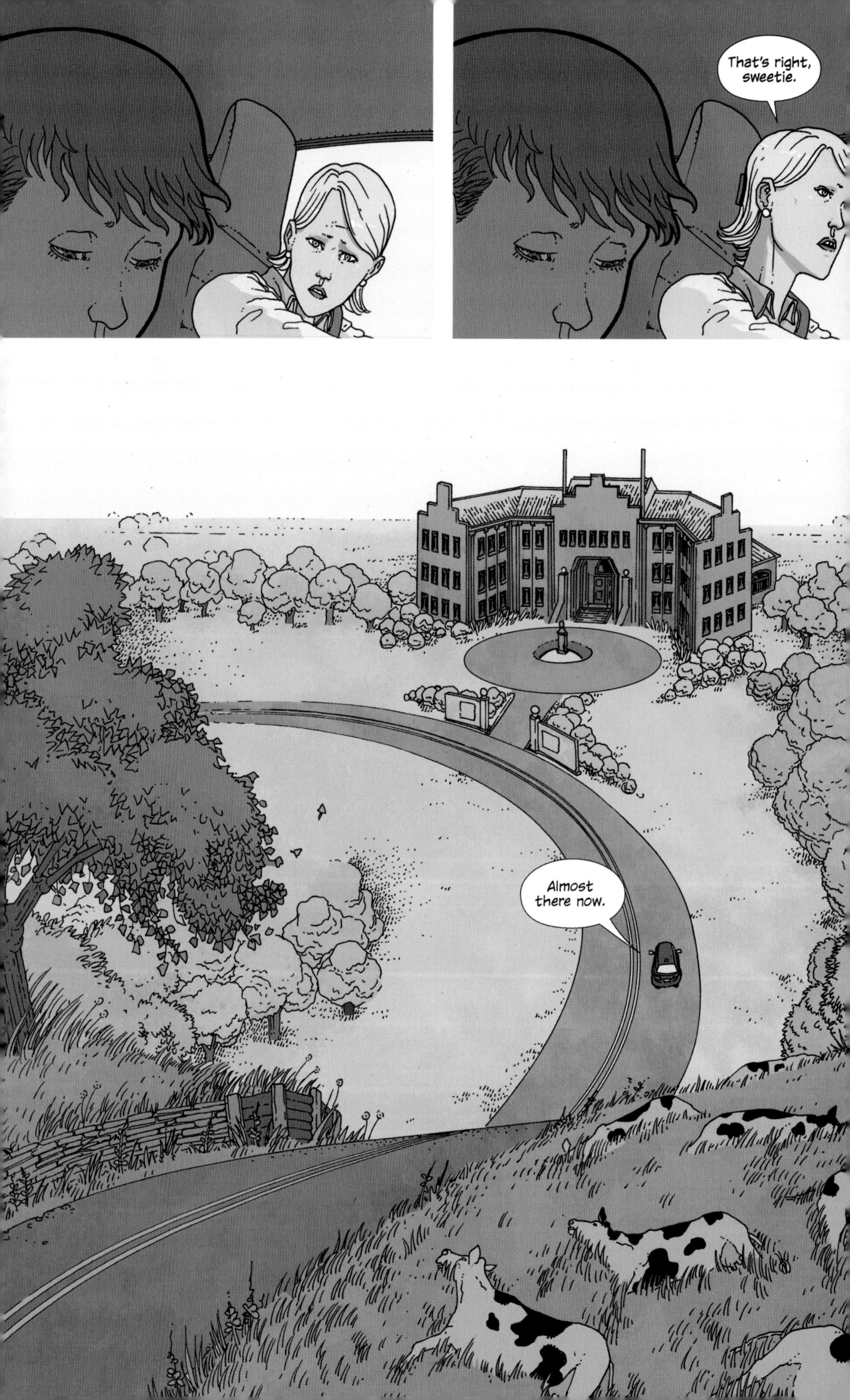
That's right, sweetie.
Almost there now.

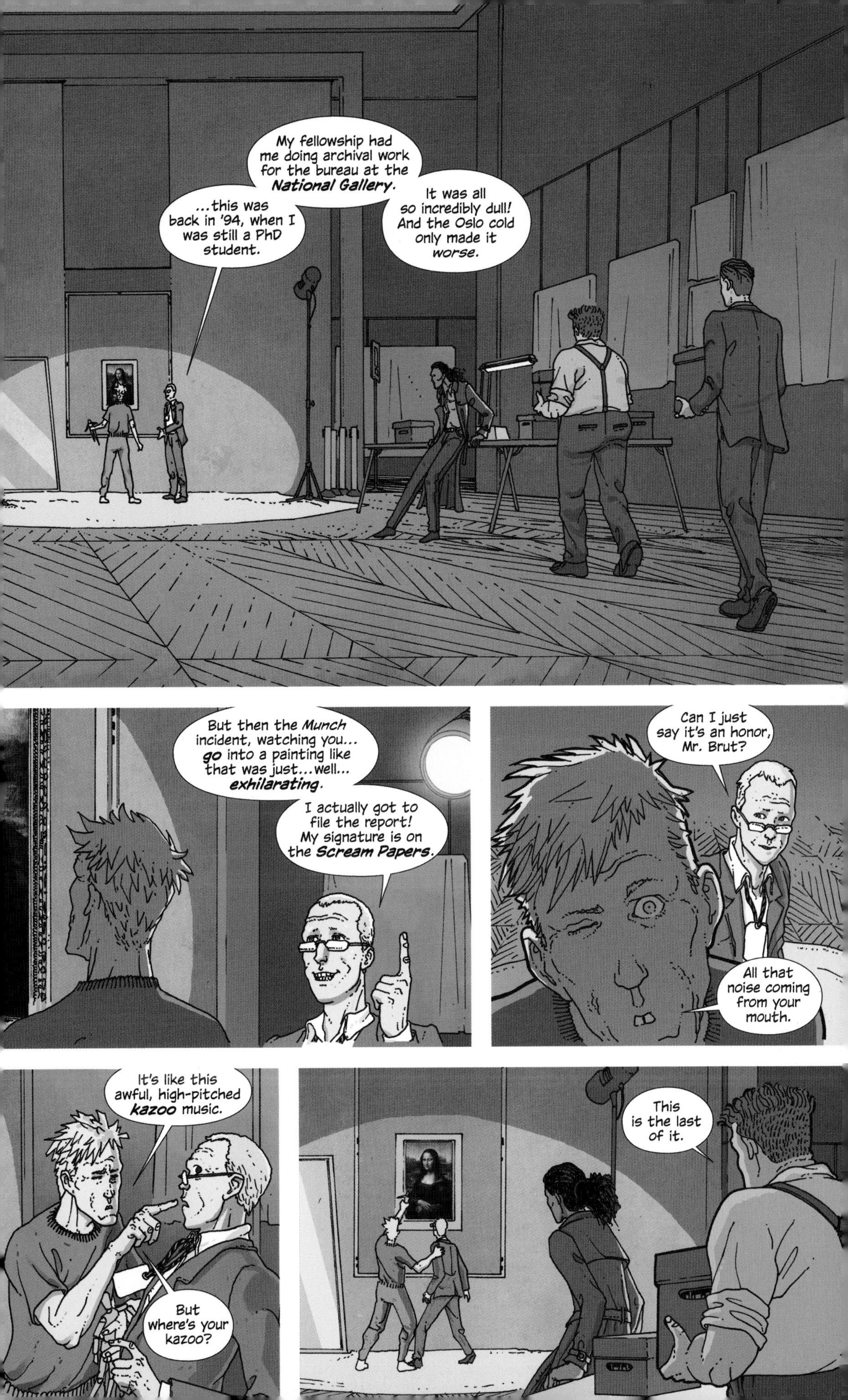
My fellowship had me doing archival work for the bureau at the **National Gallery**.
...this was back in '94, when I was still a PhD student.
It was all so incredibly dull! And the Oslo cold only made it *worse*.
But then the *Munch* incident, watching you... **go** into a painting like that was just...well... **exhilarating**.
I actually got to file the report! My signature is on the **Scream Papers**.
Can I just say it's an honor, Mr. Brut?
All that noise coming from your mouth.
It's like this awful, high-pitched **kazoo** music.
But where's your kazoo?
This is the last of it.

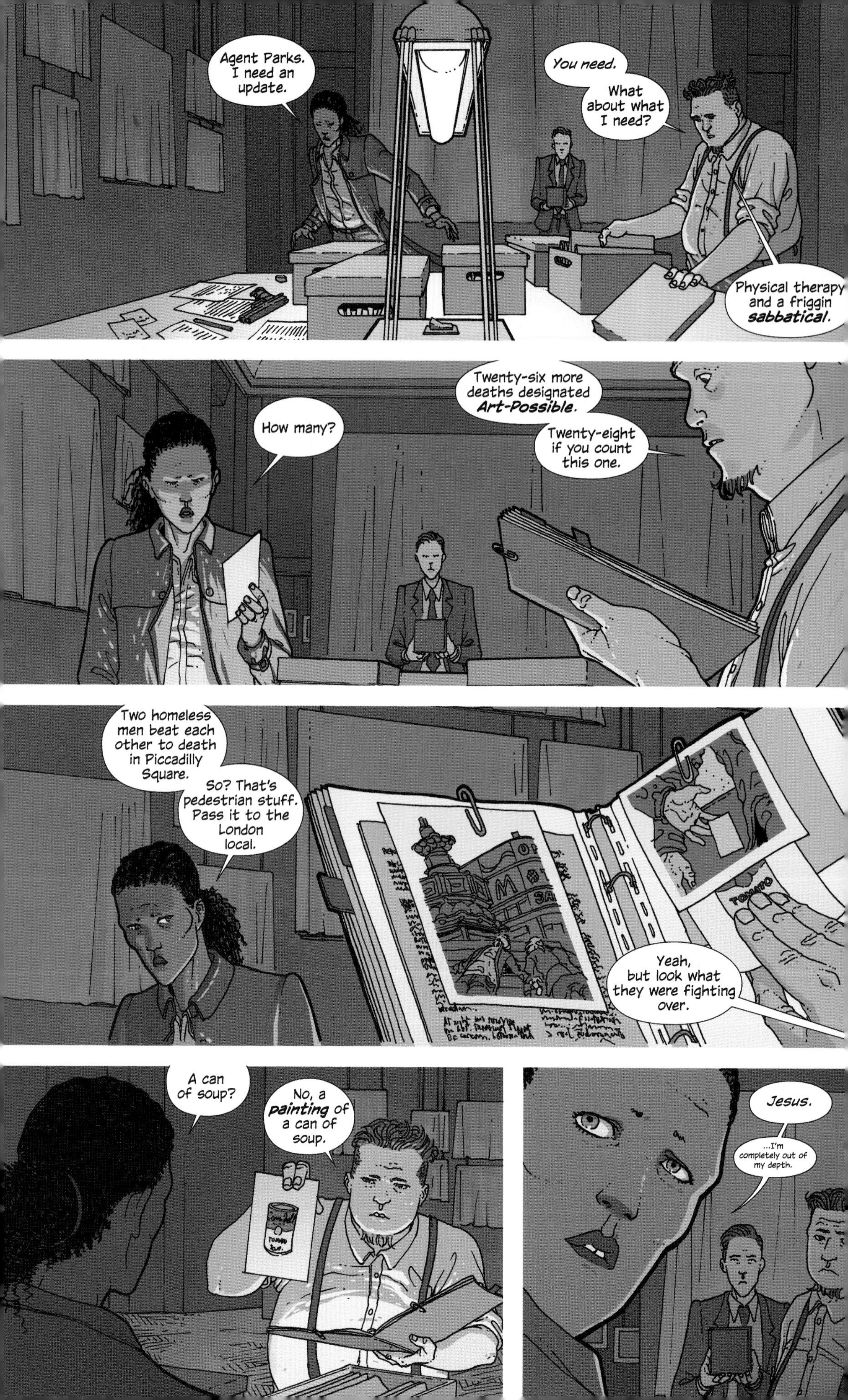
Agent Parks. I need an update.
You need.
What about what I need?
Physical therapy and a friggin *sabbatical*.
How many?
Twenty-six more deaths designated ***Art-Possible***.
Twenty-eight if you count this one.
Two homeless men beat each other to death in Piccadilly Square.
So? That's pedestrian stuff. Pass it to the London local.
Yeah, but look what they were fighting over.
A can of soup?
No, a ***painting*** of a can of soup.
Jesus.
...I'm completely out of my depth.

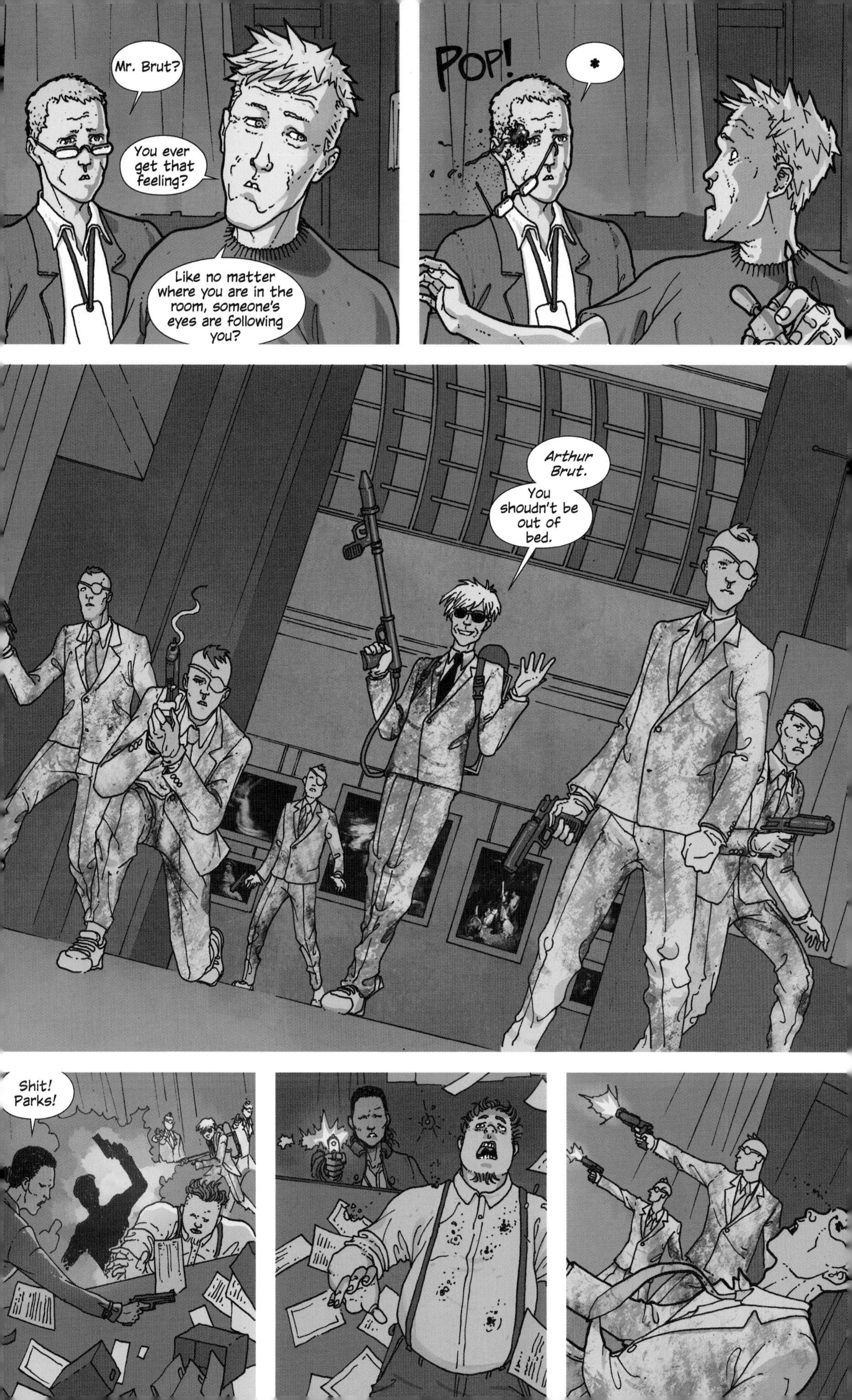
Mr. Brut?
You ever get that feeling?
Like no matter where you are in the room, someone's eyes are following you?
POP!
*
Arthur Brut.
You shoudn't be out of bed.
Shit! Parks!

Art is anything you can get away with...

Destroy it all.

Shitshit shitshit shit.

Hey...

Come on!

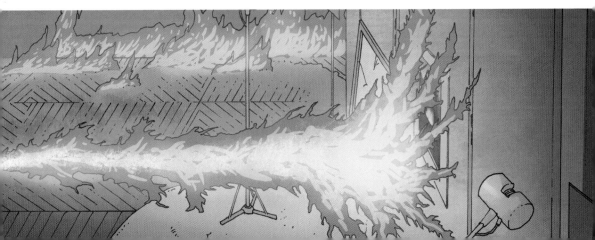

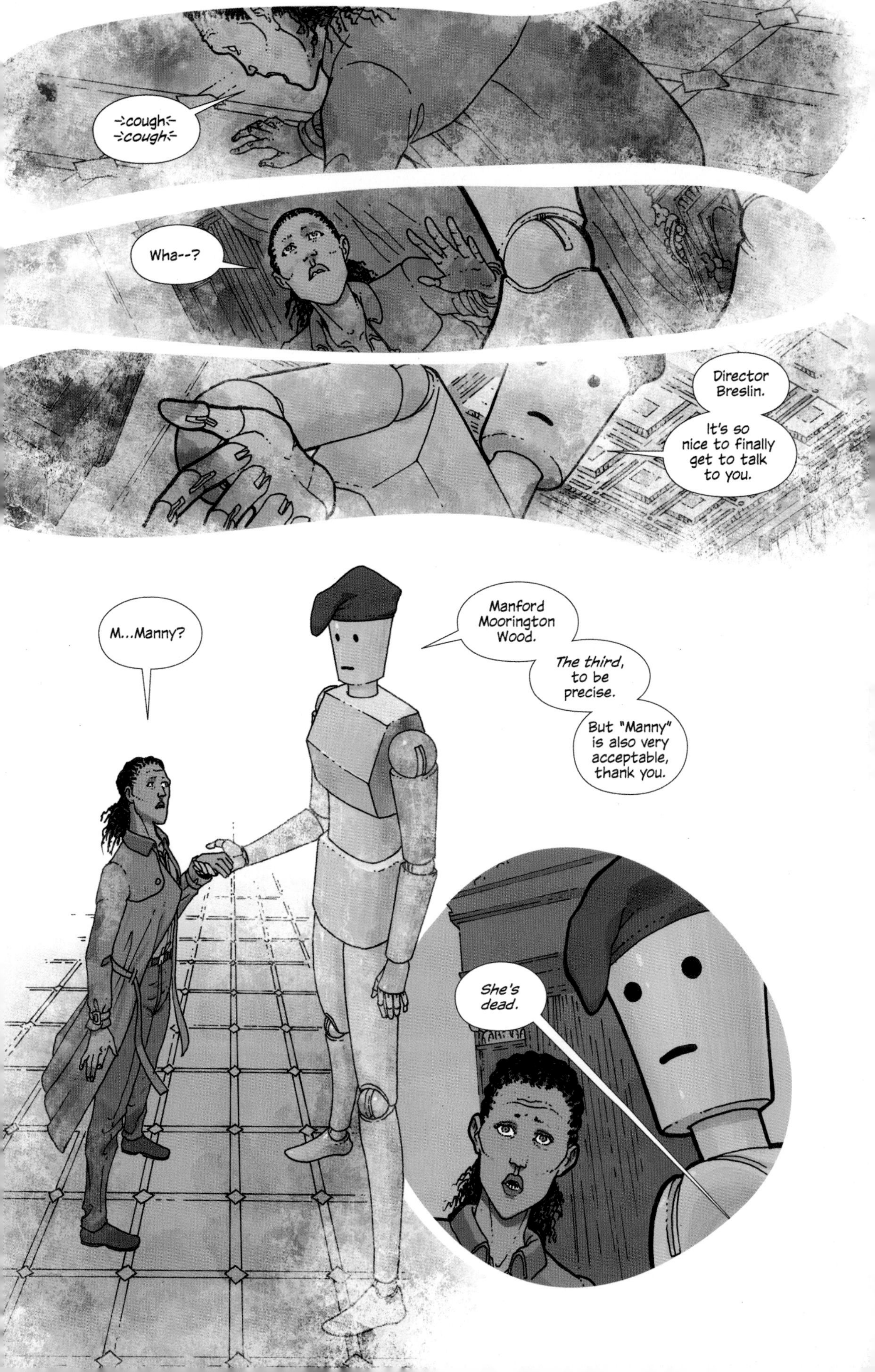

-cough-
-cough-
Wha--?
Director Breslin.
It's so nice to finally get to talk to you.
M...Manny?
Manford Moorington Wood.
The third, to be precise.
But "Manny" is also very acceptable, thank you.
She's dead.

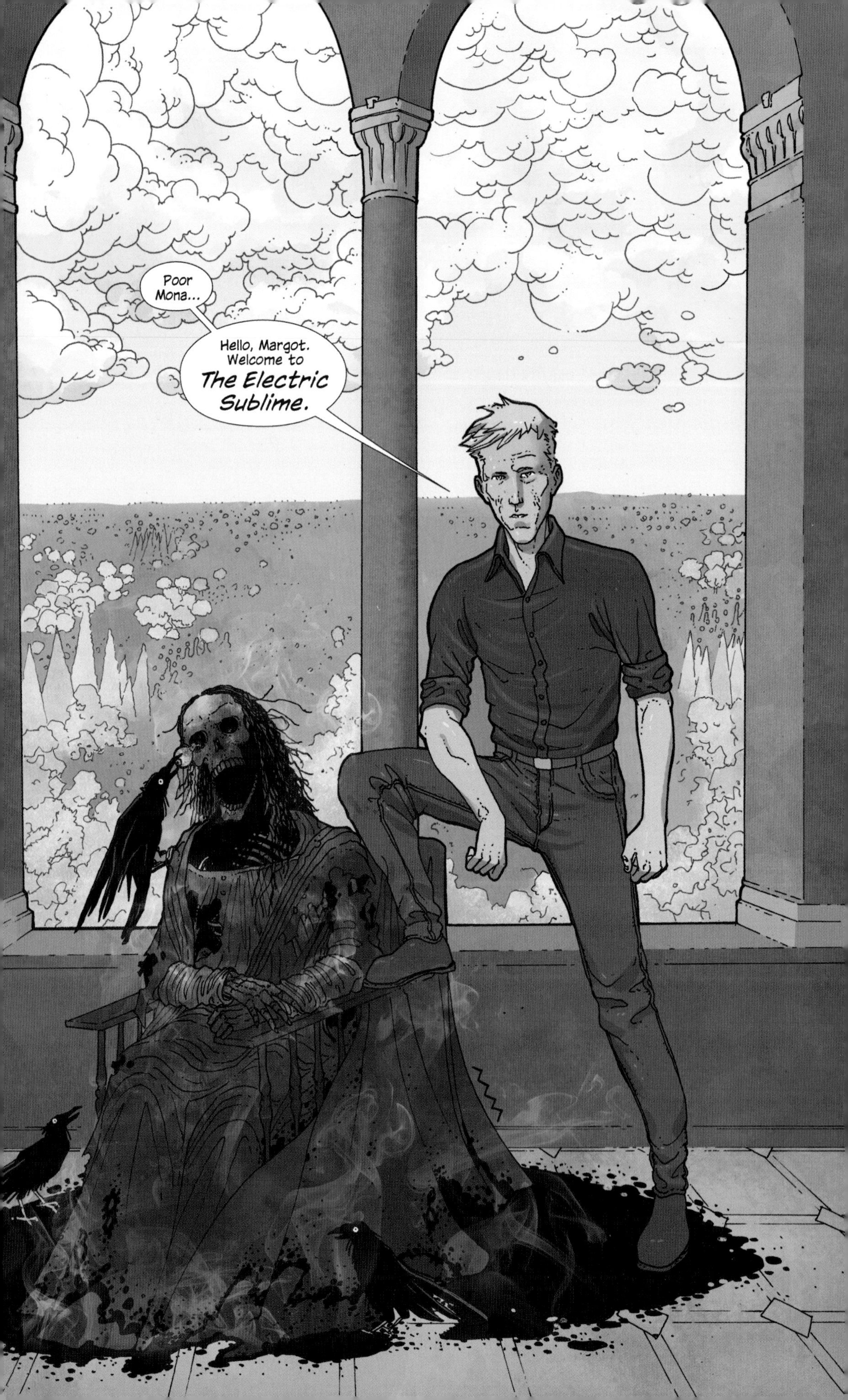
Poor Mona...
Hello, Margot. Welcome to *The Electric Sublime.*

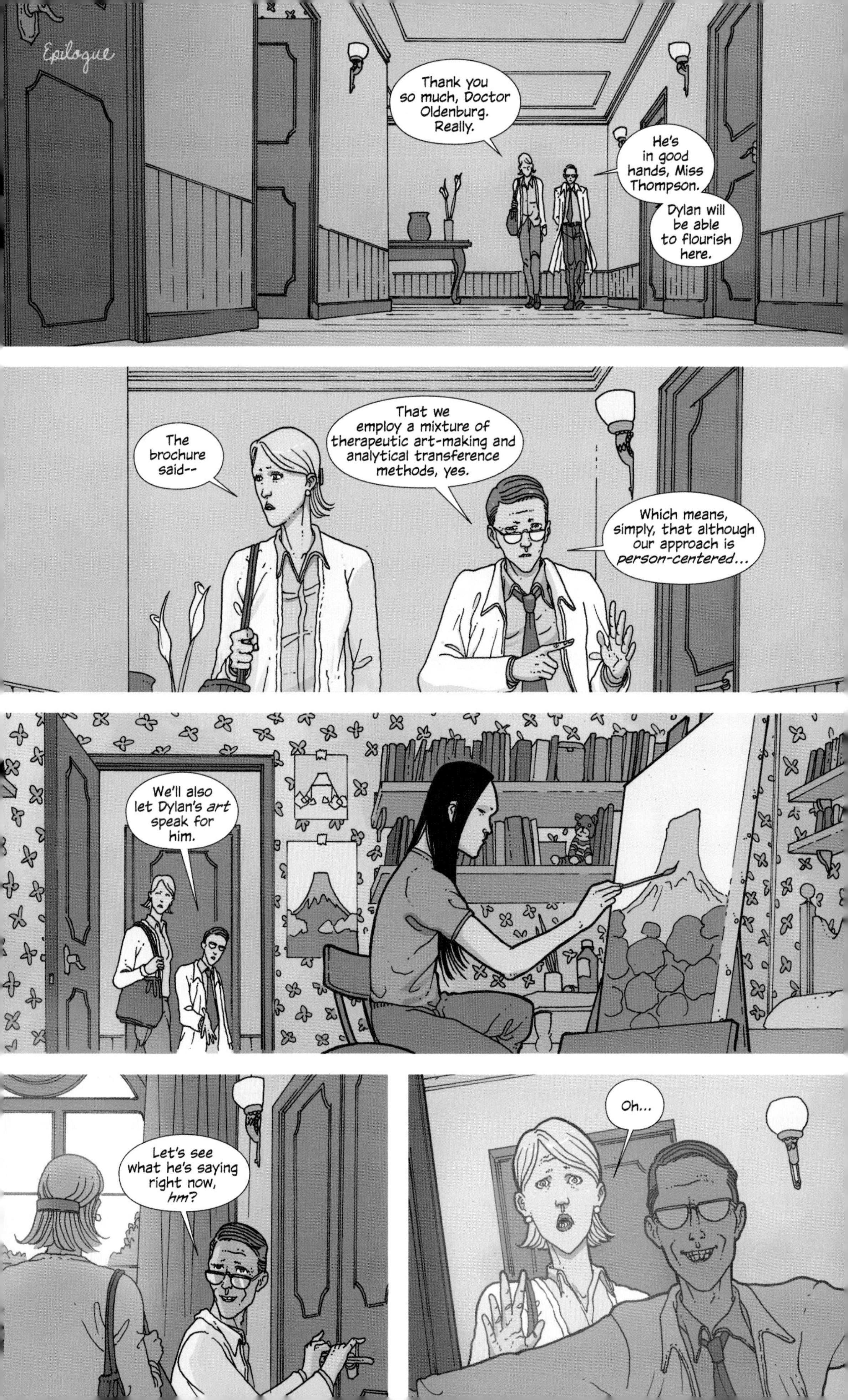
Epilogue
Thank you so much, Doctor Oldenburg. Really.
He's in good hands, Miss Thompson.
Dylan will be able to flourish here.
The brochure said--
That we employ a mixture of therapeutic art-making and analytical transference methods, yes.
Which means, simply, that although our approach is person-centered...
We'll also let Dylan's art speak for him.
Let's see what he's saying right now, hm?
Oh...

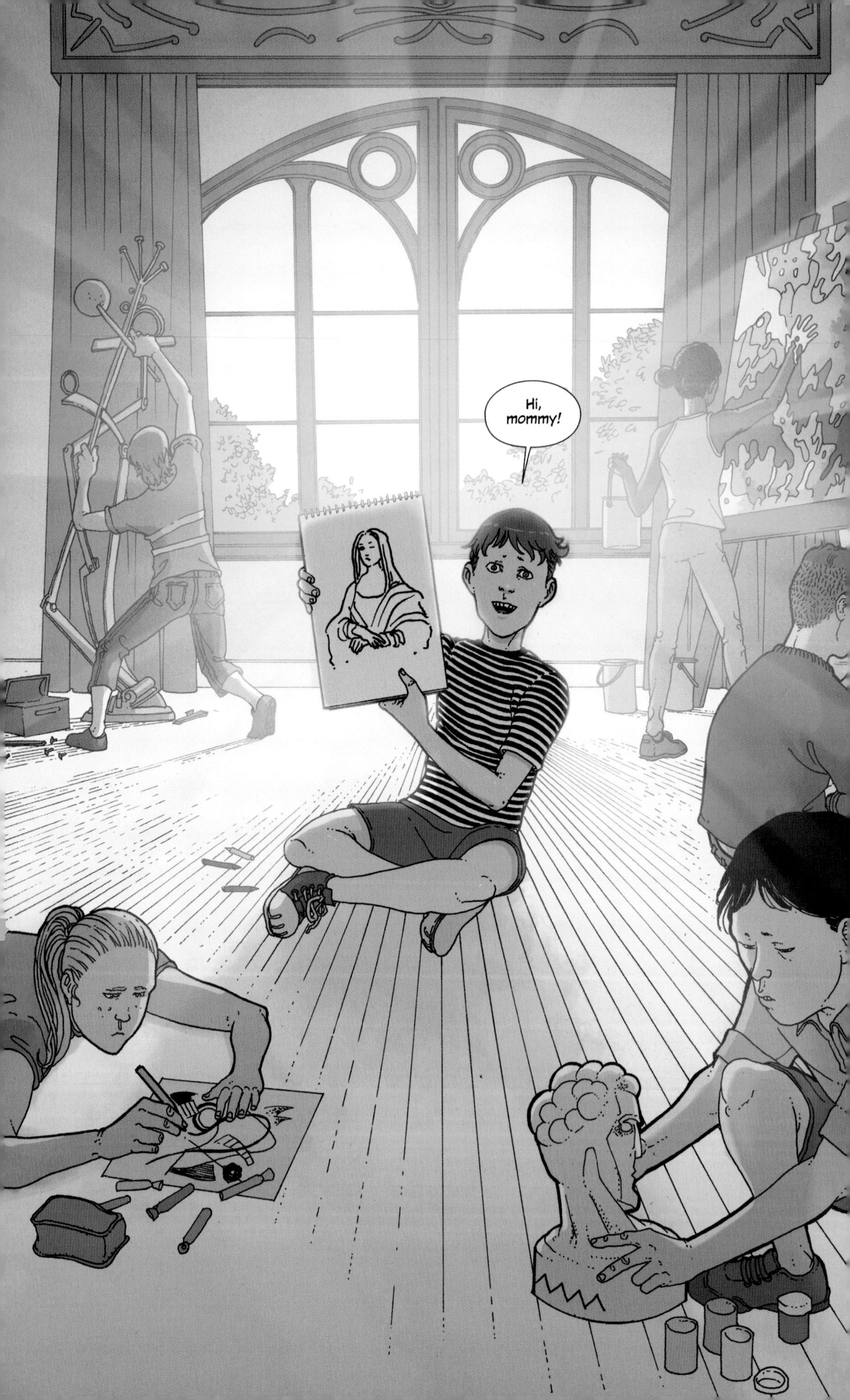
Hi, mommy!

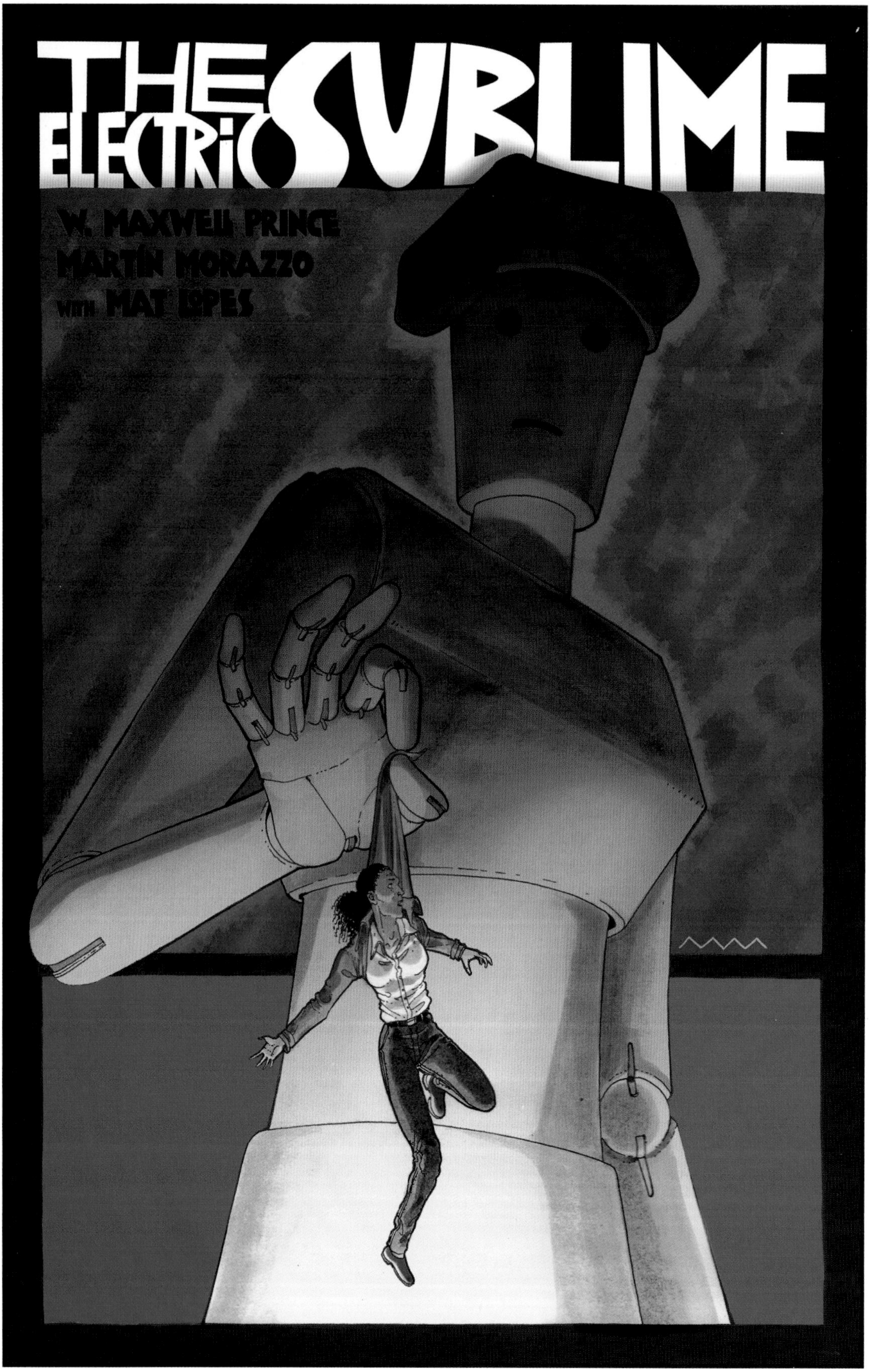
THE ELECTRIC SUBLIME
W. MAXWELL PRINCE
MARTÍN MORAZZO
WITH MAT LOPES

COVER ART BY Martín Morazzo COLORS BY Mat Lopes

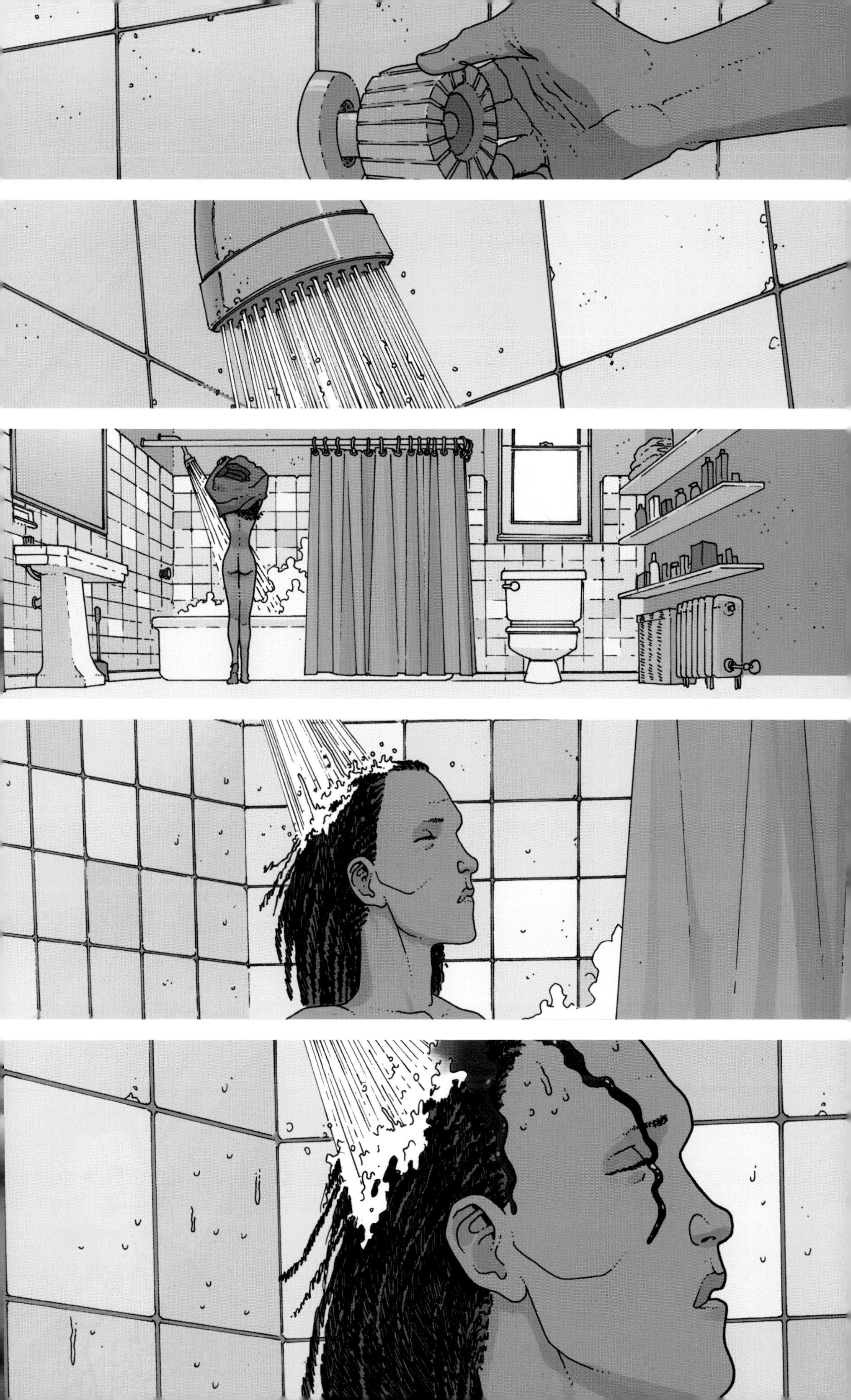

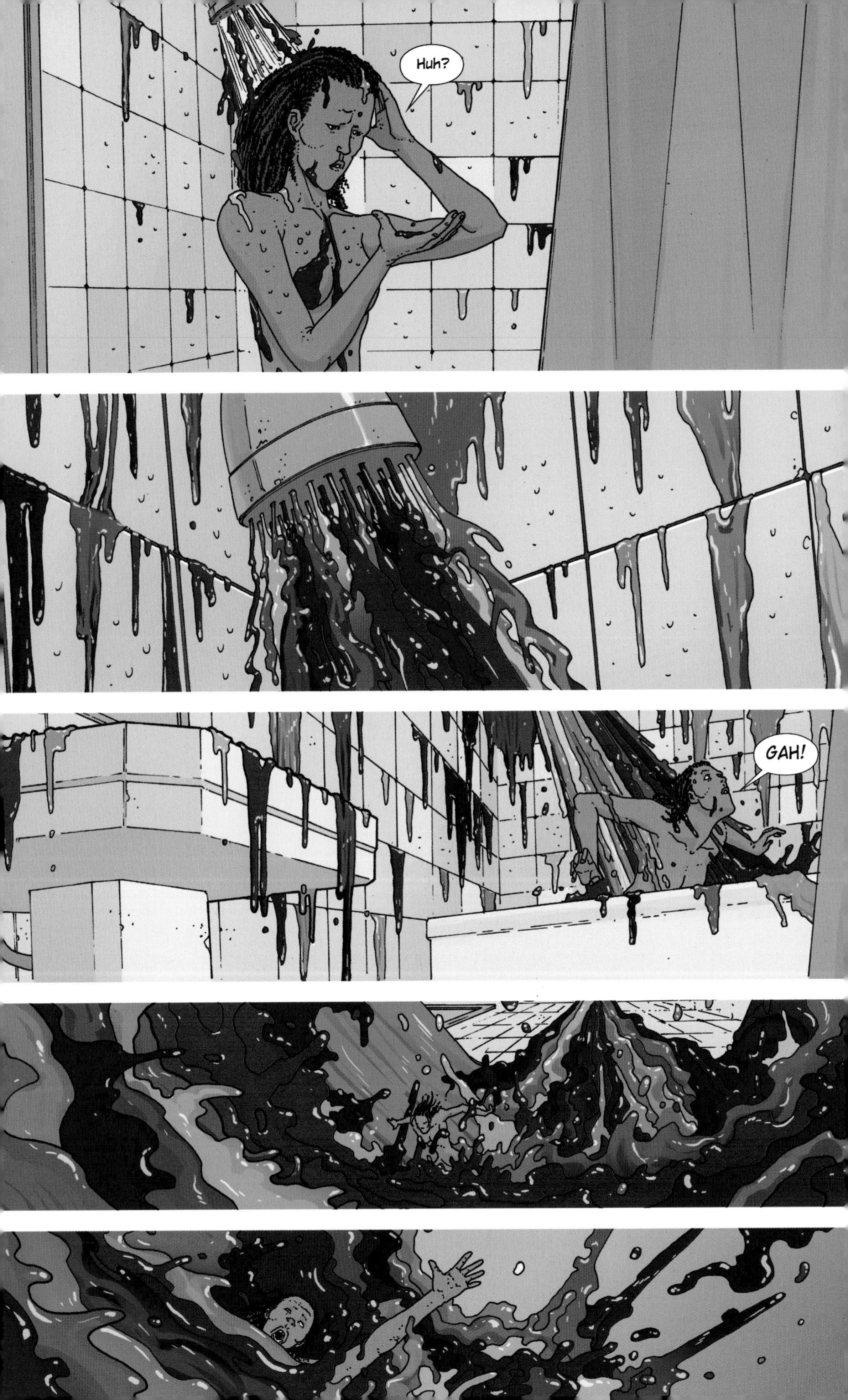
Huh?
GAH!

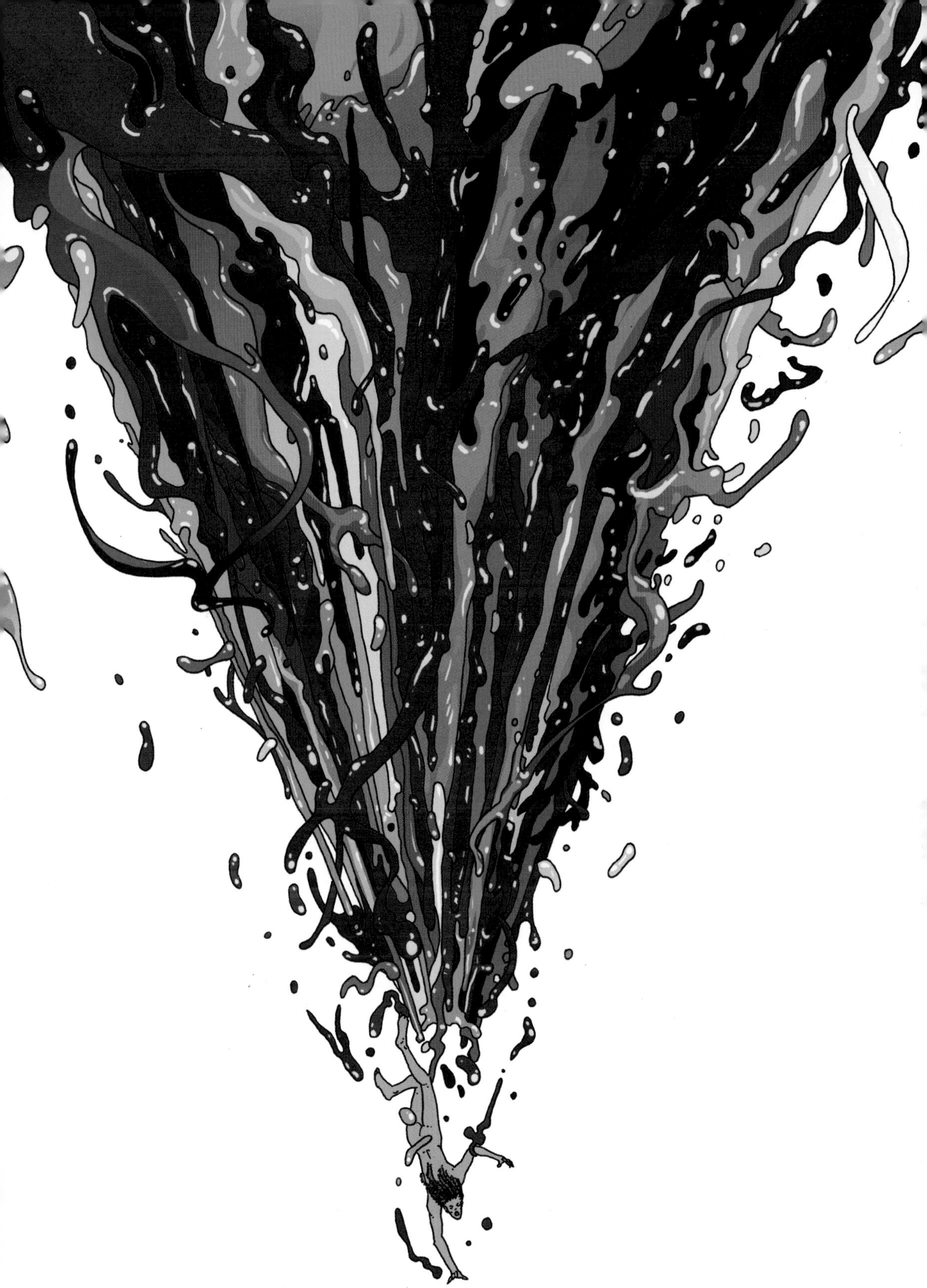

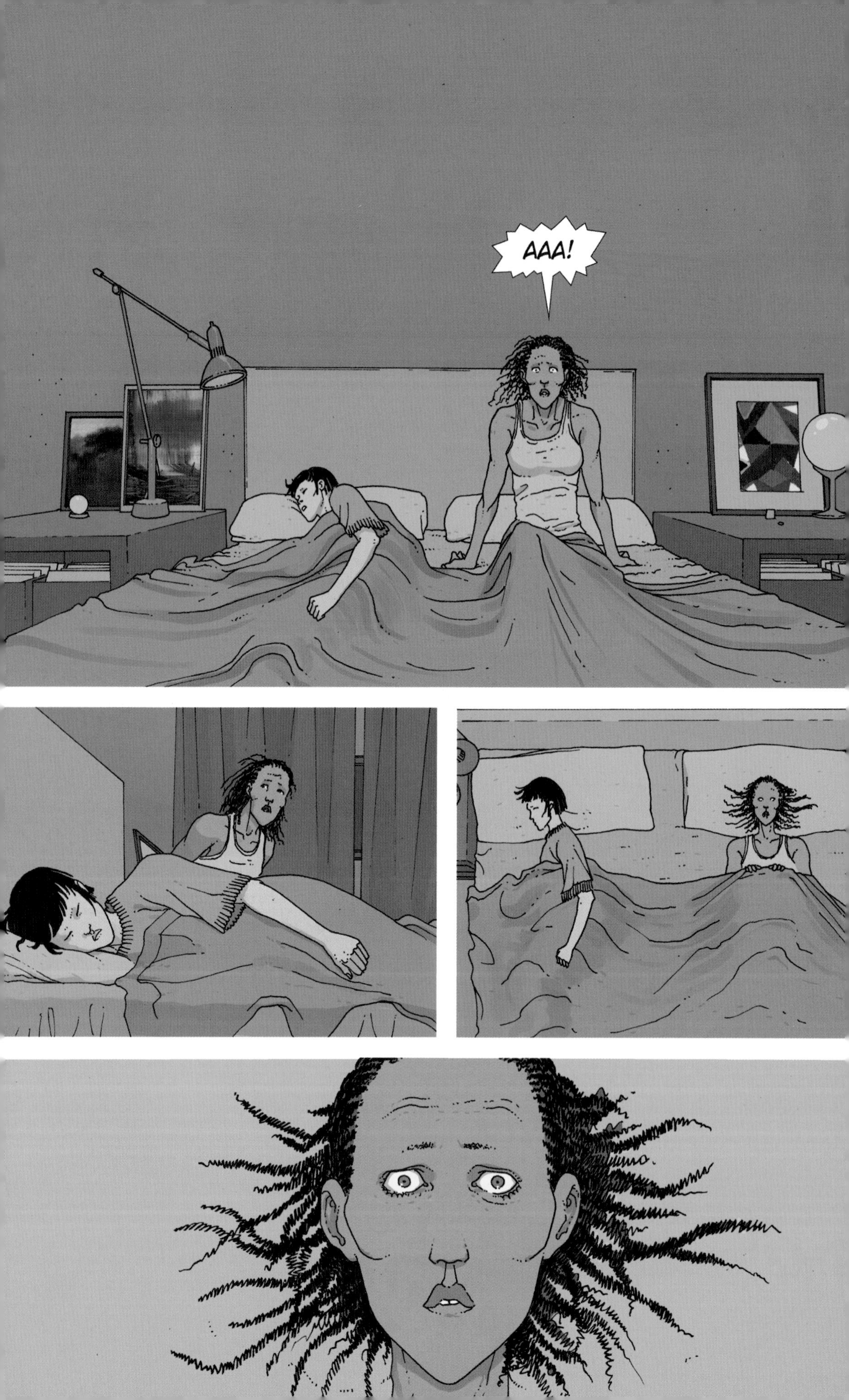
AAA!

KEY OF DREAMS

Chapter 2

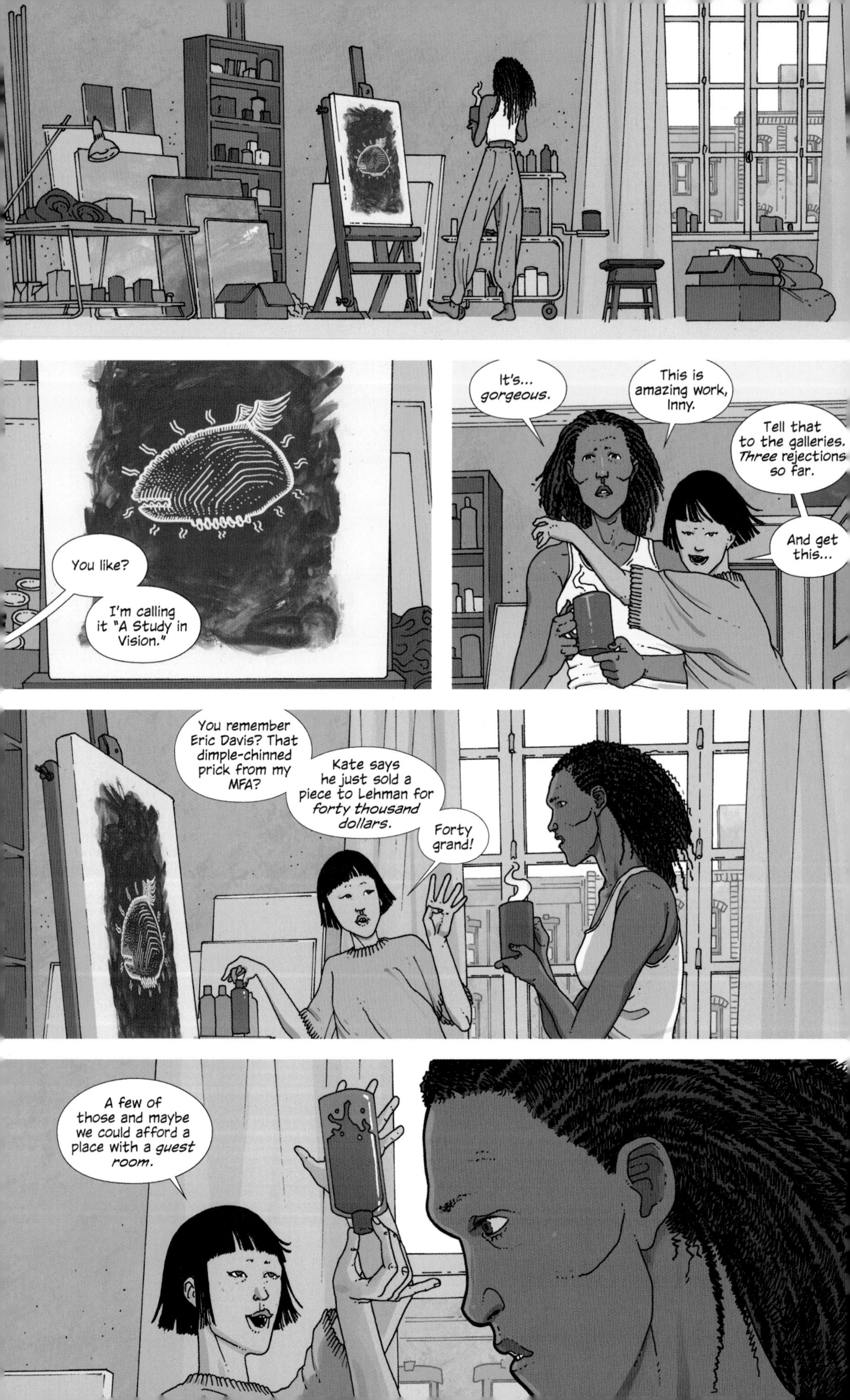

You like?
I'm calling it "A Study in Vision."
It's... *gorgeous.*
This is amazing work, Inny.
Tell that to the galleries. *Three* rejections so far.
And get this...
You remember Eric Davis? That dimple-chinned prick from my MFA?
Kate says he just sold a piece to Lehman for *forty thousand dollars.*
Forty grand!
A few of those and maybe we could afford a place with a *guest room.*

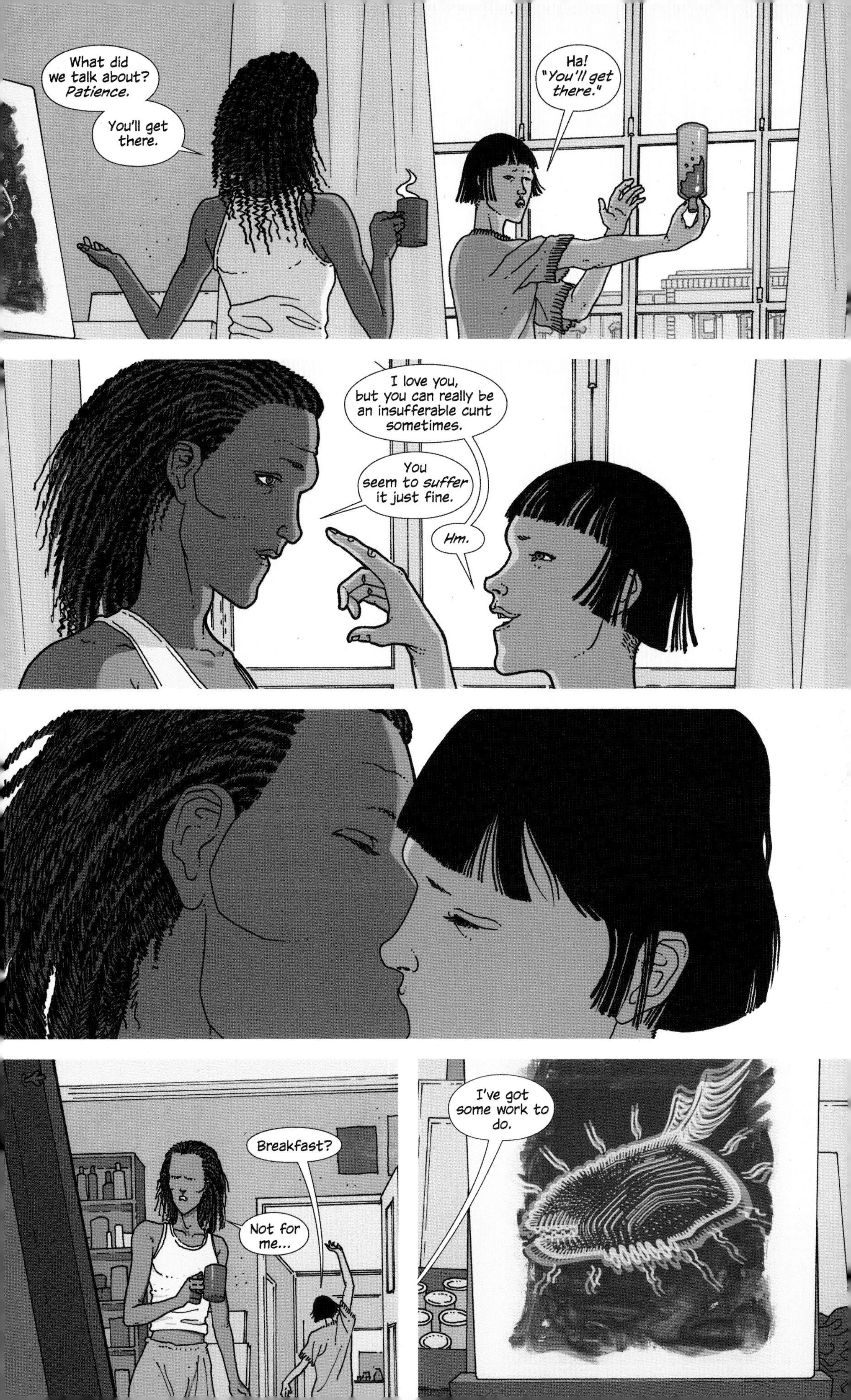
What did we talk about? *Patience.*
You'll get there.
Ha! *"You'll get there."*
I love you, but you can really be an insufferable cunt sometimes.
You seem to *suffer* it just fine.
Hm.
Breakfast?
Not for me...
I've got some work to do.

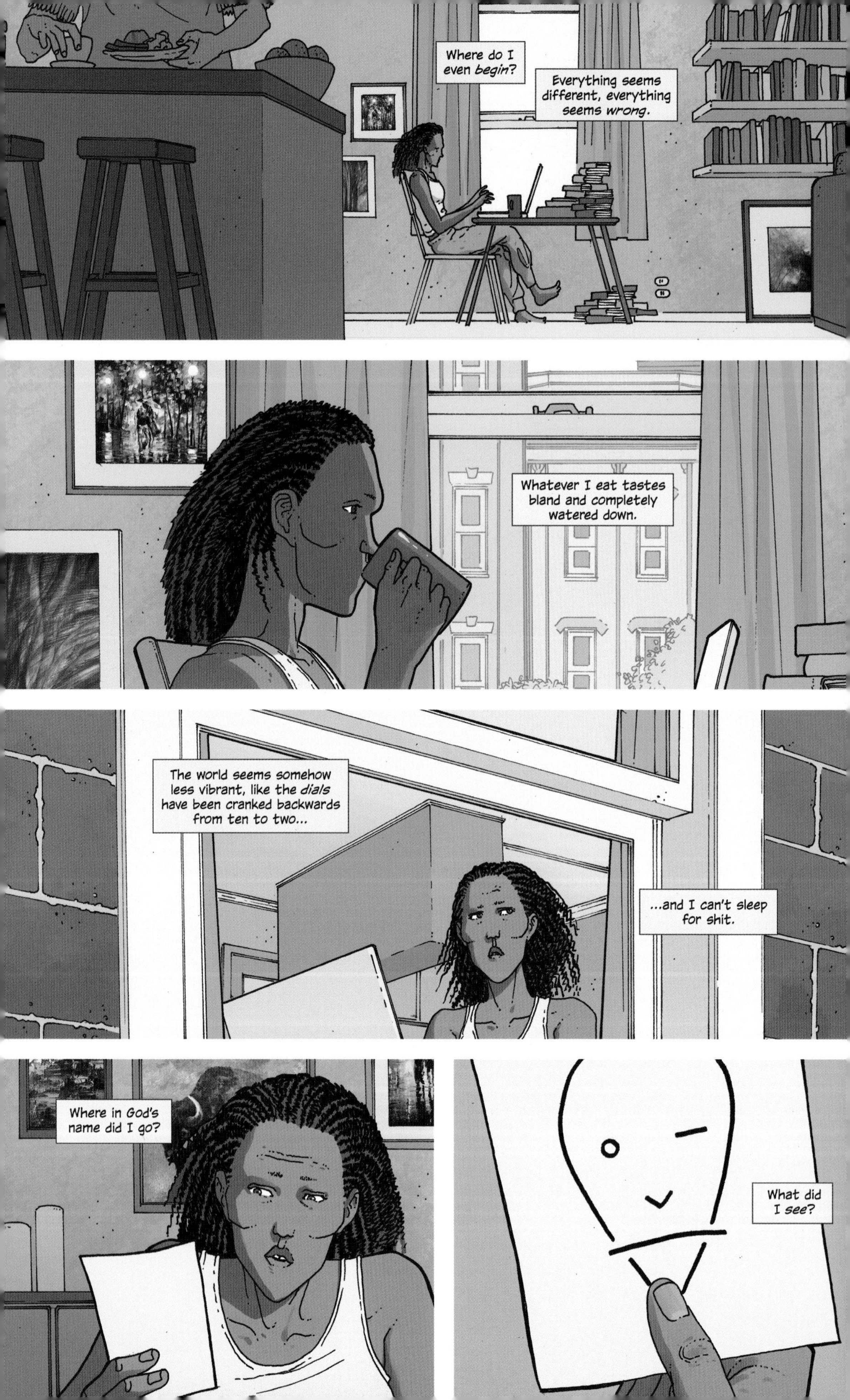
Where do I even *begin*?
Everything seems different, everything seems *wrong*.
Whatever I eat tastes bland and completely watered down.
The world seems somehow less vibrant, like the *dials* have been cranked backwards from ten to two...
...and I can't sleep for shit.
Where in God's name did I go?
What did I *see*?

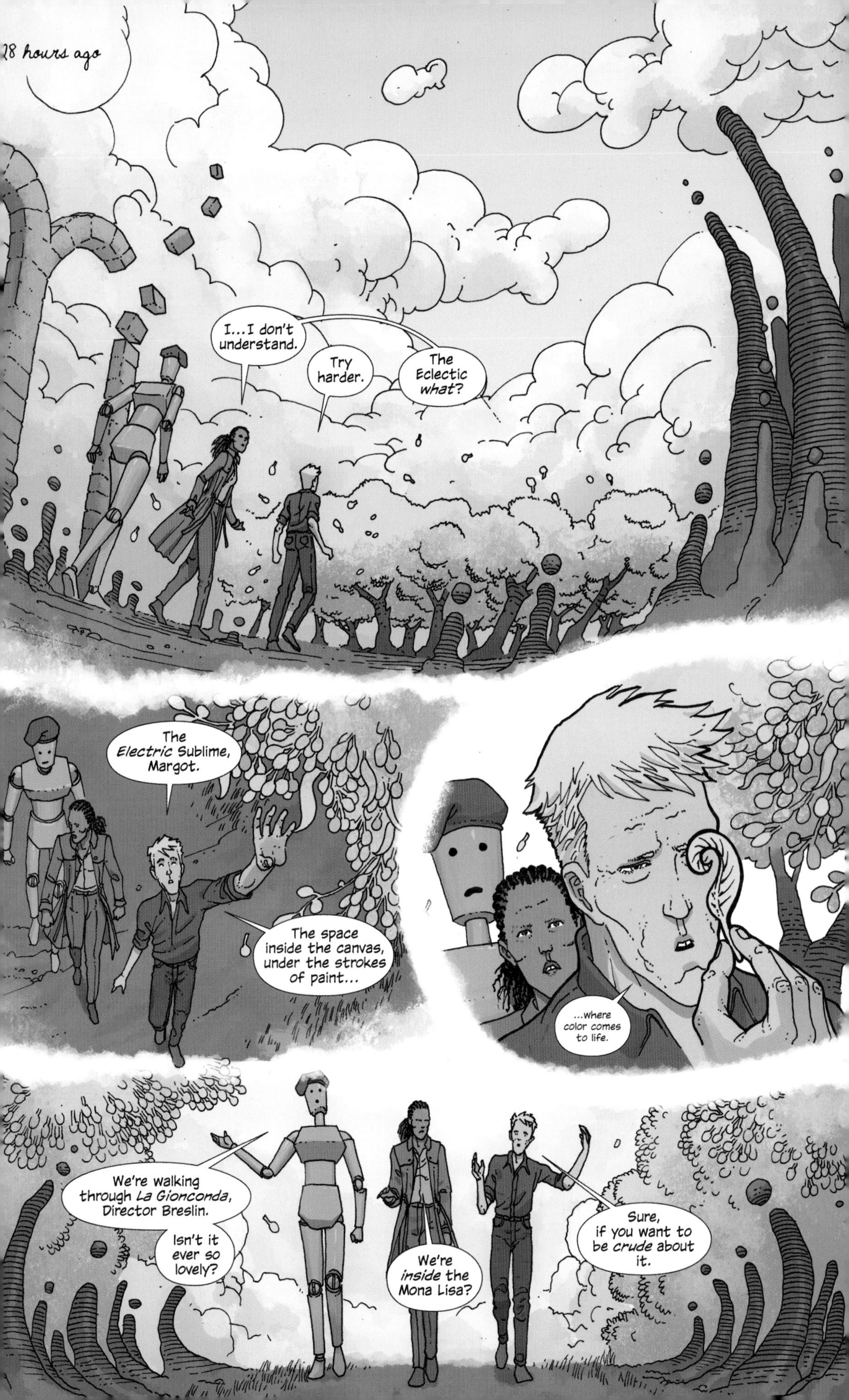
18 hours ago
I...I don't understand.
Try harder.
The Eclectic *what?*
The *Electric* Sublime, Margot.
The space inside the canvas, under the strokes of paint...
...where color comes to life.
We're walking through *La Gioconda*, Director Breslin.
Isn't it ever so lovely?
We're *inside* the Mona Lisa?
Sure, if you want to be *crude* about it.

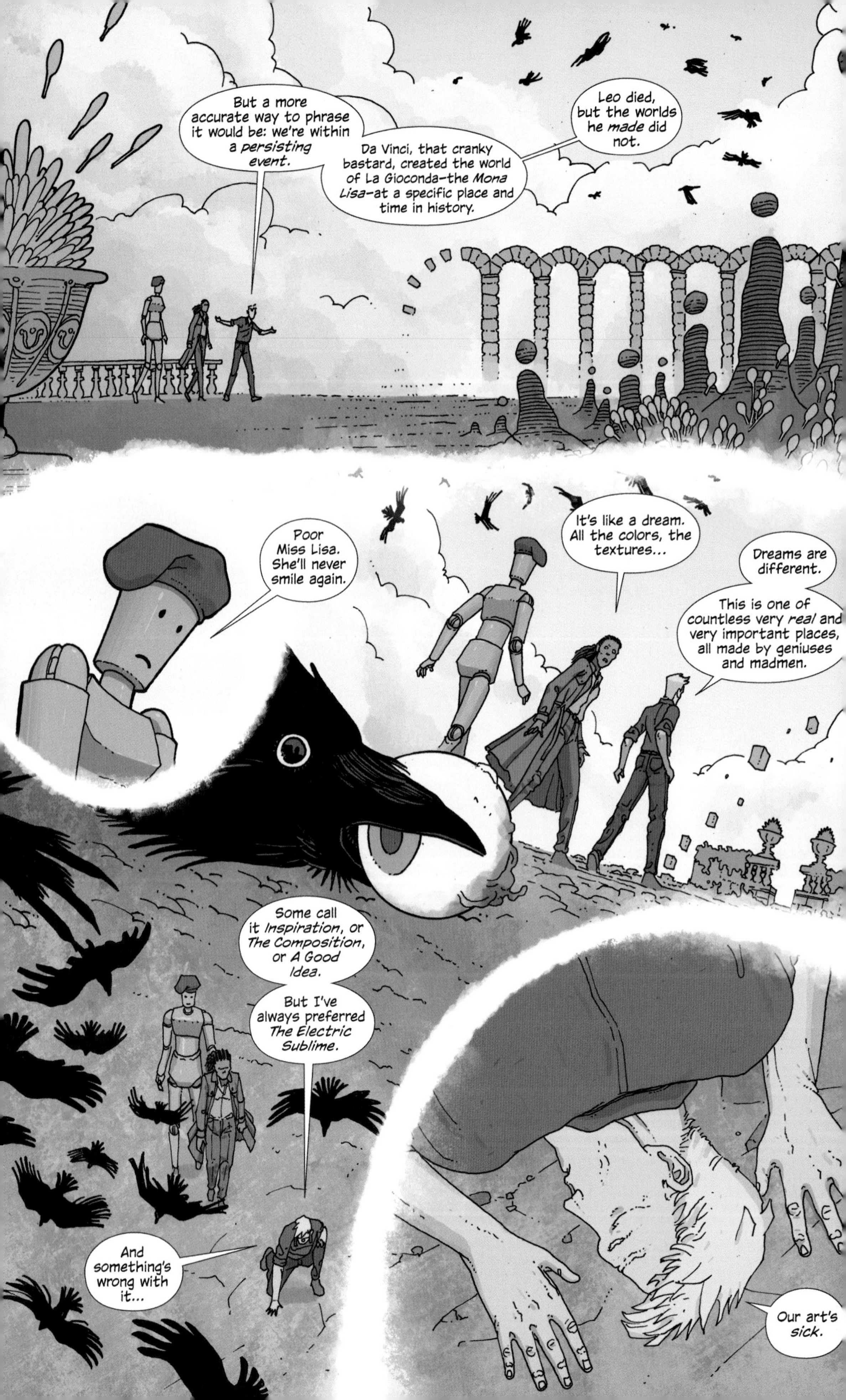
But a more accurate way to phrase it would be: we're within a *persisting event*.
Da Vinci, that cranky bastard, created the world of La Gioconda—the *Mona Lisa*—at a specific place and time in history.
Leo died, but the worlds he *made* did not.
Poor Miss Lisa. She'll never smile again.
It's like a dream. All the colors, the textures...
Dreams are different.
This is one of countless very *real* and very important places, all made by geniuses and madmen.
Some call it *Inspiration*, or *The Composition*, or *A Good Idea*.
But I've always preferred *The Electric Sublime*.
And something's wrong with it...
Our art's *sick*.

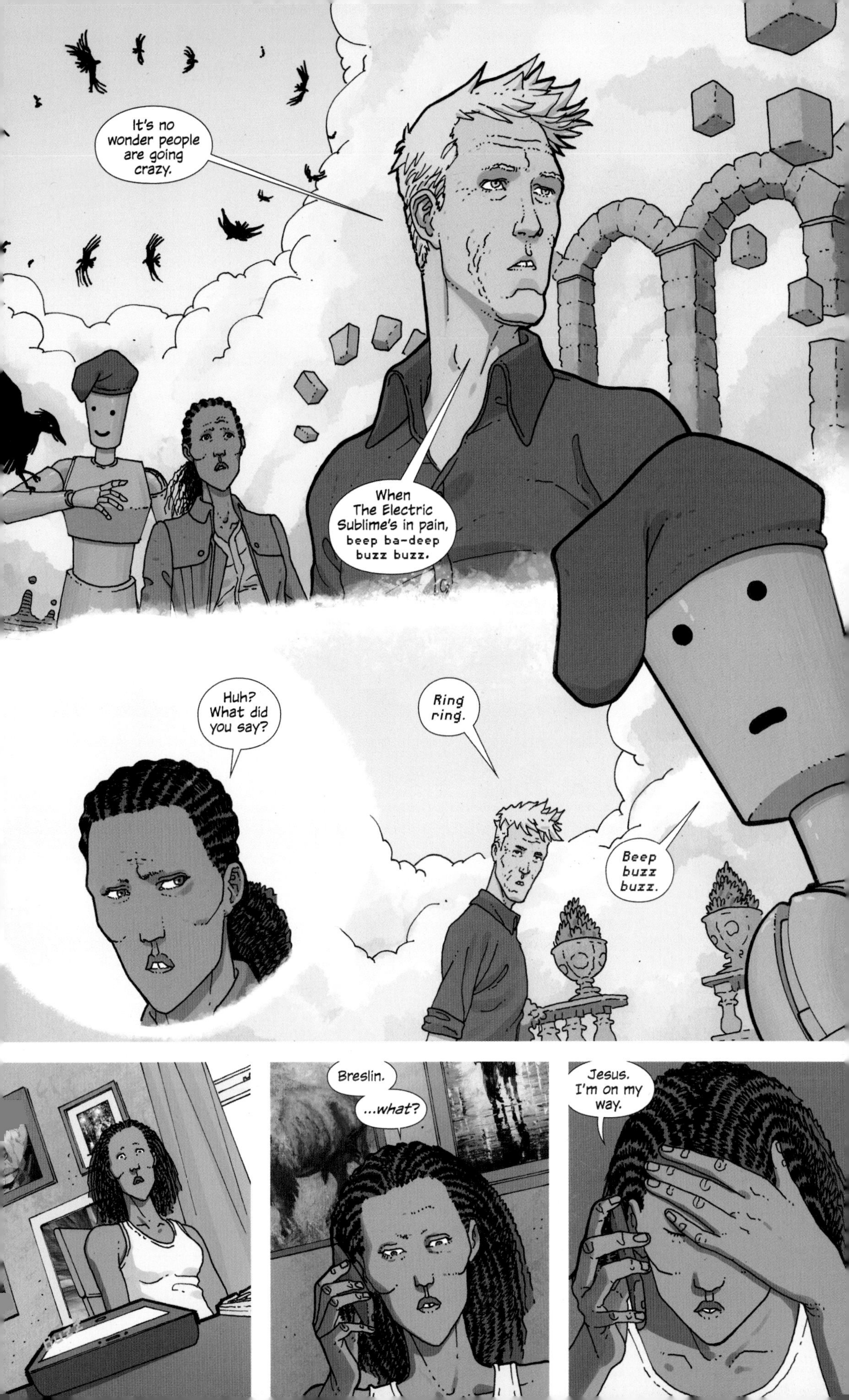
It's no wonder people are going crazy.
When The Electric Sublime's in pain, beep ba-deep buzz buzz.
Huh? What did you say?
Ring ring.
Beep buzz buzz.
Breslin.
...what?
Jesus. I'm on my way.

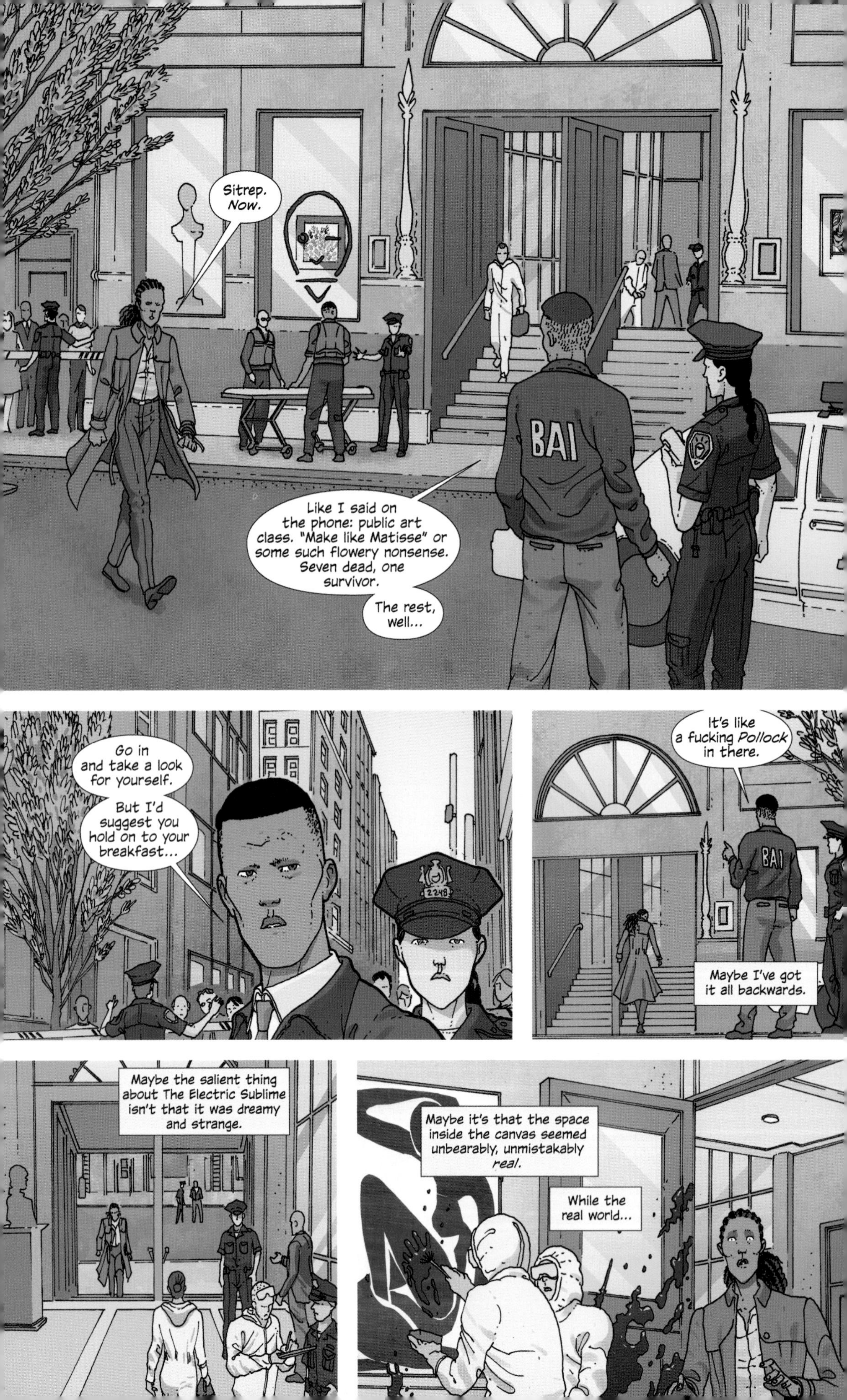

Sitrep. *Now.*
Like I said on the phone: public art class. "Make like Matisse" or some such flowery nonsense. Seven dead, one survivor.
The rest, well...
BAI
Go in and take a look for yourself.
But I'd suggest you hold on to your breakfast...
2248
It's like a fucking *Pollock* in there.
BAI
Maybe I've got it all backwards.
Maybe the salient thing about The Electric Sublime isn't that it was dreamy and strange.
Maybe it's that the space inside the canvas seemed unbearably, unmistakably *real.*
While the real world...

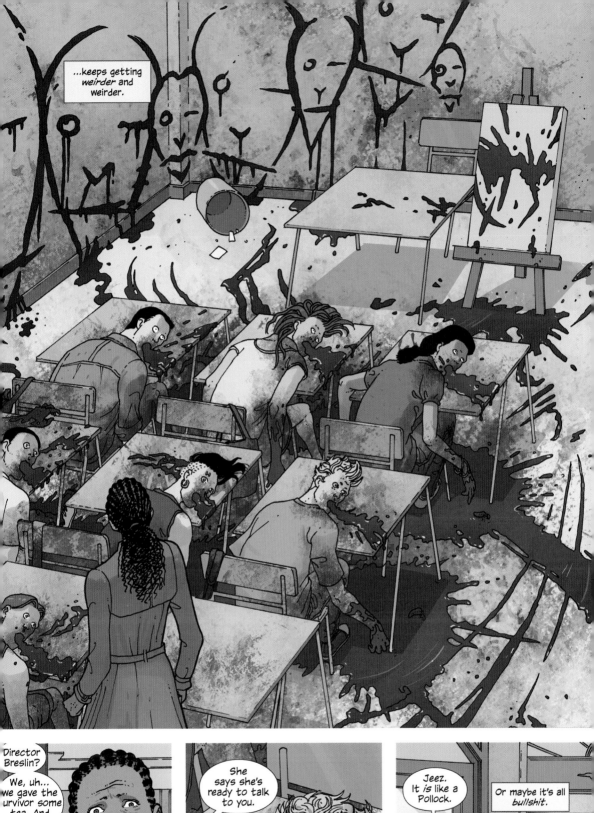

...keeps getting *weirder* and weirder.

Director Breslin?

We, uh... we gave the urvivor some tea. And Xanax.

She's calmed down some.

She says she's ready to talk to you.

Jeez. It *is* like a Pollock.

Or maybe it's all *bullshit*.

What do I know?

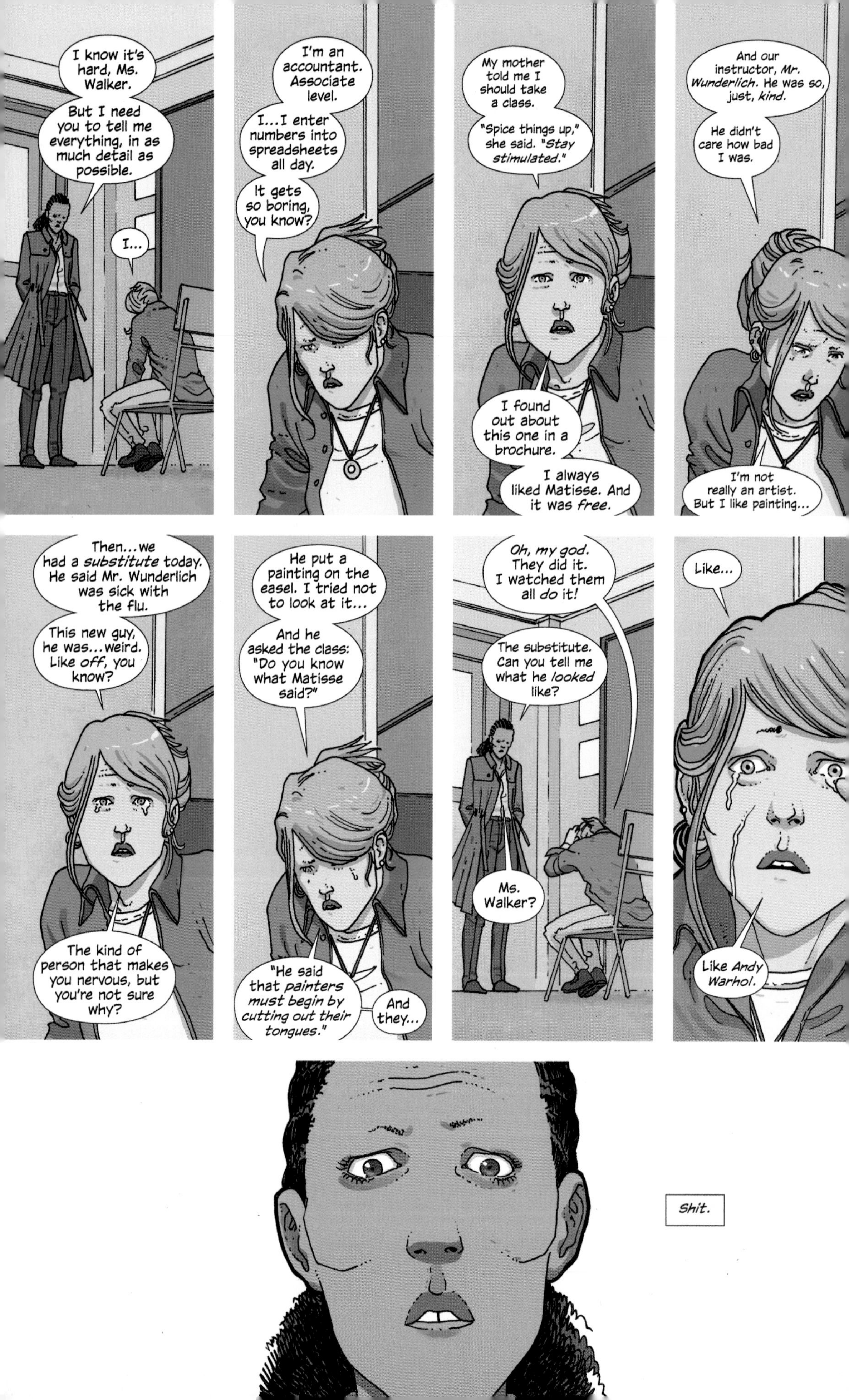
I know it's hard, Ms. Walker.
But I need you to tell me everything, in as much detail as possible.
I...
I'm an accountant. Associate level.
I...I enter numbers into spreadsheets all day.
It gets so boring, you know?
My mother told me I should take a class.
"Spice things up," she said. "*Stay stimulated.*"
I found out about this one in a brochure.
I always liked Matisse. And it was *free.*
And our instructor, *Mr. Wunderlich.* He was so, just, *kind.*
He didn't care how bad I was.
I'm not really an artist. But I like painting...
Then...we had a *substitute* today. He said Mr. Wunderlich was sick with the flu.
This new guy, he was...weird. Like *off*, you know?
The kind of person that makes you nervous, but you're not sure why?
He put a painting on the easel. I tried not to look at it...
And he asked the class: "Do you know what Matisse said?"
"He said that *painters must begin by cutting out their tongues.*"
And they...
Oh, my god. They did it. I watched them all *do* it!
The substitute. Can you tell me what he *looked* like?
Ms. Walker?
Like...
Like *Andy Warhol.*
Shit.

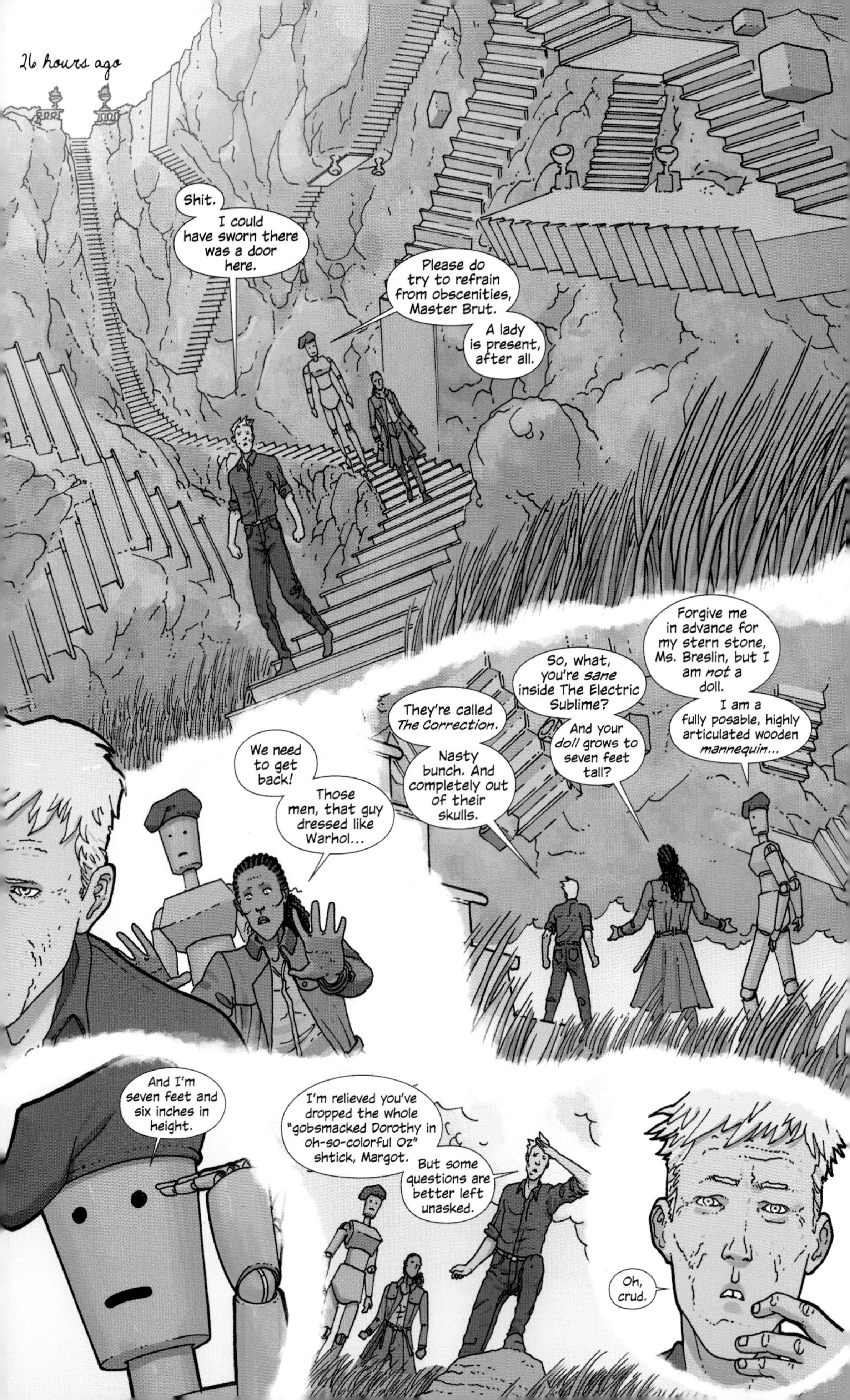
26 hours ago
Shit.
I could have sworn there was a door here.
Please do try to refrain from obscenities, Master Brut.
A lady is present, after all.
We need to get back!
Those men, that guy dressed like Warhol...
They're called *The Correction.*
Nasty bunch. And completely out of their skulls.
So, what, you're *sane* inside The Electric Sublime?
And your *doll* grows to seven feet tall?
Forgive me in advance for my stern stone, Ms. Breslin, but I am *not* a doll.
I am a fully posable, highly articulated wooden *mannequin*...
And I'm seven feet and six inches in height.
I'm relieved you've dropped the whole "gobsmacked Dorothy in oh-so-colorful Oz" shtick, Margot.
But some questions are better left unasked.
Oh, crud.

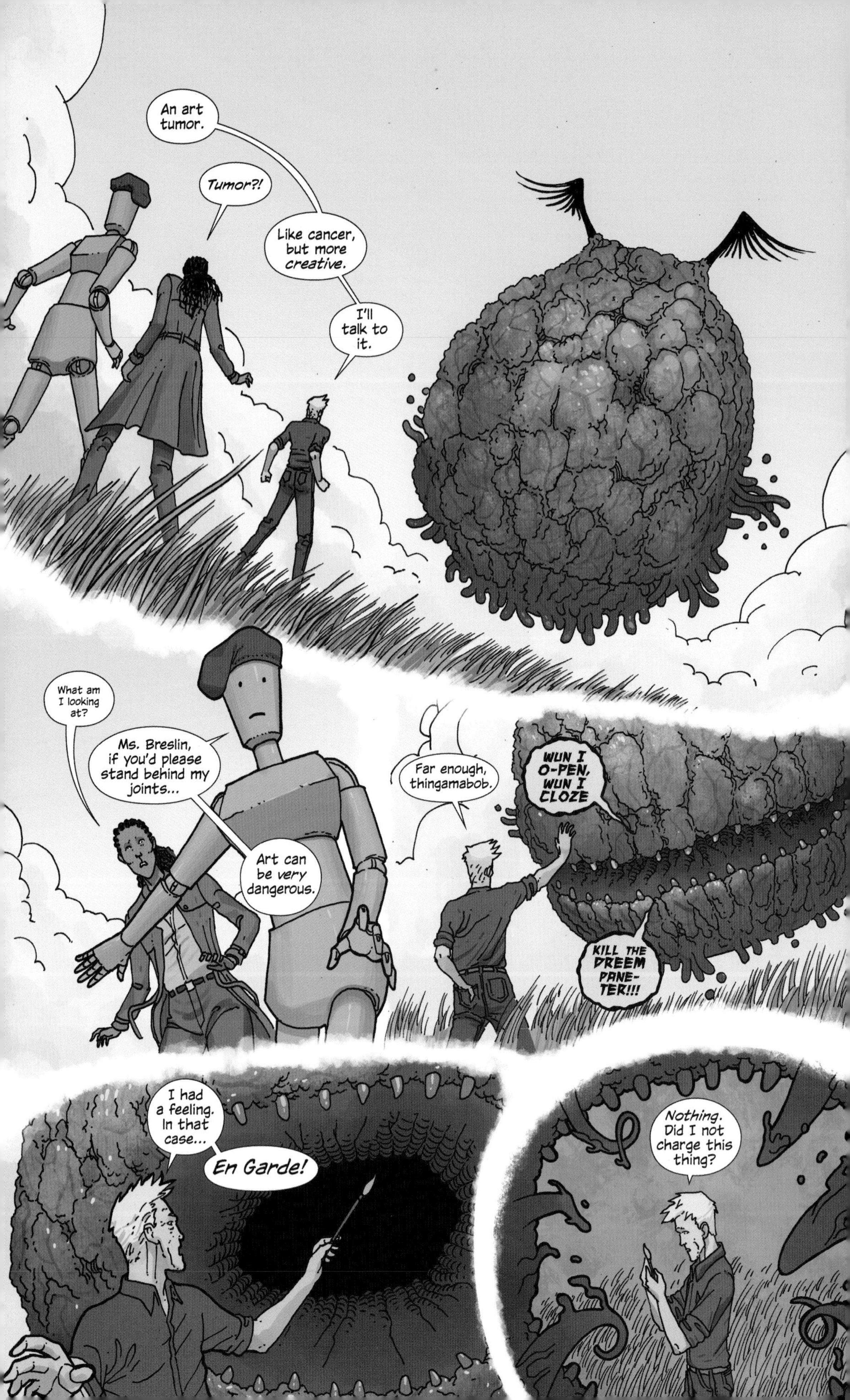
An art tumor.
Tumor?!
Like cancer, but more *creative*.
I'll talk to it.
What am I looking at?
Ms. Breslin, if you'd please stand behind my joints...
Art can be *very* dangerous.
Far enough, thingamabob.
WUN I O-PEN, WUN I CLOZE
KILL THE DREEM PANE-TER!!!
I had a feeling. In that case...
En Garde!
Nothing. Did I not charge this thing?

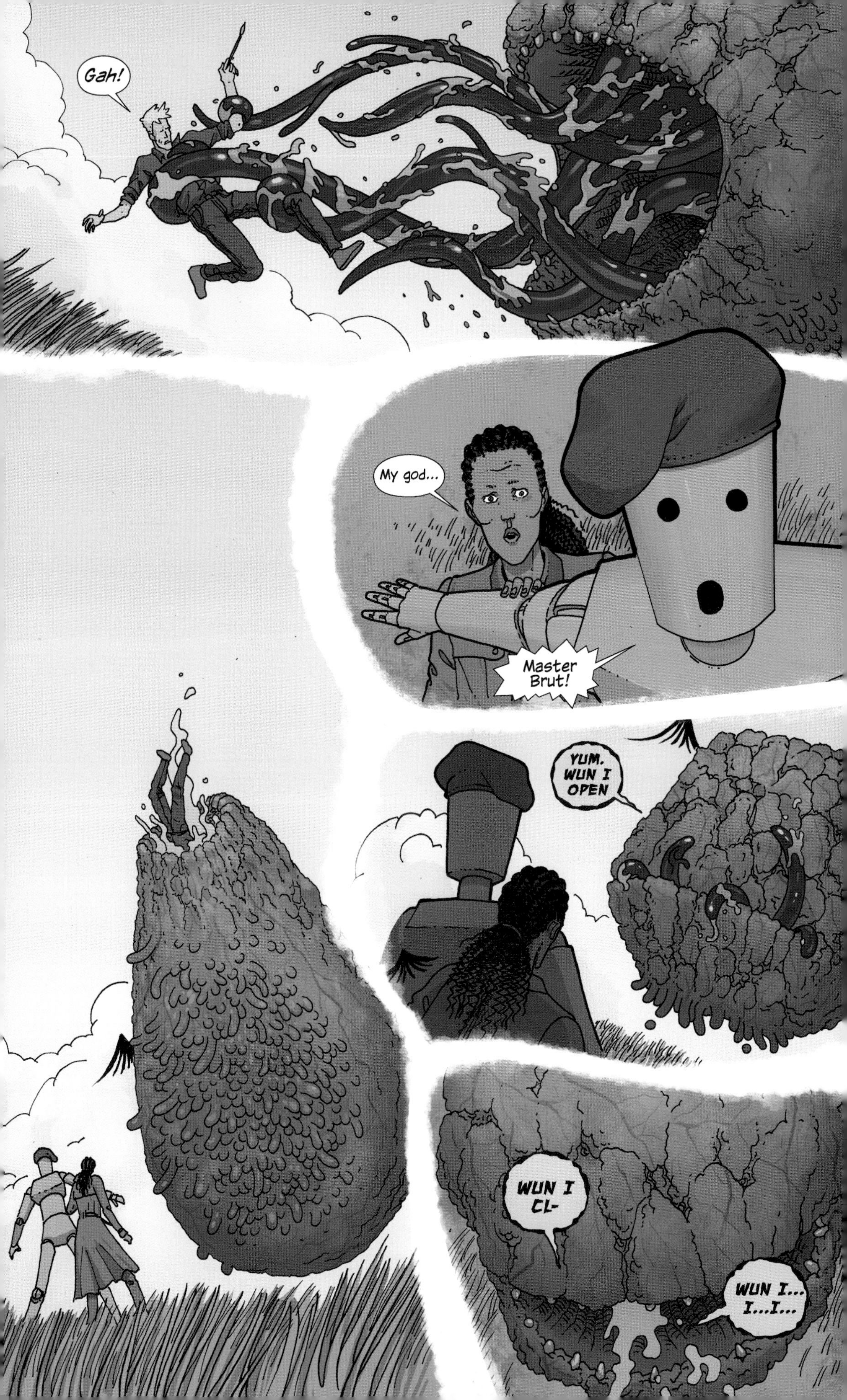
Gah!
My god...
Master Brut!
YUM. WUN I OPEN
WUN I CL-
WUN I... I...I...

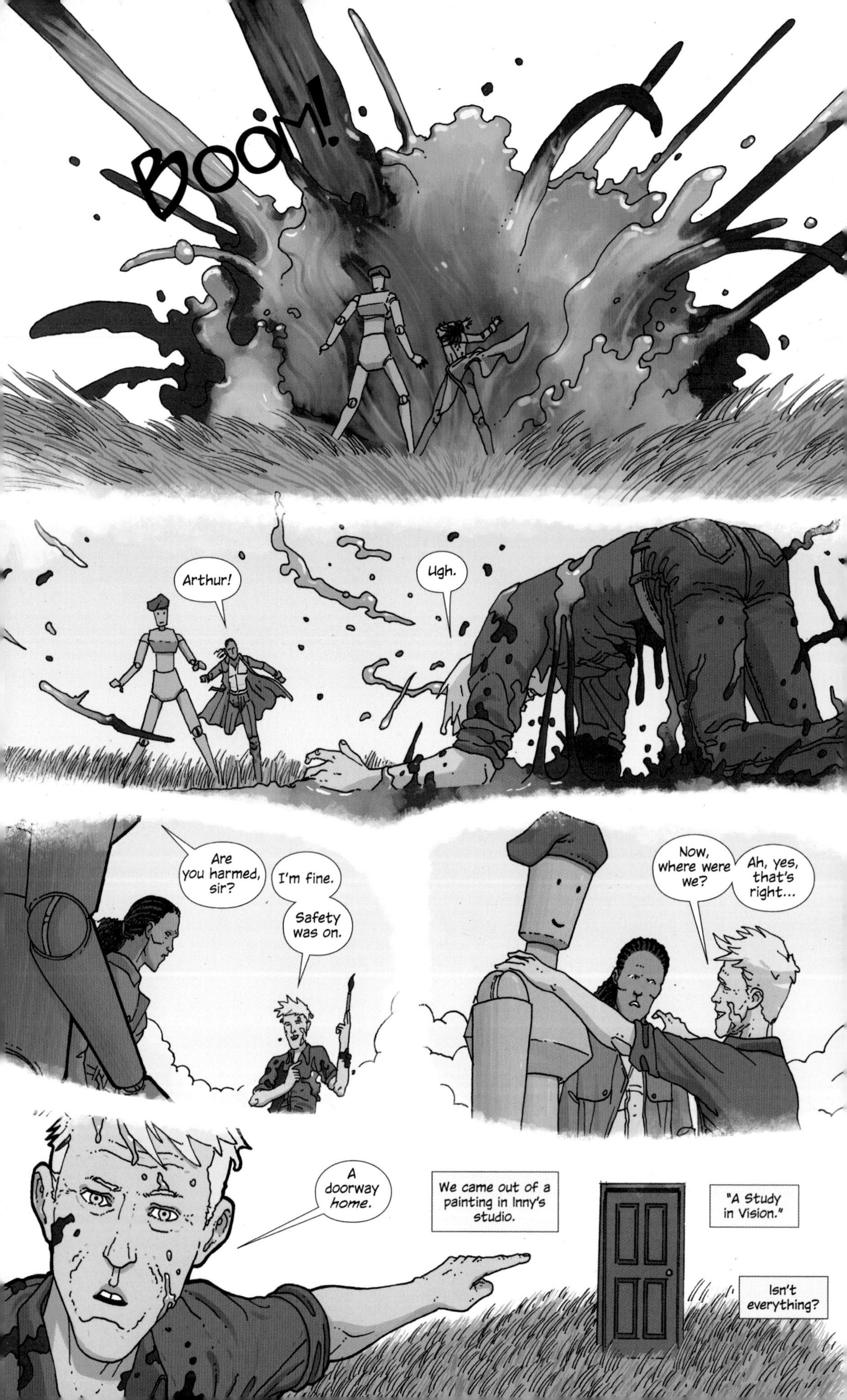
BOOM!
Arthur!
Ugh.
Are you harmed, sir?
I'm fine.
Safety was on.
Now, where were we?
Ah, yes, that's right...
A doorway *home.*
We came out of a painting in Inny's studio.
"A Study in Vision."
Isn't everything?

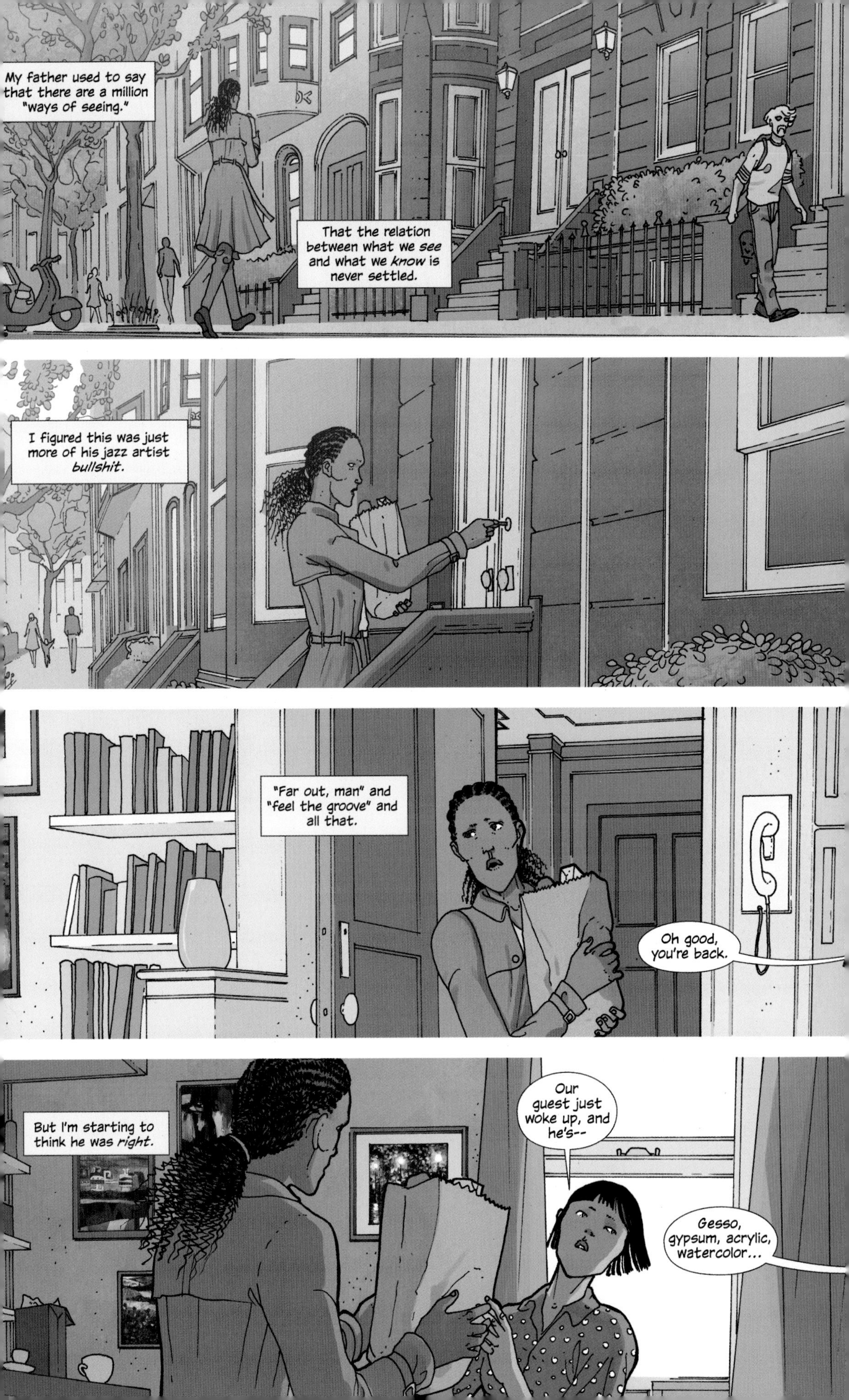

My father used to say that there are a million "ways of seeing."
That the relation between what we *see* and what we *know* is never settled.
I figured this was just more of his jazz artist *bullshit*.
"Far out, man" and "feel the groove" and all that.
Oh good, you're back.
But I'm starting to think he was *right*.
Our guest just woke up, and he's--
Gesso, gypsum, acrylic, watercolor...

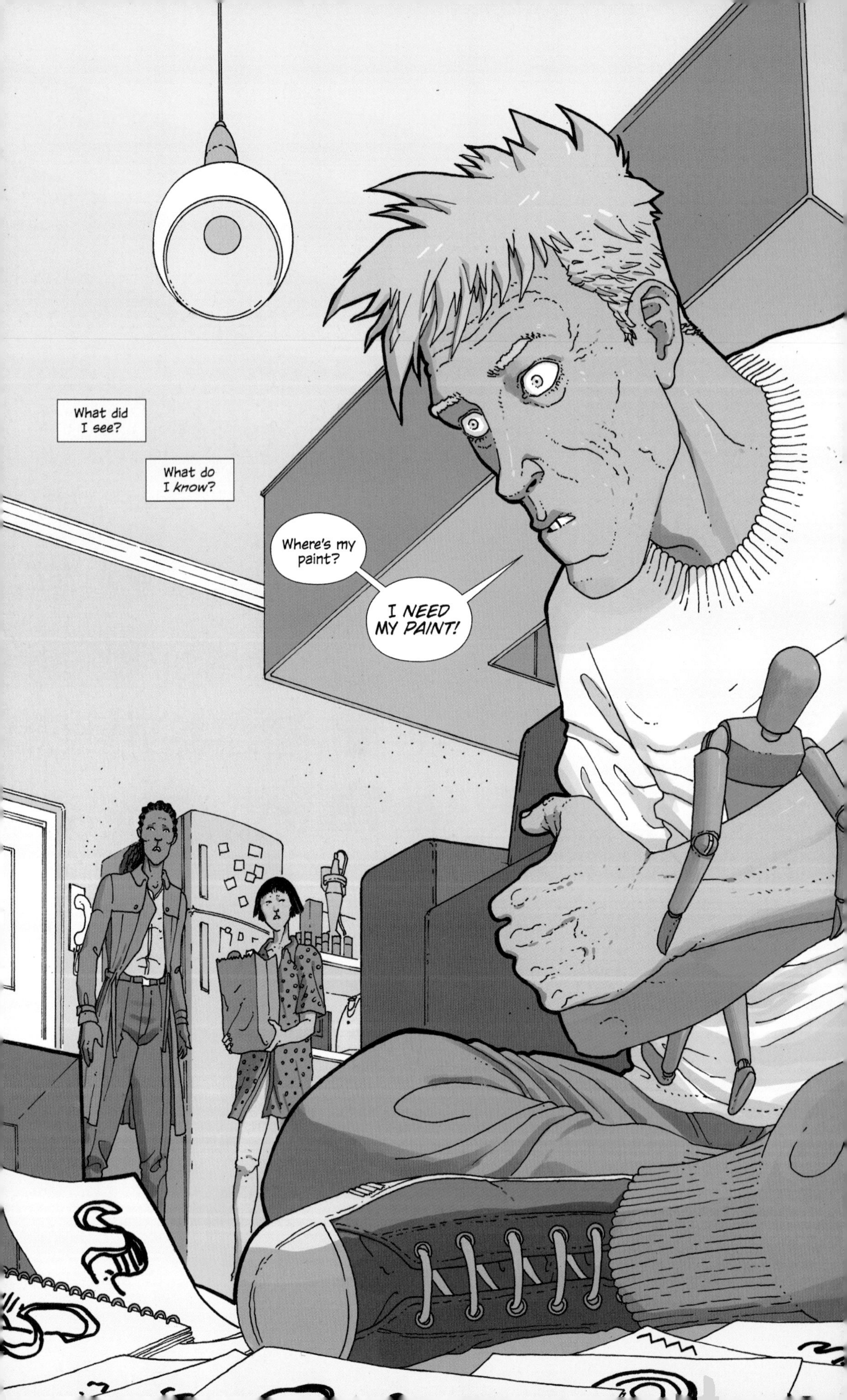
What did I see?
What do I *know*?
Where's my paint?
I NEED MY PAINT!

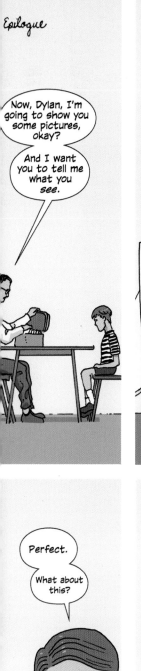

Epilogue

Now, Dylan, I'm going to show you some pictures, okay?

And I want you to tell me what you see.

Dylan?

I see a ...door.

Very good.

And this one?

The wind.

Perfect.

What about this?

A birdie.

Great, Dylan. Just great.

What about this one? What do you see?

I see...

kaboom.

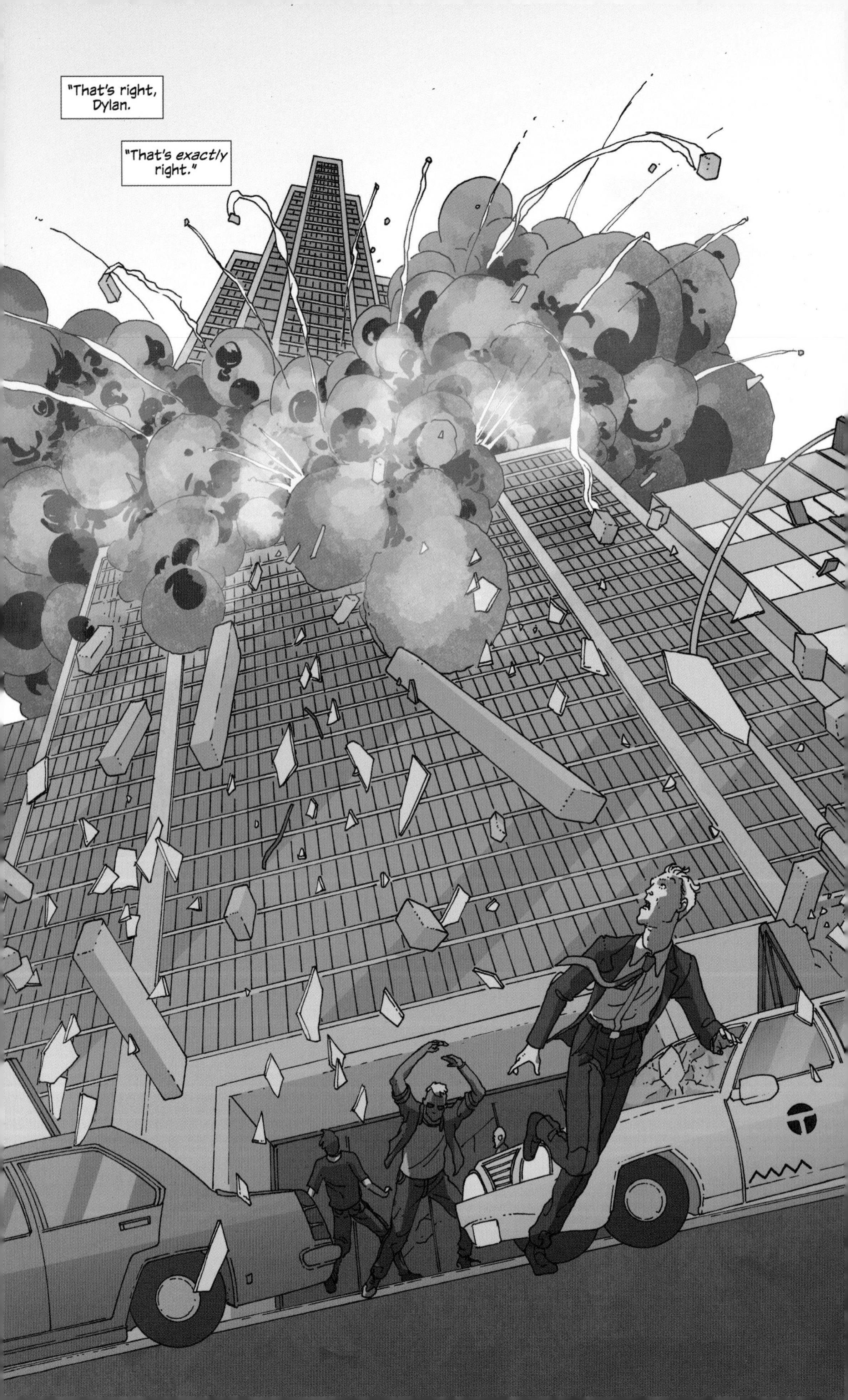
"That's right,
Dylan.
"That's *exactly*
right."

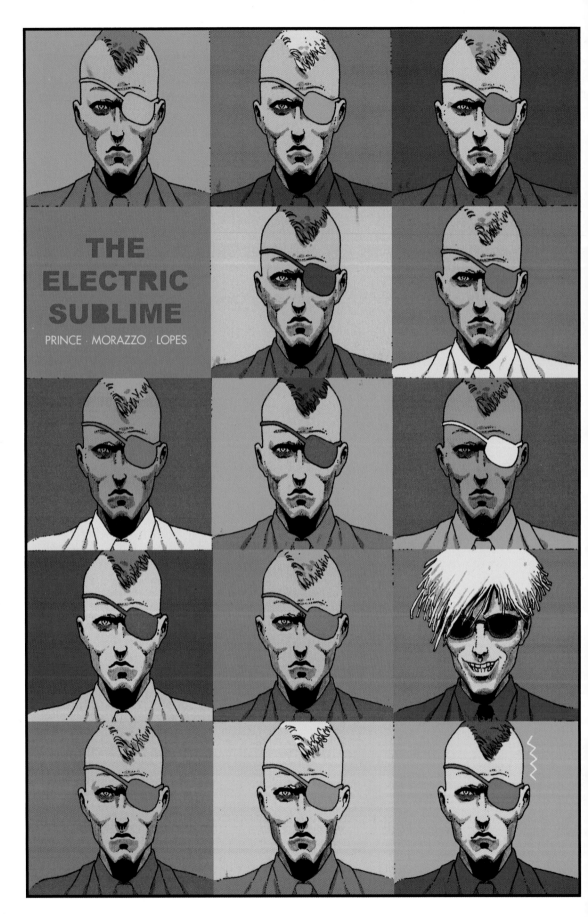

THE ELECTRIC SUBLIME

PRINCE · MORAZZO · LOPES

COVER ART BY *Martin Morazzo*

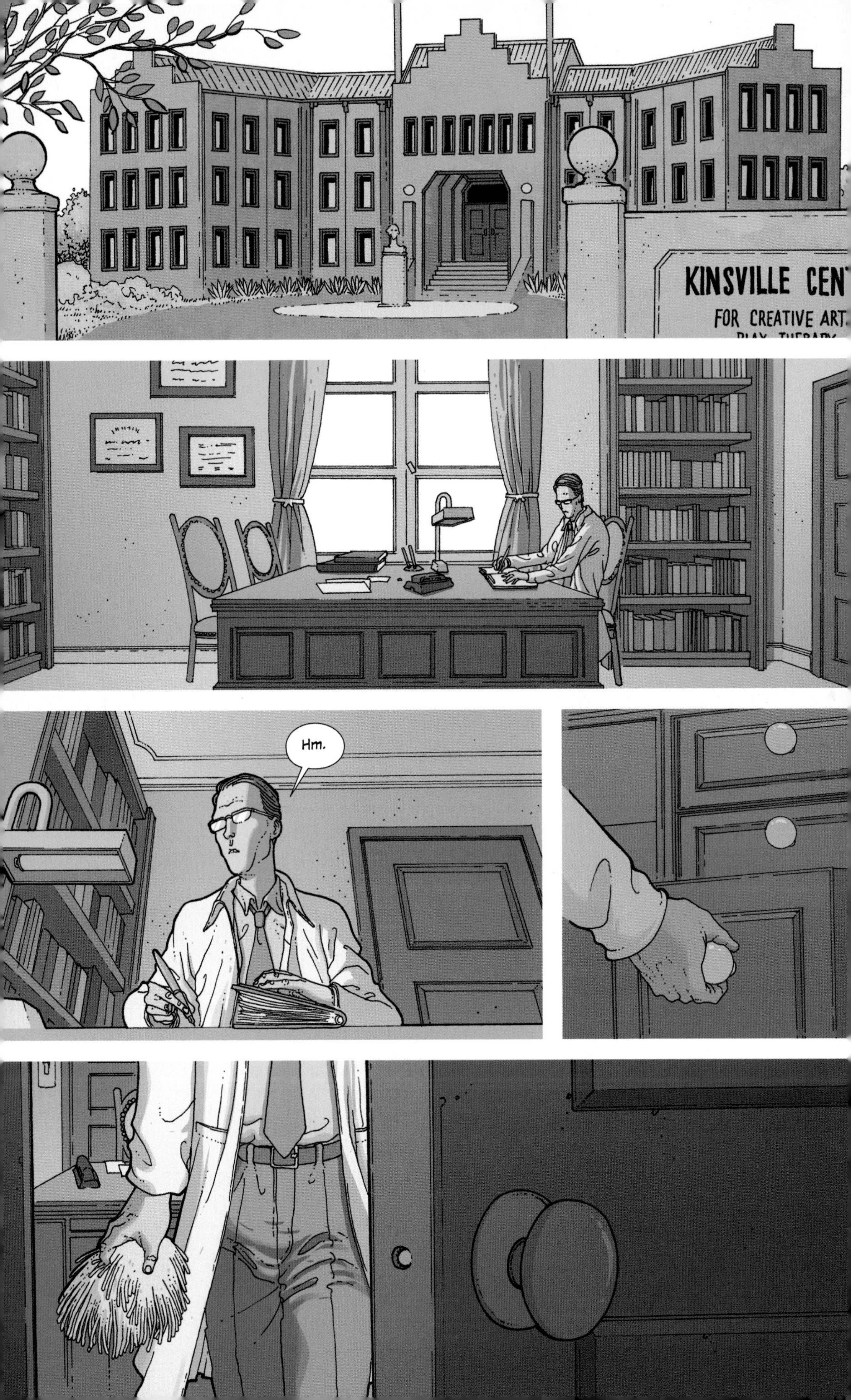
KINSVILLE CENT
FOR CREATIVE ART.
Hm.

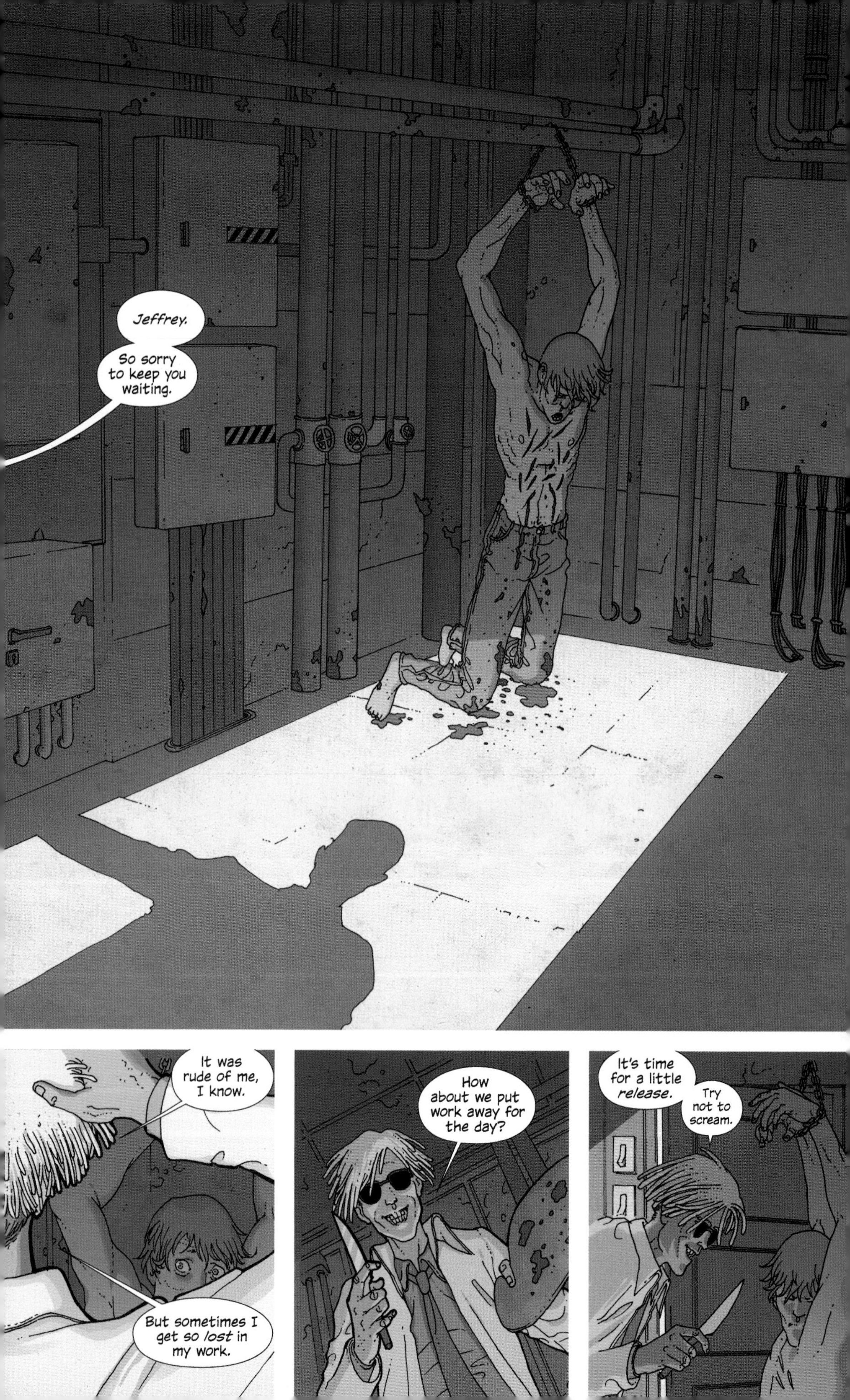

Jeffrey.
So sorry to keep you waiting.
It was rude of me, I know.
But sometimes I get so *lost* in my work.
How about we put work away for the day?
It's time for a little *release.*
Try not to scream.

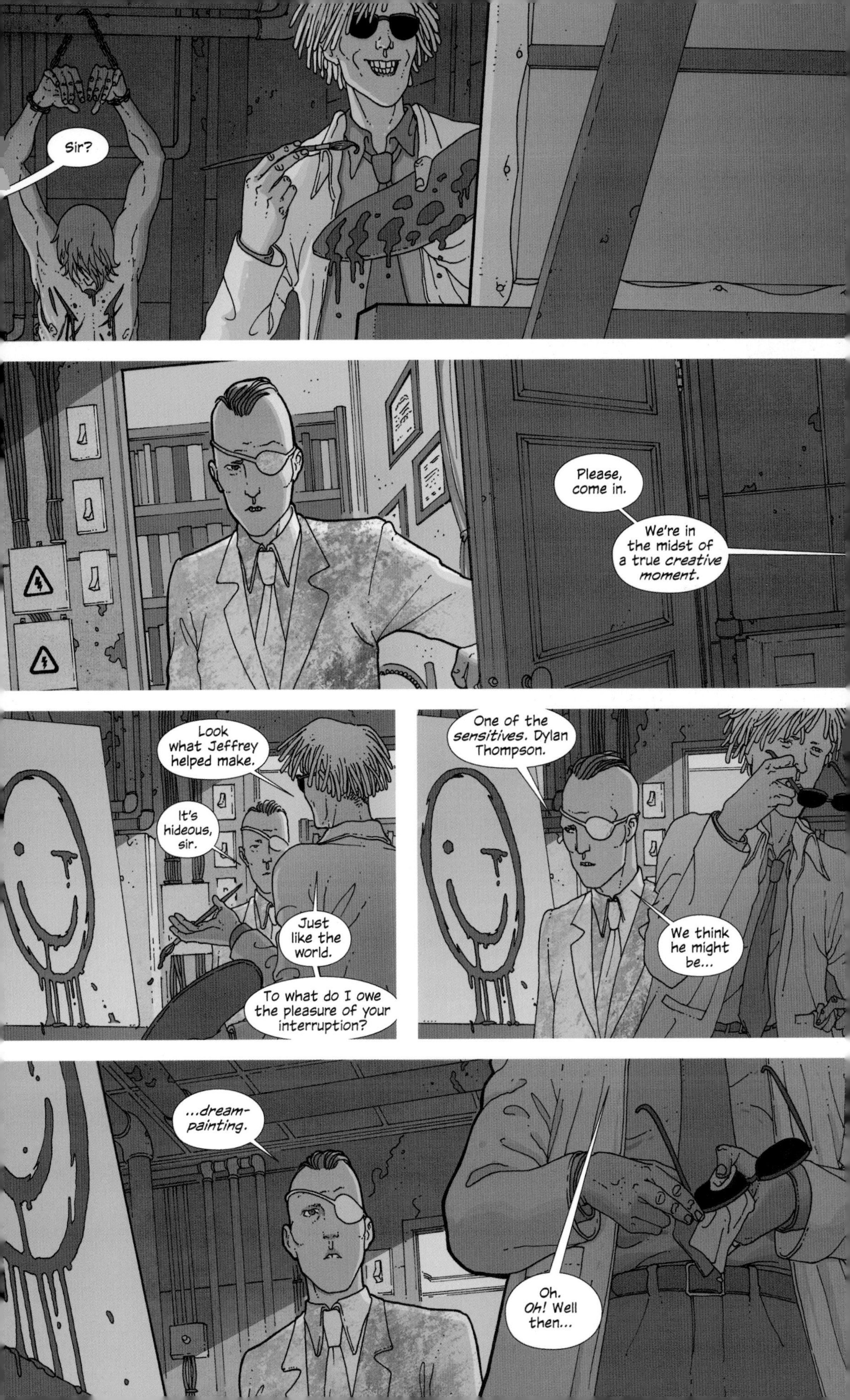
Sir?
Please, come in.
We're in the midst of a true *creative moment.*
Look what Jeffrey helped make.
It's hideous, sir.
Just like the world.
To what do I owe the pleasure of your interruption?
One of the *sensitives.* Dylan Thompson.
We think he might be...
...*dream-painting.*
Oh. *Oh!* Well then...

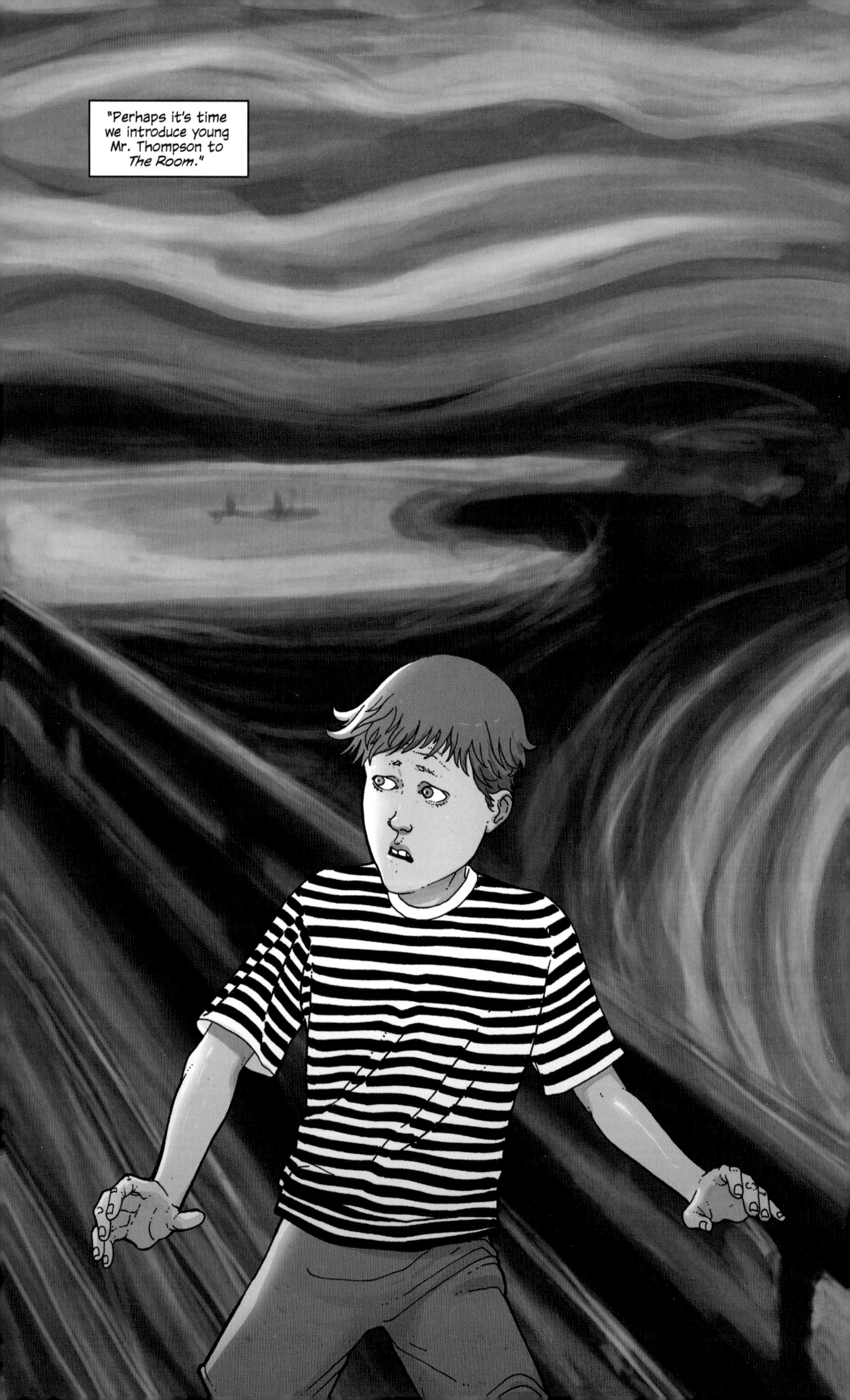
"Perhaps it's time we introduce young Mr. Thompson to *The Room.*"

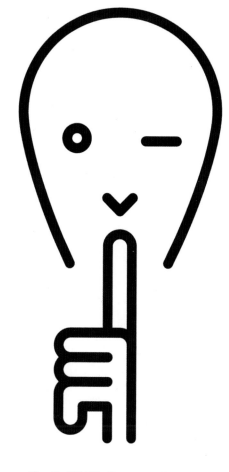

SOTTO VOCE

Chapter 3

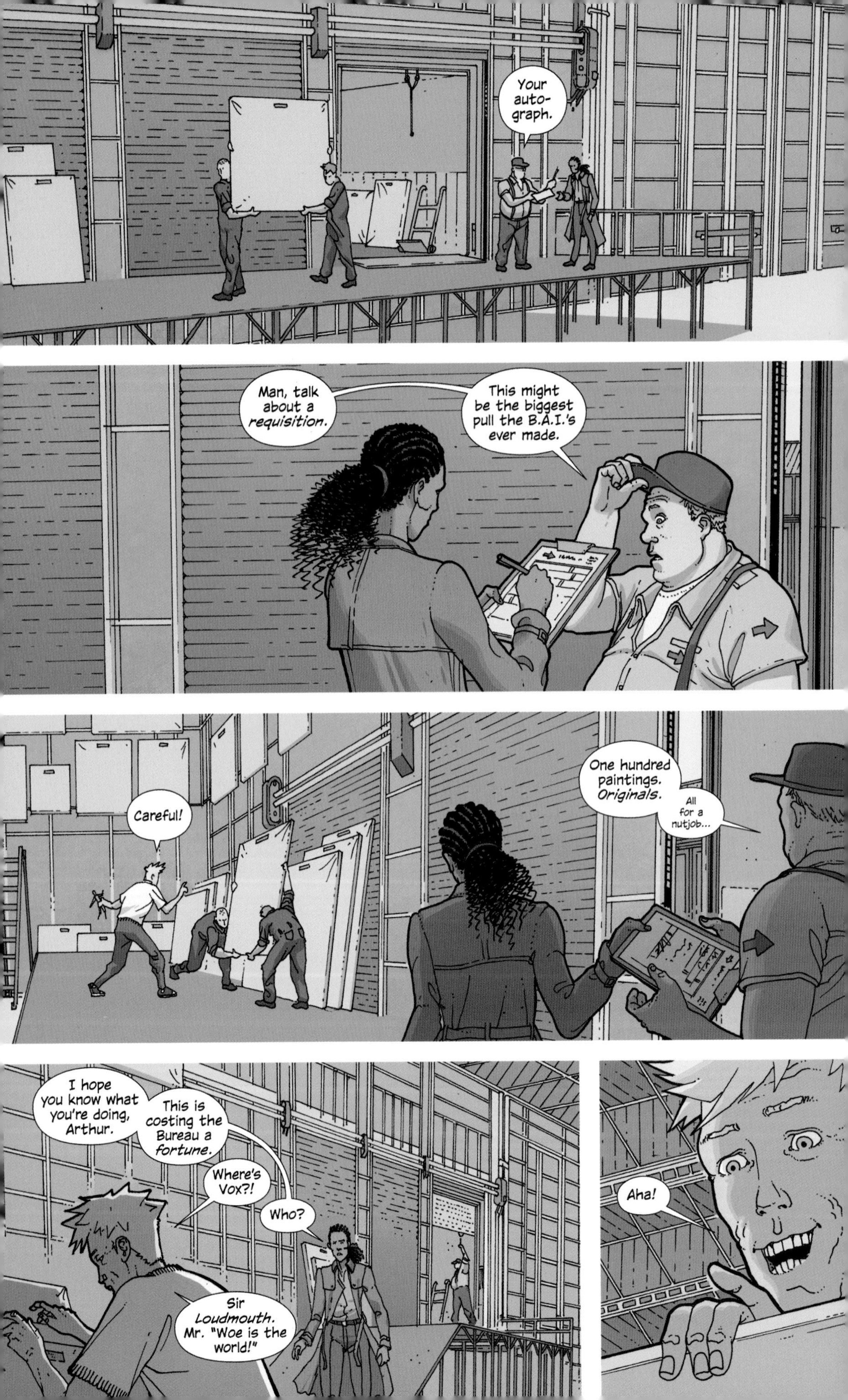

Your autograph.
Man, talk about a *requisition*.
This might be the biggest pull the B.A.I.'s ever made.
Careful!
One hundred paintings. *Originals*.
All for a nutjob...
I hope you know what you're doing, Arthur.
This is costing the Bureau a *fortune*.
Where's Vox?!
Who?
Sir *Loudmouth*. Mr. "Woe is the world!"
Aha!

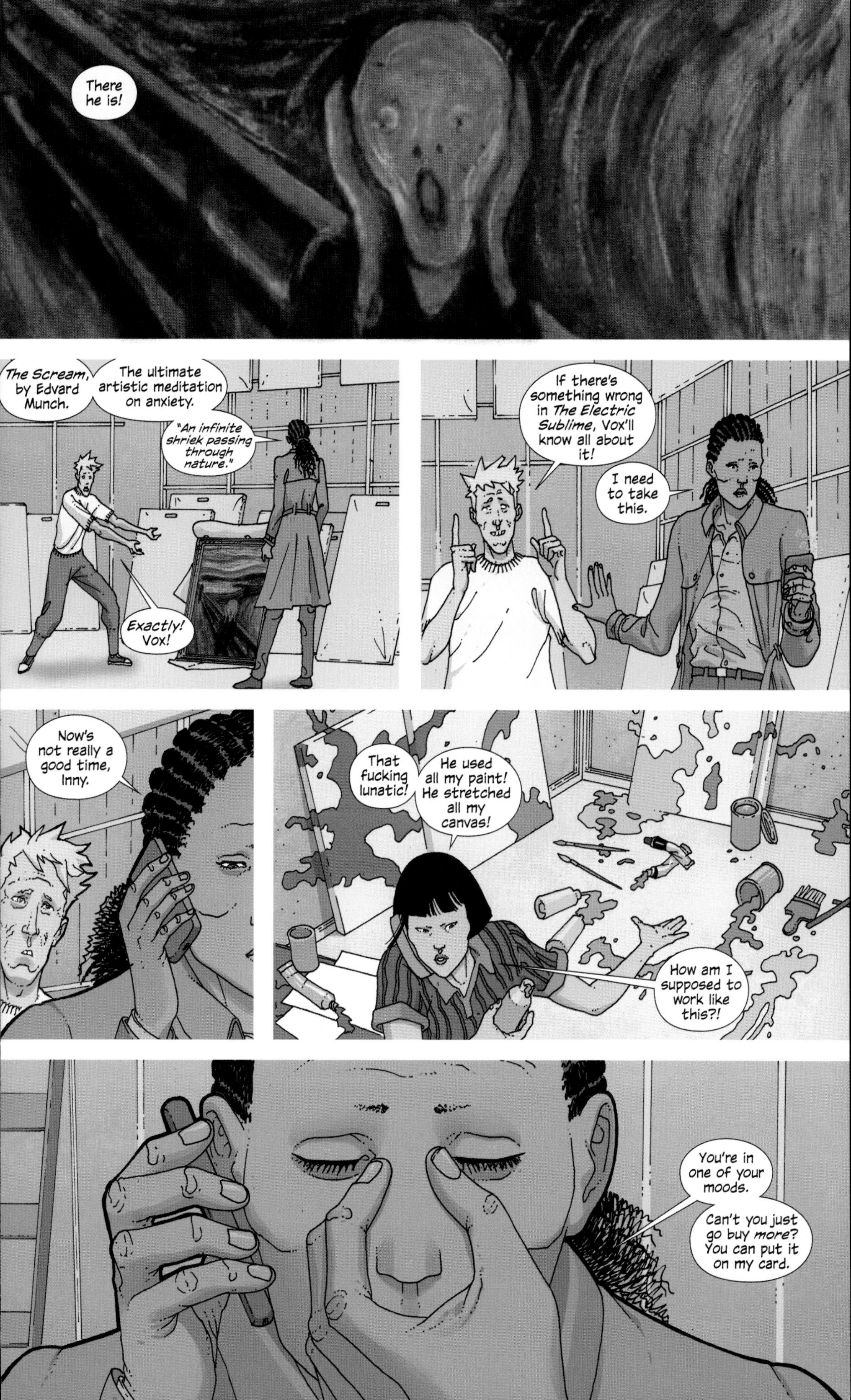
There he is!
The Scream, by Edvard Munch.
The ultimate artistic meditation on anxiety.
"An infinite shriek passing through nature."
Exactly! Vox!
If there's something wrong in The Electric Sublime, Vox'll know all about it!
I need to take this.
Now's not really a good time, Inny.
That fucking lunatic!
He used all my paint! He stretched all my canvas!
How am I supposed to work like this?!
You're in one of your moods.
Can't you just go buy more? You can put it on my card.

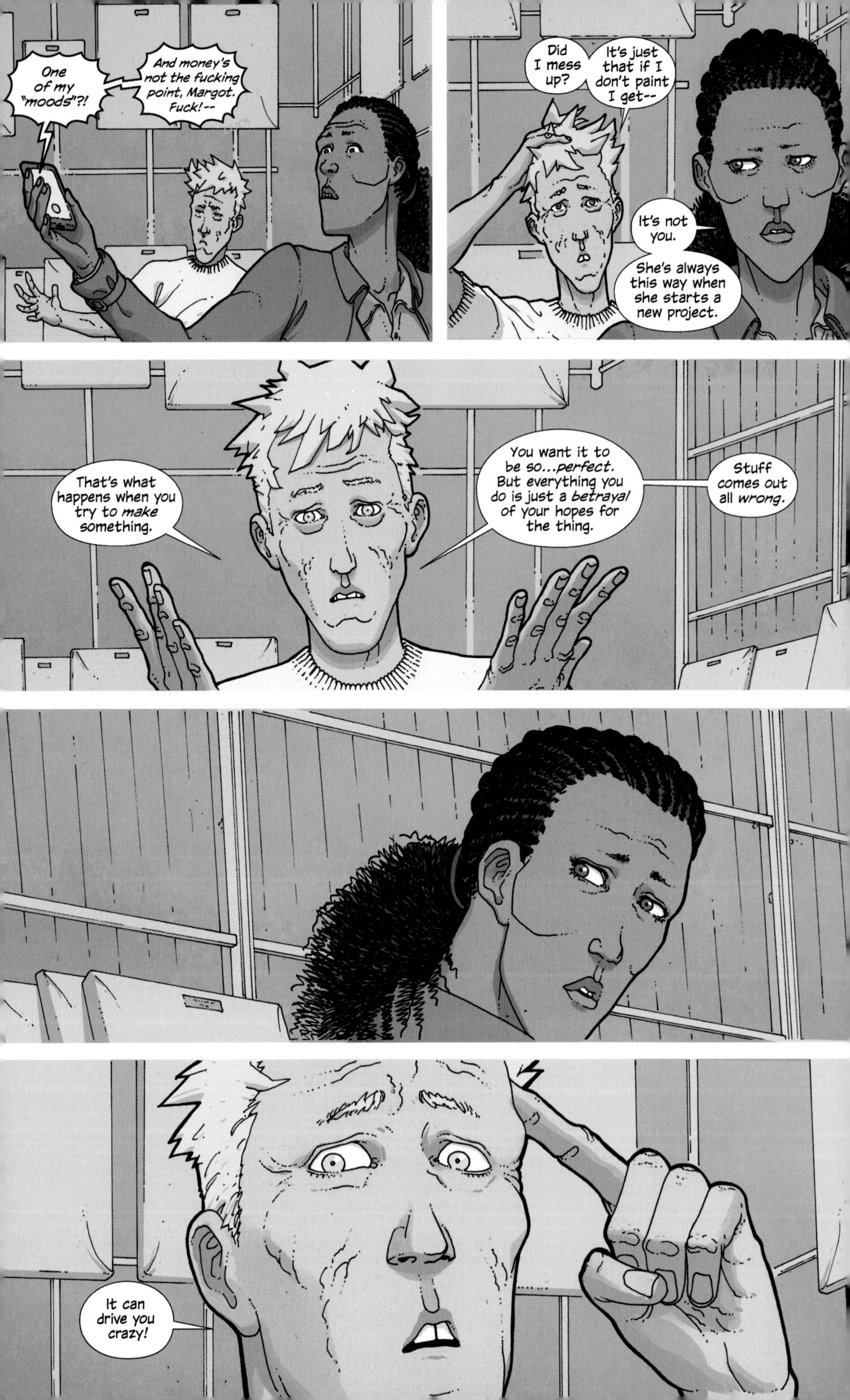
One of my "moods"?!
And money's not the fucking point, Margot. Fuck!--
Did I mess up?
It's just that if I don't paint I get--
It's not you.
She's always this way when she starts a new project.
That's what happens when you try to *make* something.
You want it to be so...*perfect*. But everything you do is just a *betrayal* of your hopes for the thing.
Stuff comes out all *wrong*.
It can drive you crazy!

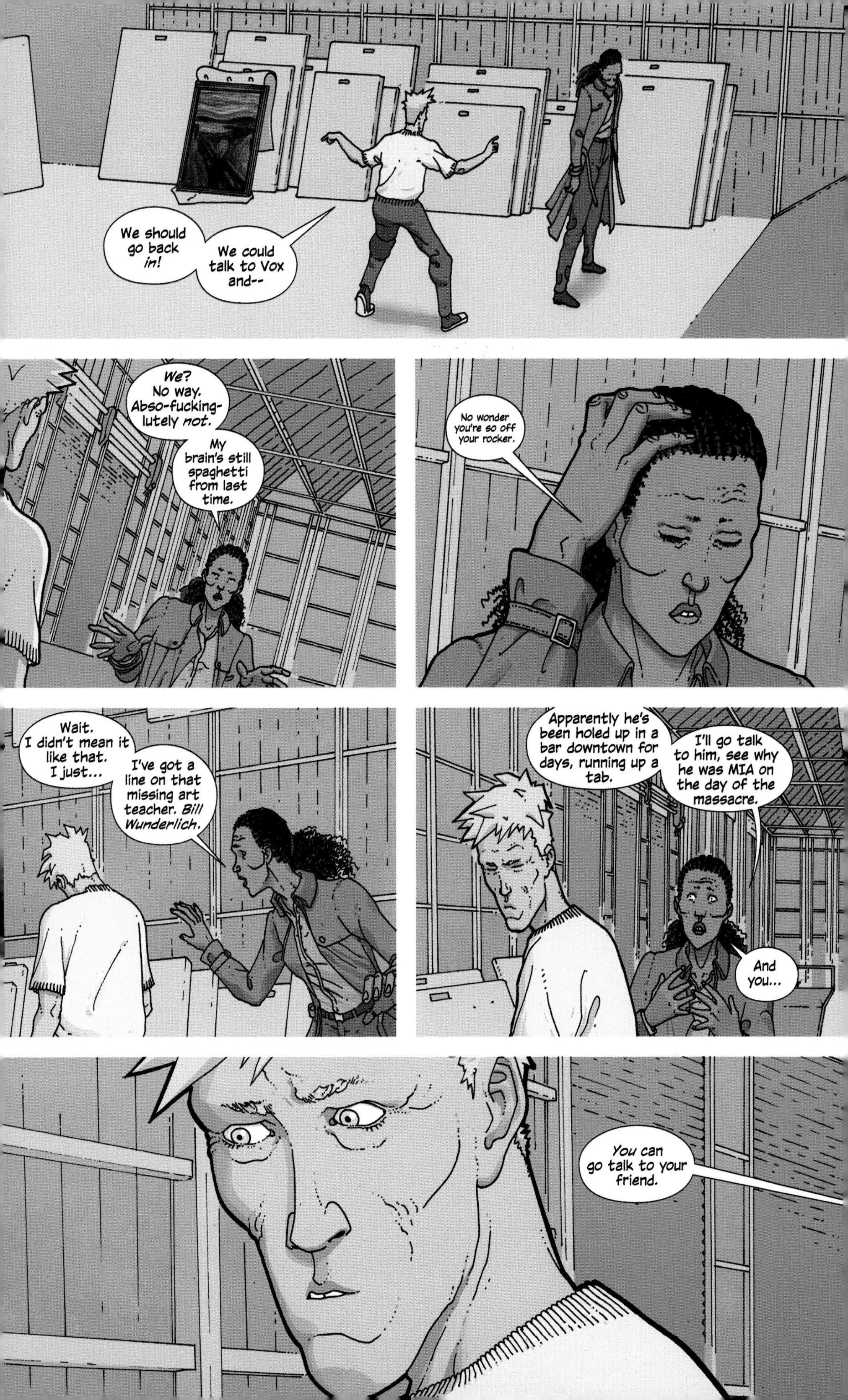
We should go back *in!*
We could talk to Vox and--
We? No way. Abso-fucking-lutely *not.*
My brain's still spaghetti from last time.
No wonder you're so off your rocker.
Wait. I didn't mean it like that. I just...
I've got a line on that missing art teacher. *Bill Wunderlich.*
Apparently he's been holed up in a bar downtown for days, running up a tab.
I'll go talk to him, see why he was MIA on the day of the massacre.
And you...
You can go talk to your friend.

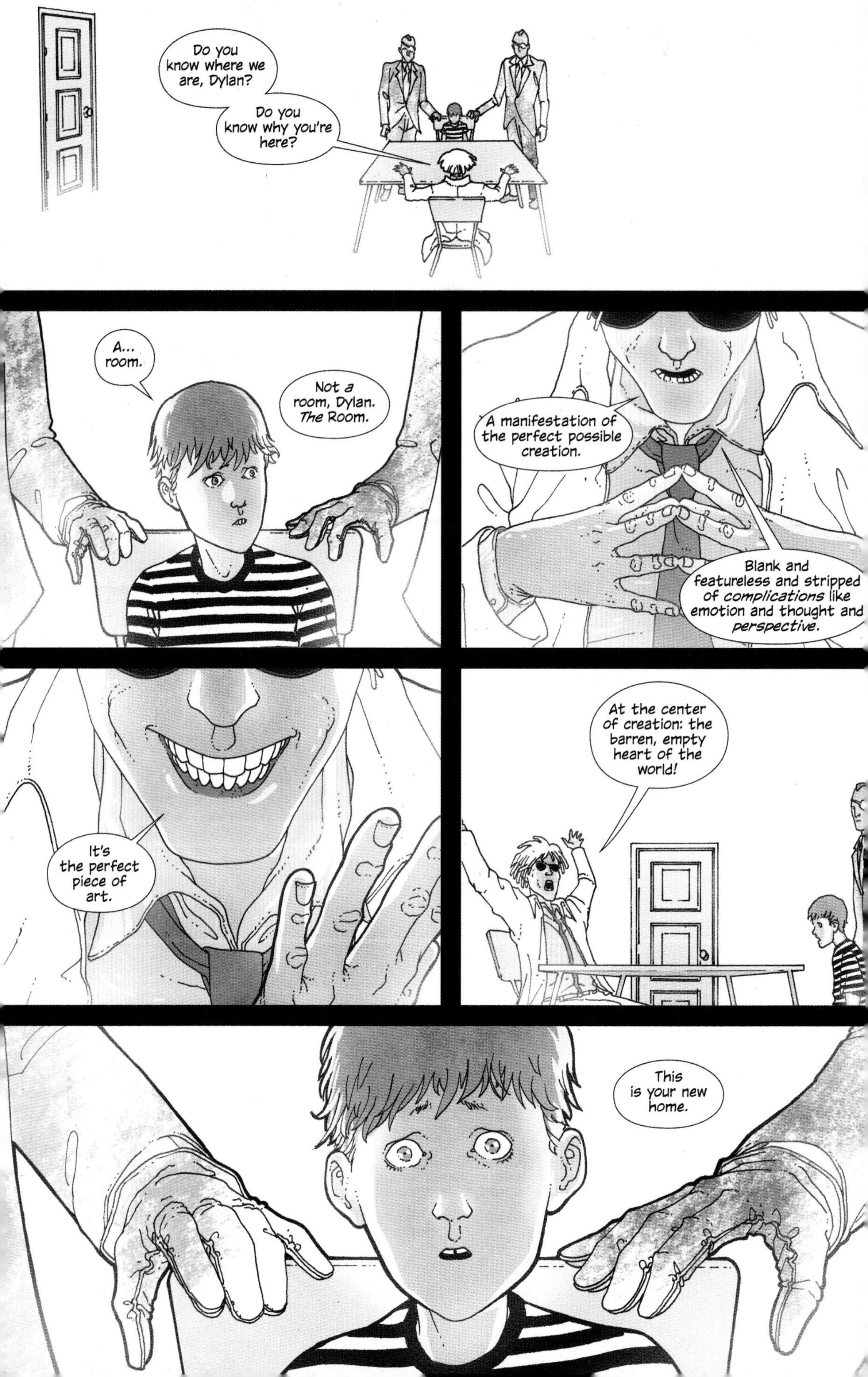
Do you know where we are, Dylan?
Do you know why you're here?
A... room.
Not *a* room, Dylan. *The* Room.
A manifestation of the perfect possible creation.
Blank and featureless and stripped of *complications* like emotion and thought and *perspective.*
It's the perfect piece of art.
At the center of creation: the barren, empty heart of the world!
This is your new home.

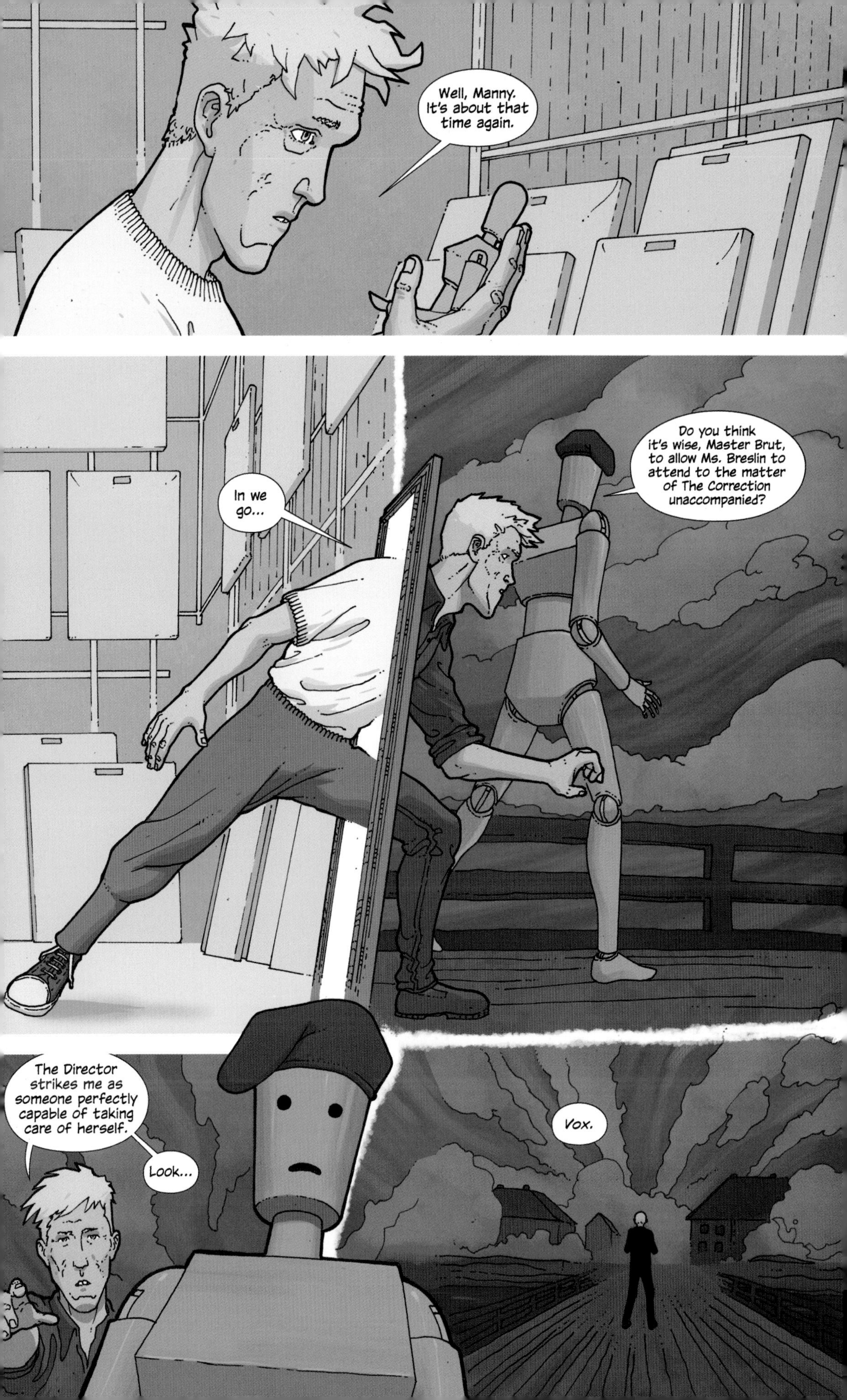
Well, Manny. It's about that time again.
In we go...
Do you think it's wise, Master Brut, to allow Ms. Breslin to attend to the matter of The Correction unaccompanied?
The Director strikes me as someone perfectly capable of taking care of herself.
Look...
Vox.

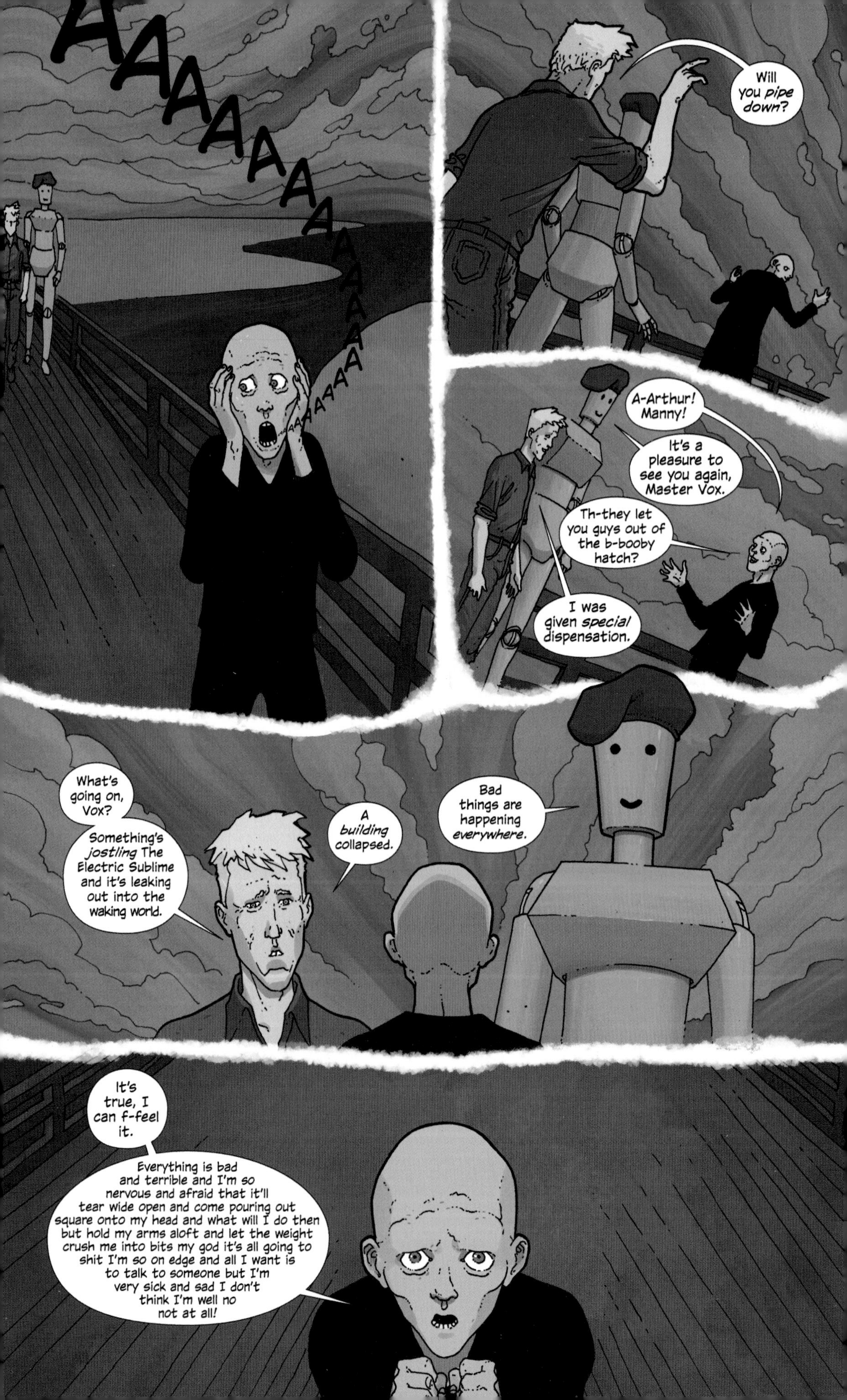
AAAAAAAAAAAAAAAAAA
Will you *pipe* down?
A-Arthur! Manny!
It's a pleasure to see you again, Master Vox.
Th-they let you guys out of the b-booby hatch?
I was given *special* dispensation.
What's going on, Vox?
Something's *jostling* The Electric Sublime and it's leaking out into the waking world.
A *building* collapsed.
Bad things are happening *everywhere*.
It's true, I can f-feel it.
Everything is bad and terrible and I'm so nervous and afraid that it'll tear wide open and come pouring out square onto my head and what will I do then but hold my arms aloft and let the weight crush me into bits my god it's all going to shit I'm so on edge and all I want is to talk to someone but I'm very sick and sad I don't think I'm well no not at all!

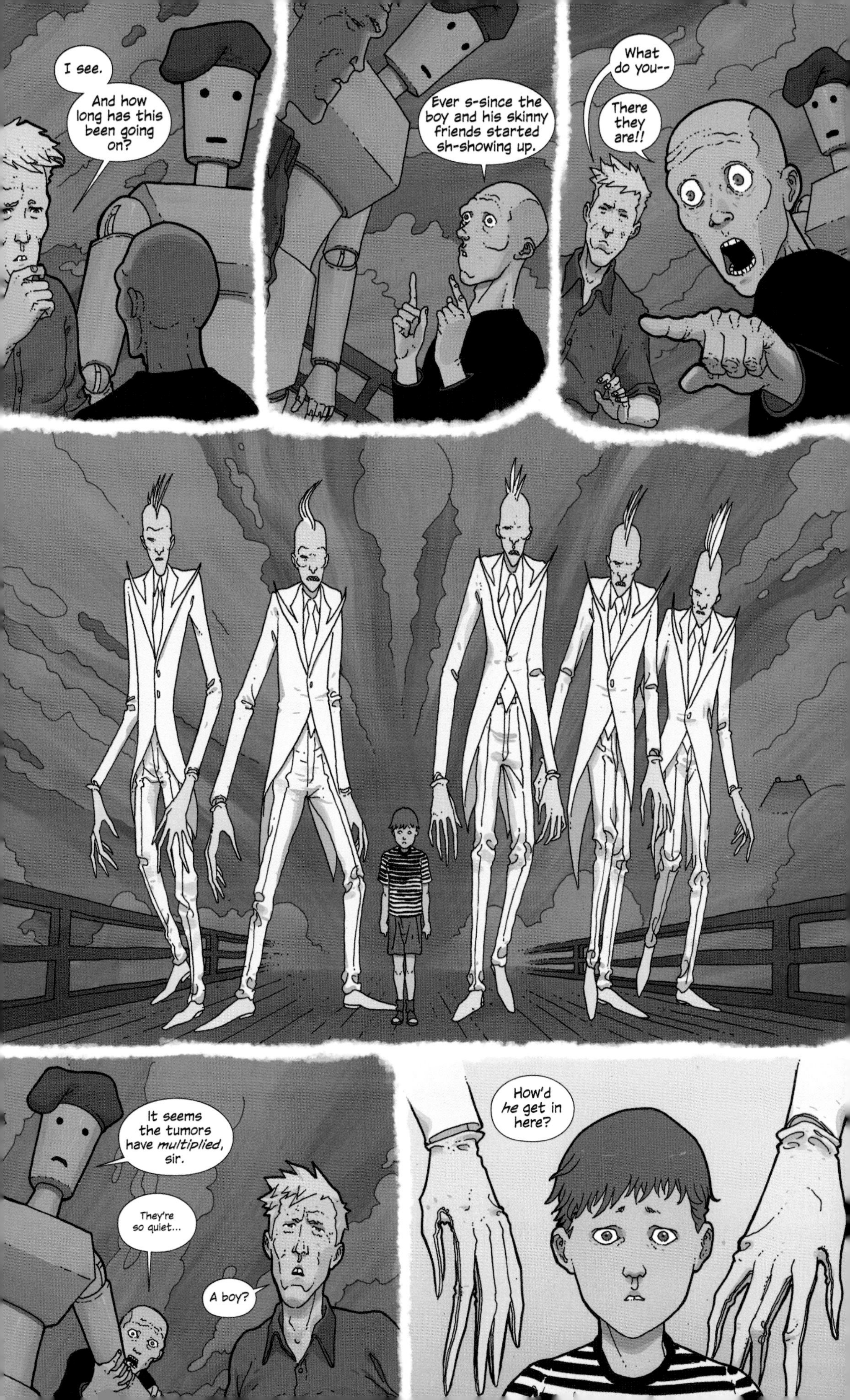
I see.
And how long has this been going on?
Ever s-since the boy and his skinny friends started sh-showing up.
What do you--
There they are!!
It seems the tumors have *multiplied*, sir.
They're so quiet...
A boy?
How'd *he* get in here?

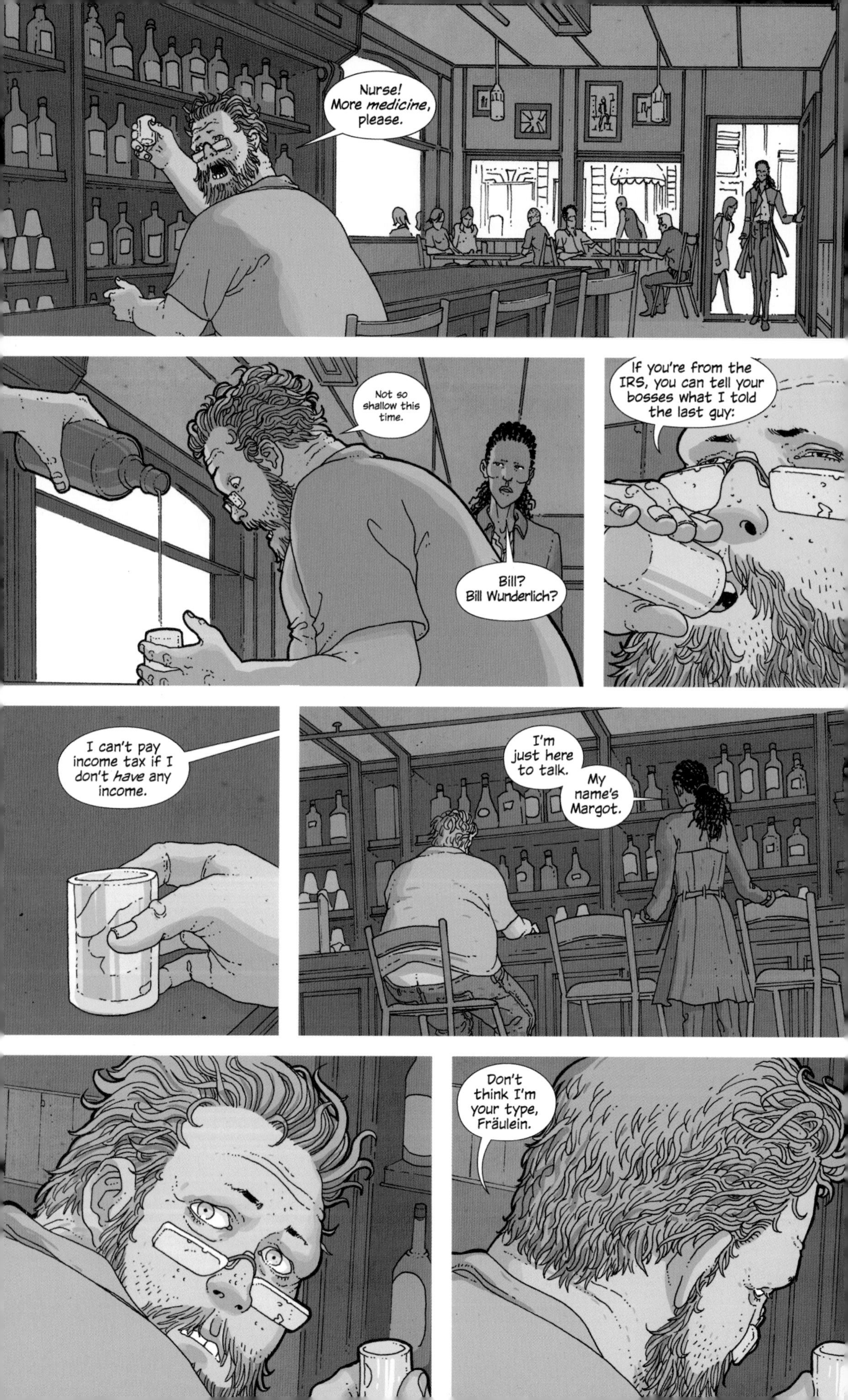
Nurse!
More *medicine*, please.
Not so shallow this time.
Bill?
Bill Wunderlich?
If you're from the IRS, you can tell your bosses what I told the last guy:
I can't pay income tax if I don't *have* any income.
I'm just here to talk.
My name's Margot.
Don't think I'm your type, Fräulein.

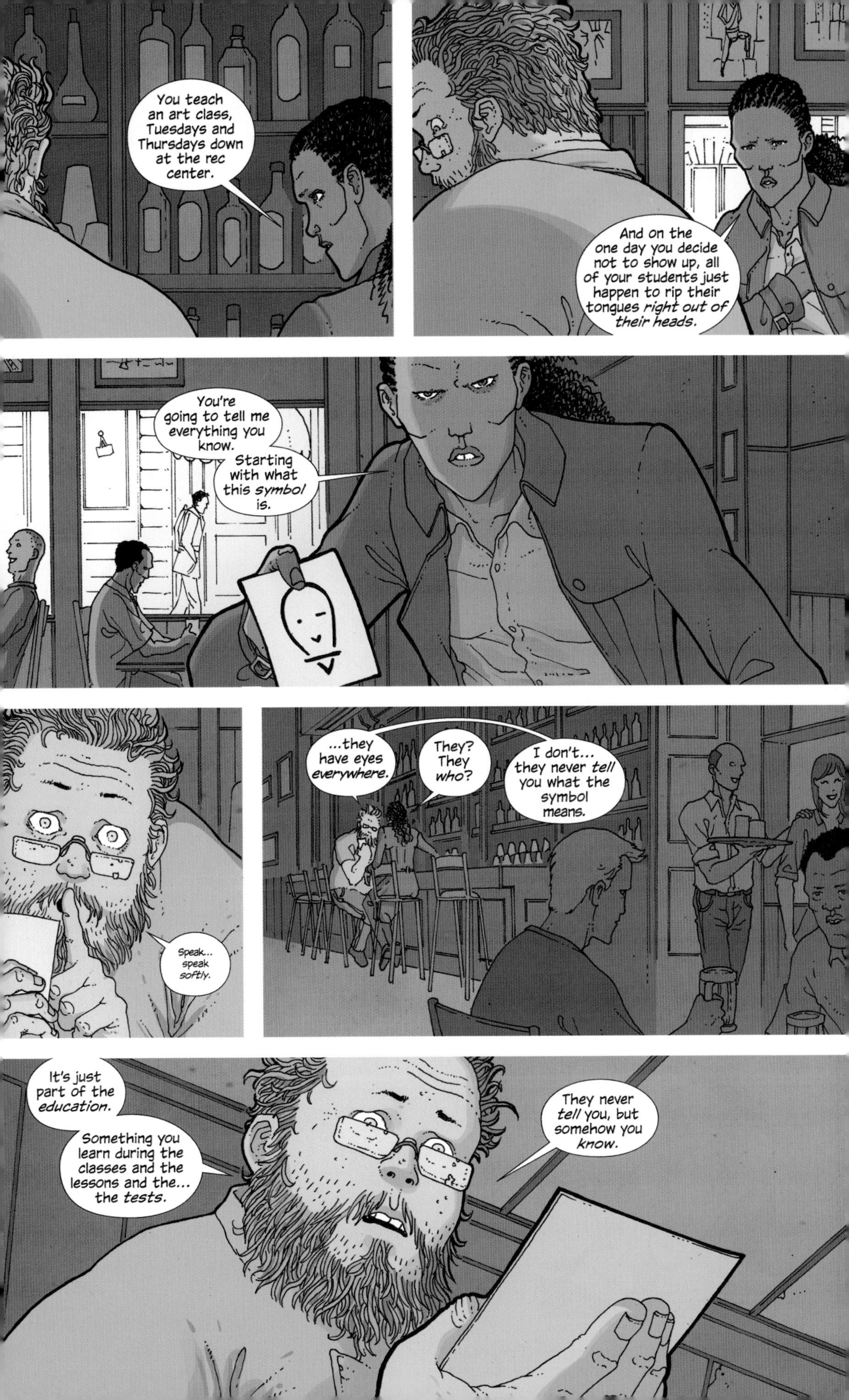
You teach an art class, Tuesdays and Thursdays down at the rec center.
And on the one day you decide not to show up, all of your students just happen to rip their tongues *right out of their heads.*
You're going to tell me everything you know.
Starting with what this *symbol* is.
Speak... speak *softly.*
...they have eyes *everywhere.*
They? They *who?*
I don't... they never *tell* you what the symbol means.
It's just part of the *education.*
Something you learn during the classes and the lessons and the... the *tests.*
They never *tell* you, but somehow you *know.*

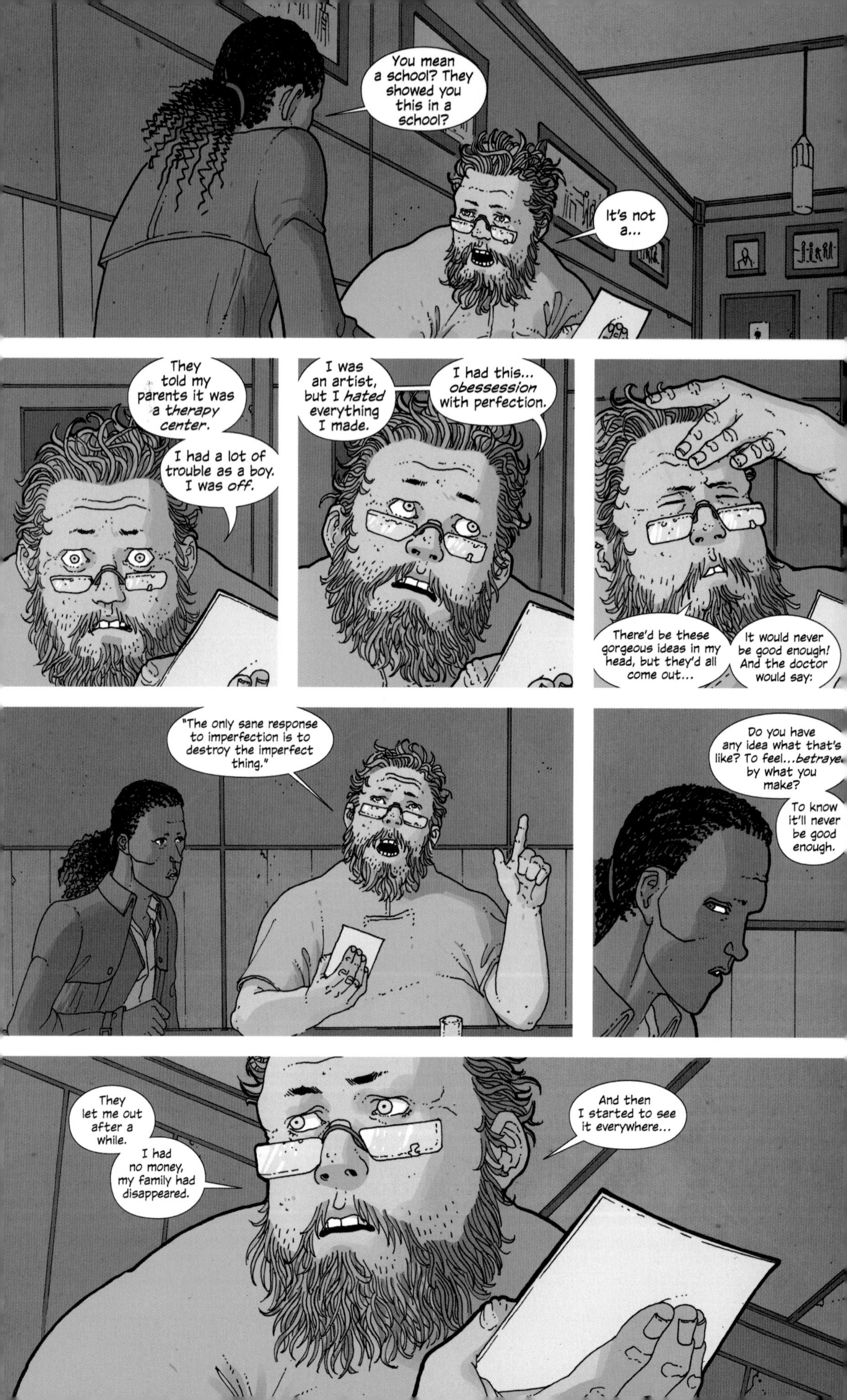
You mean a school? They showed you this in a school?
It's not a...
They told my parents it was a *therapy center*.
I had a lot of trouble as a boy. I was *off*.
I was an artist, but I *hated* everything I made.
I had this... *obsession* with perfection.
There'd be these gorgeous ideas in my head, but they'd all come out...
It would never be good enough! And the doctor would say:
"The only sane response to imperfection is to destroy the imperfect thing."
Do you have any idea what that's like? To feel...*betraye* by what you make?
To know it'll never be good enough.
They let me out after a while.
I had no money, my family had disappeared.
And then I started to see it everywhere...

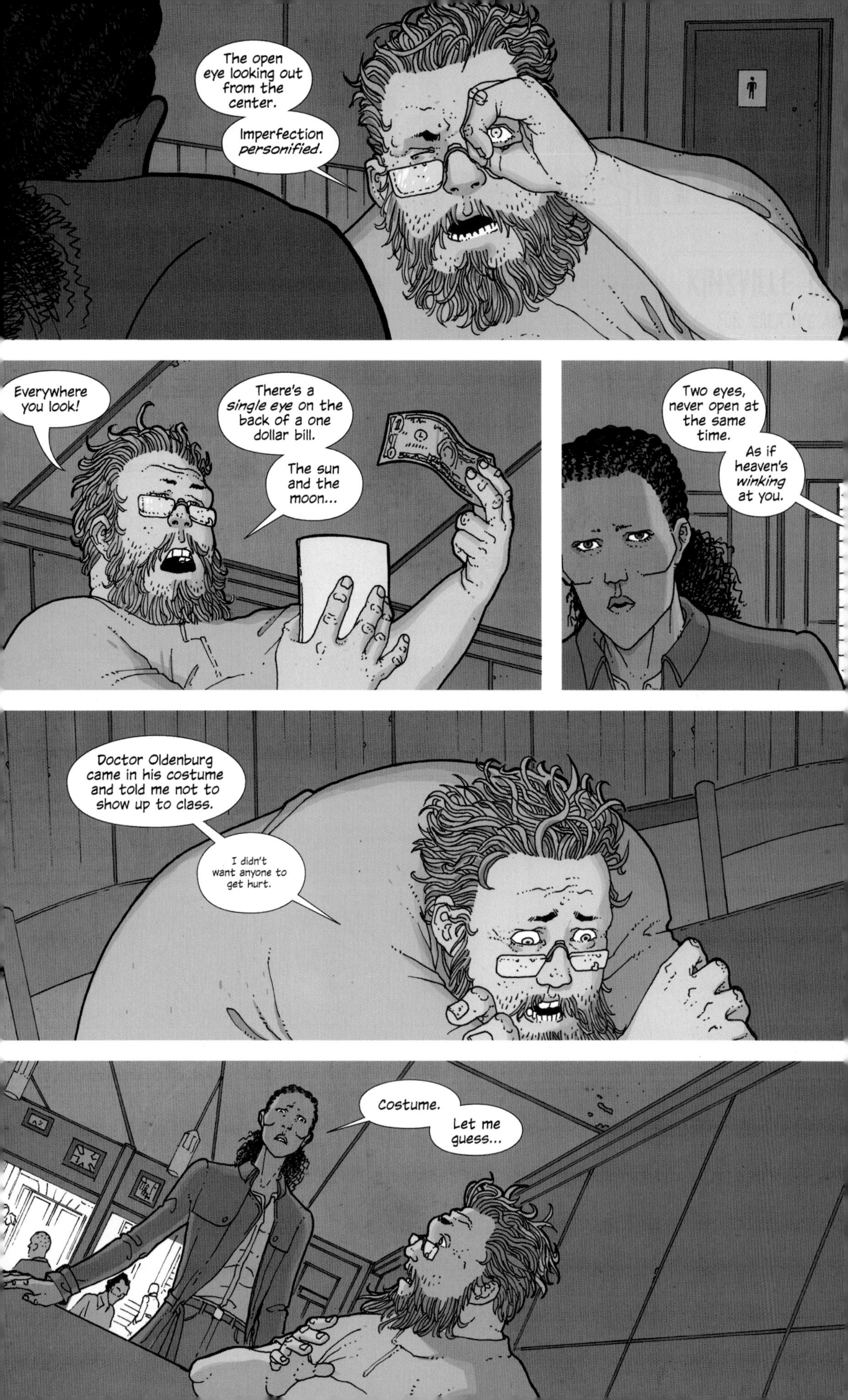
The open eye looking out from the center.
Imperfection *personified.*
Everywhere you look!
There's a *single eye* on the back of a one dollar bill.
The sun and the moon...
Two eyes, never open at the same time.
As if heaven's *winking* at you.
Doctor Oldenburg came in his costume and told me not to show up to class.
I didn't want anyone to get hurt.
Costume.
Let me guess...

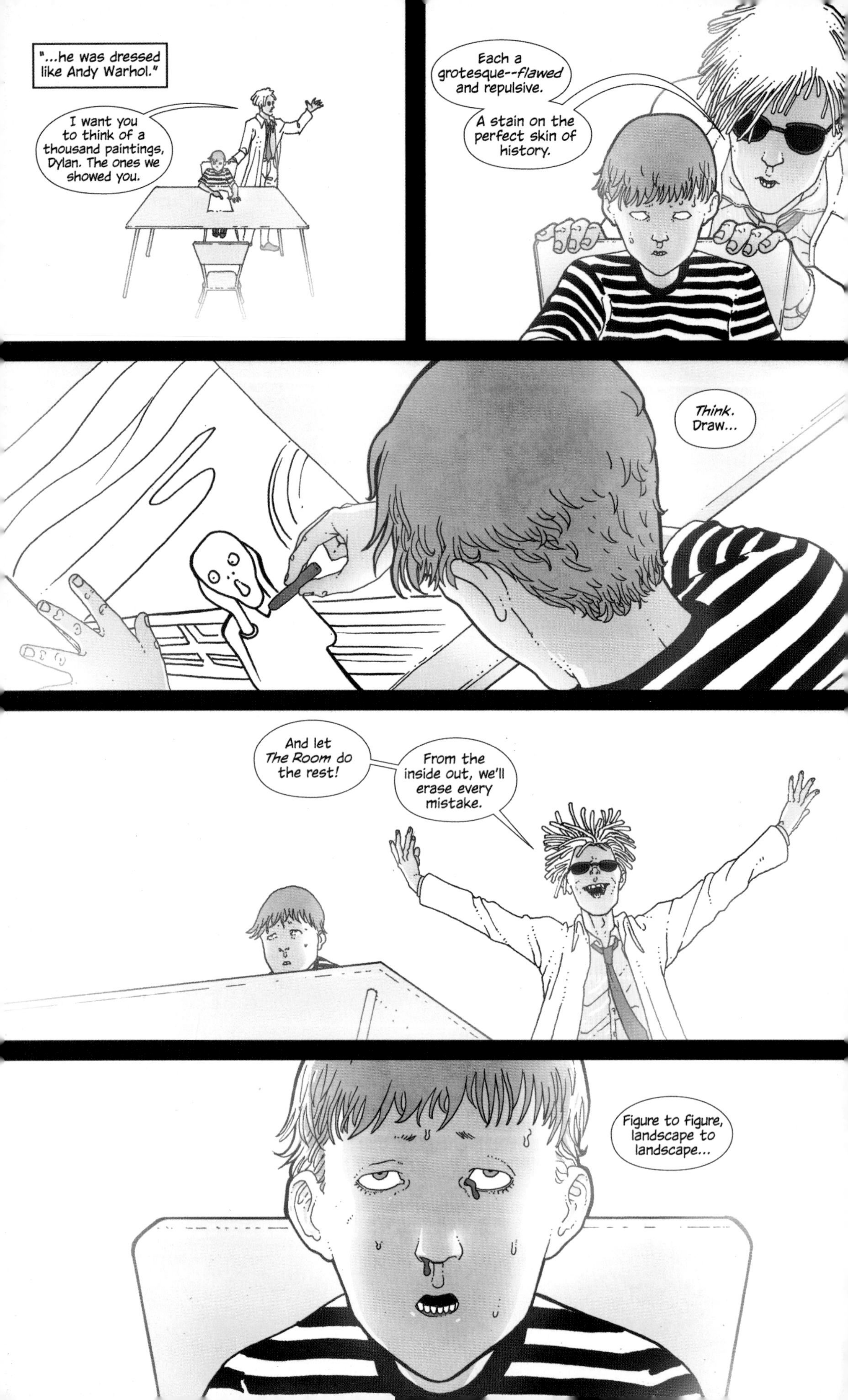
"...he was dressed like Andy Warhol."
I want you to think of a thousand paintings, Dylan. The ones we showed you.
Each a grotesque--*flawed* and repulsive.
A stain on the perfect skin of history.
Think. Draw...
And let *The Room* do the rest!
From the inside out, we'll erase every mistake.
Figure to figure, landscape to landscape...

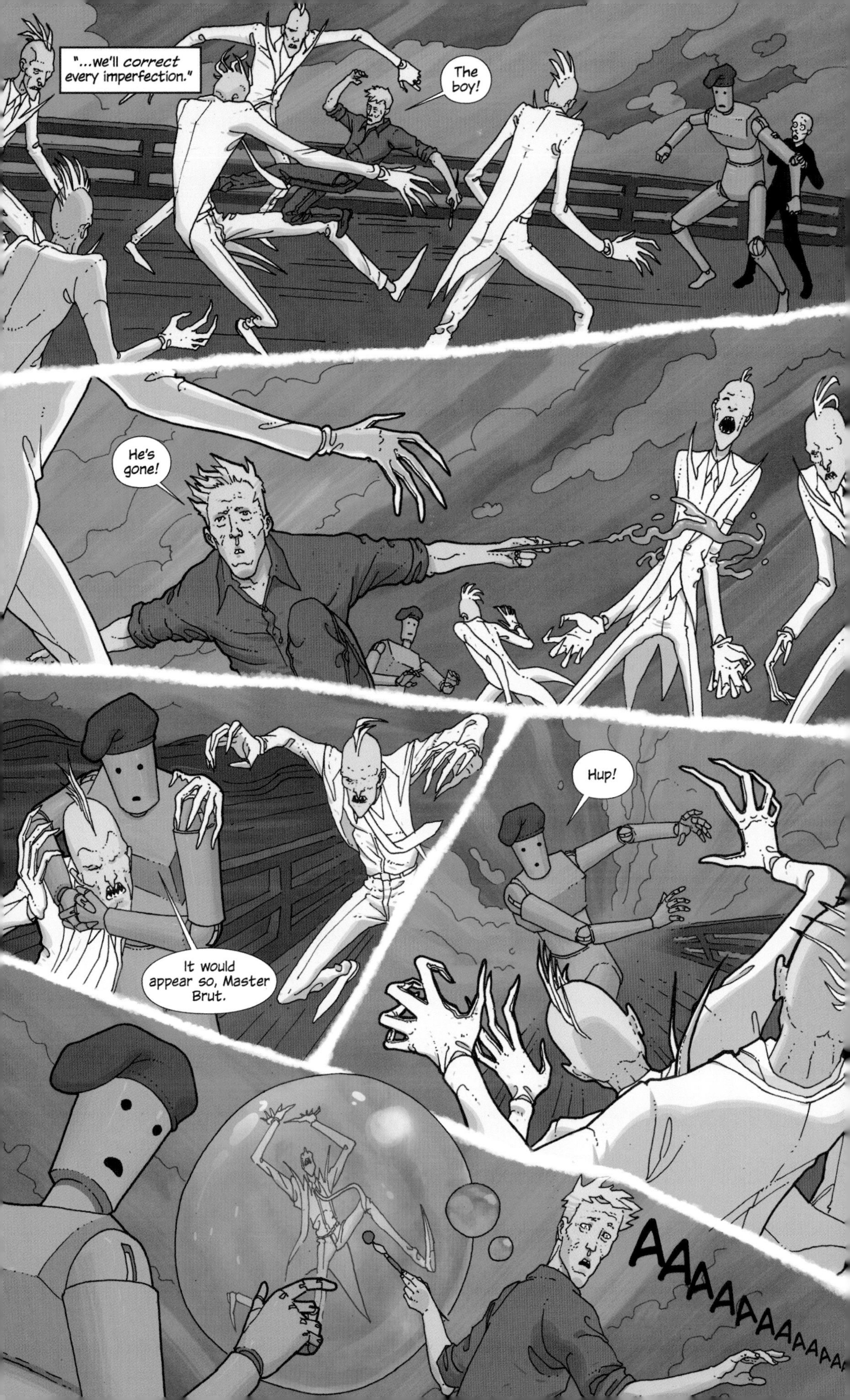
"...we'll correct every imperfection."
The boy!
He's gone!
It would appear so, Master Brut.
Hup!
AAAAAAAAAAAA

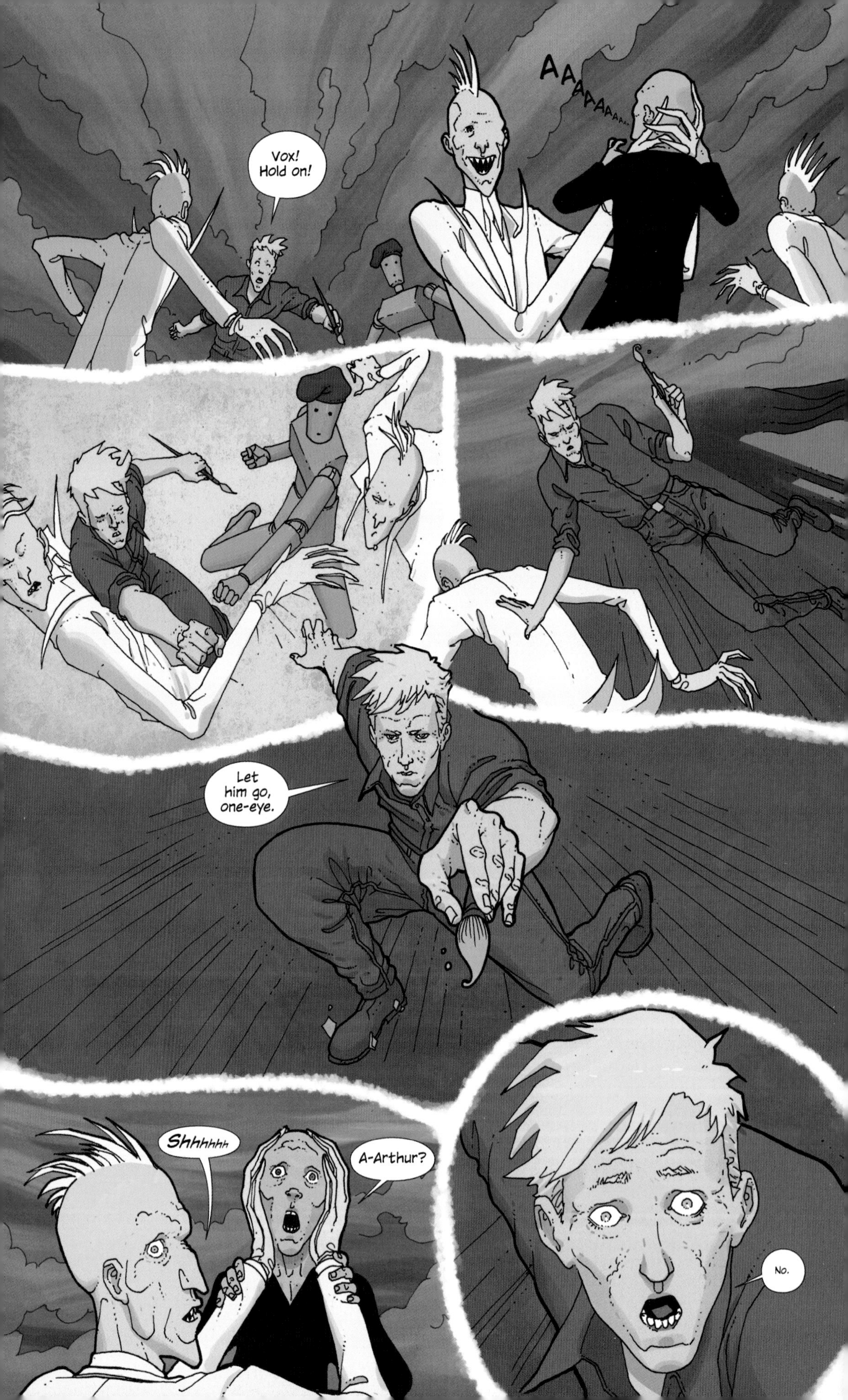
Vox! Hold on!
AAAAAAAA...
Let him go, one-eye.
Shhhhhh
A-Arthur?
No.

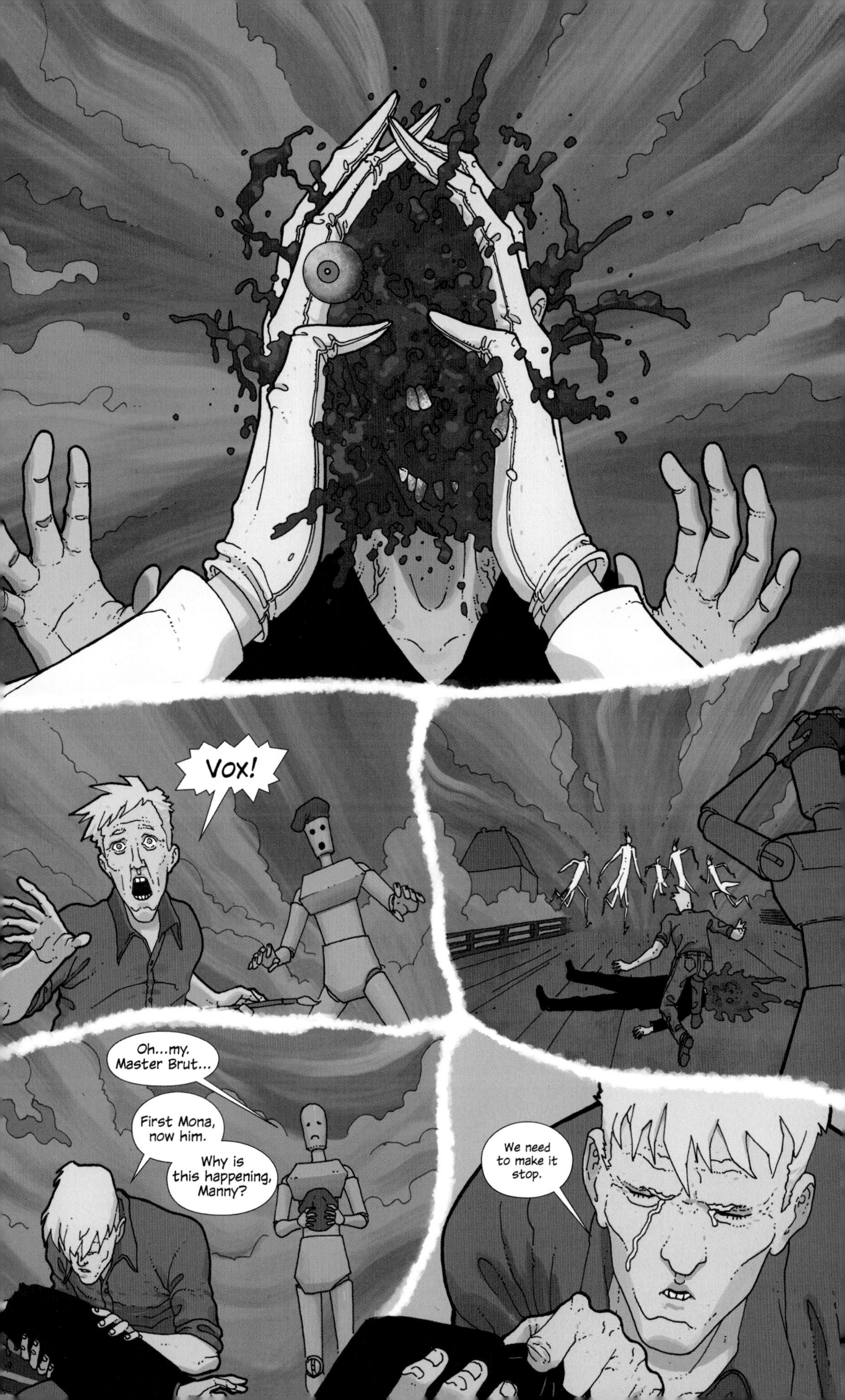
VOX!
Oh...my. Master Brut...
First Mona, now him.
Why is this happening, Manny?
We need to make it stop.

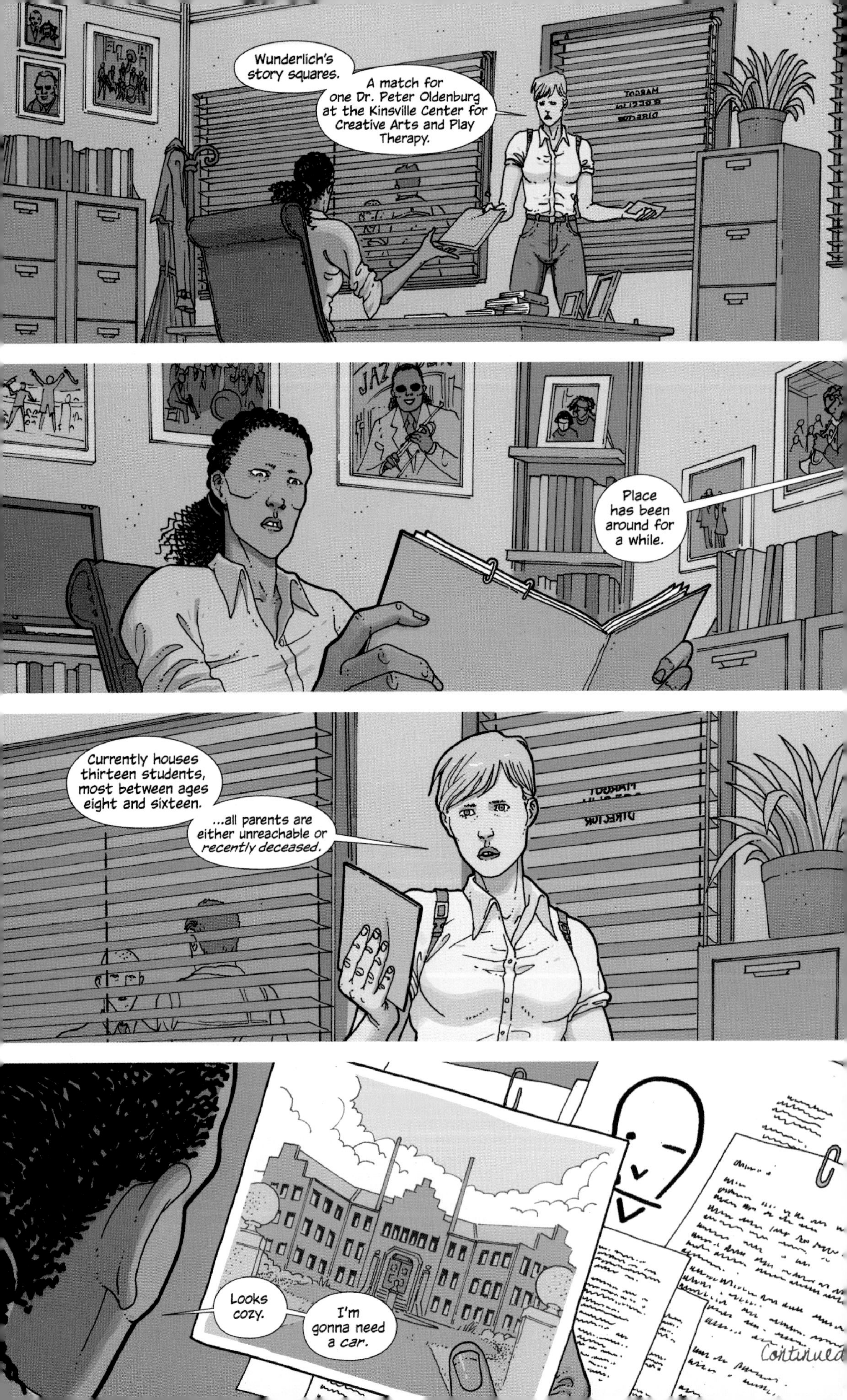
Wunderlich's story squares.
A match for one Dr. Peter Oldenburg at the Kinsville Center for Creative Arts and Play Therapy.
Place has been around for a while.
Currently houses thirteen students, most between ages eight and sixteen.
...all parents are either unreachable or *recently deceased.*
Looks cozy.
I'm gonna need a *car.*
Continued

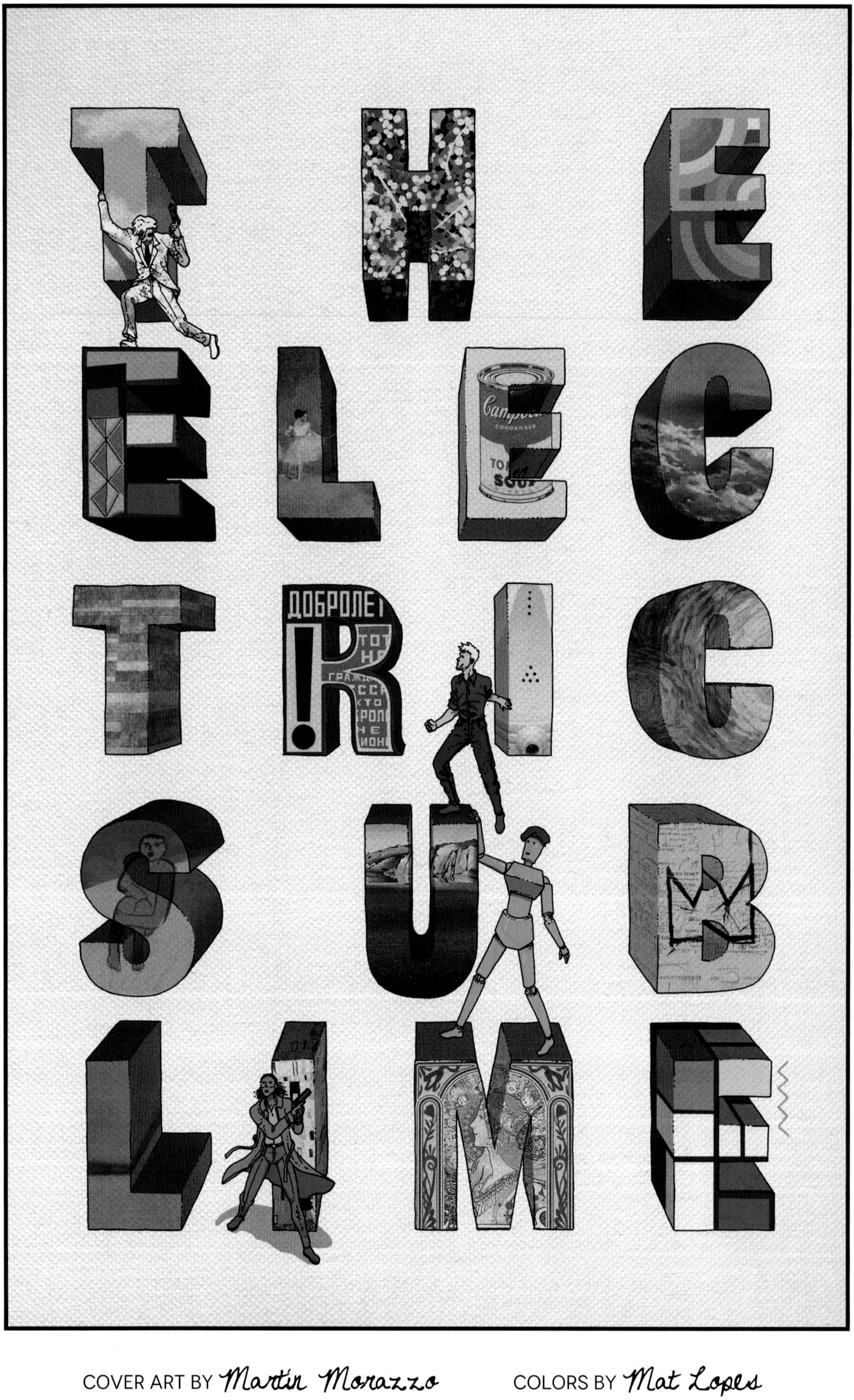
THE ELECTRIC SUBLIME
ДОБРОЛЕТ
CONDENSED

COVER ART BY *Martin Morazzo* COLORS BY *Mat Lopes*

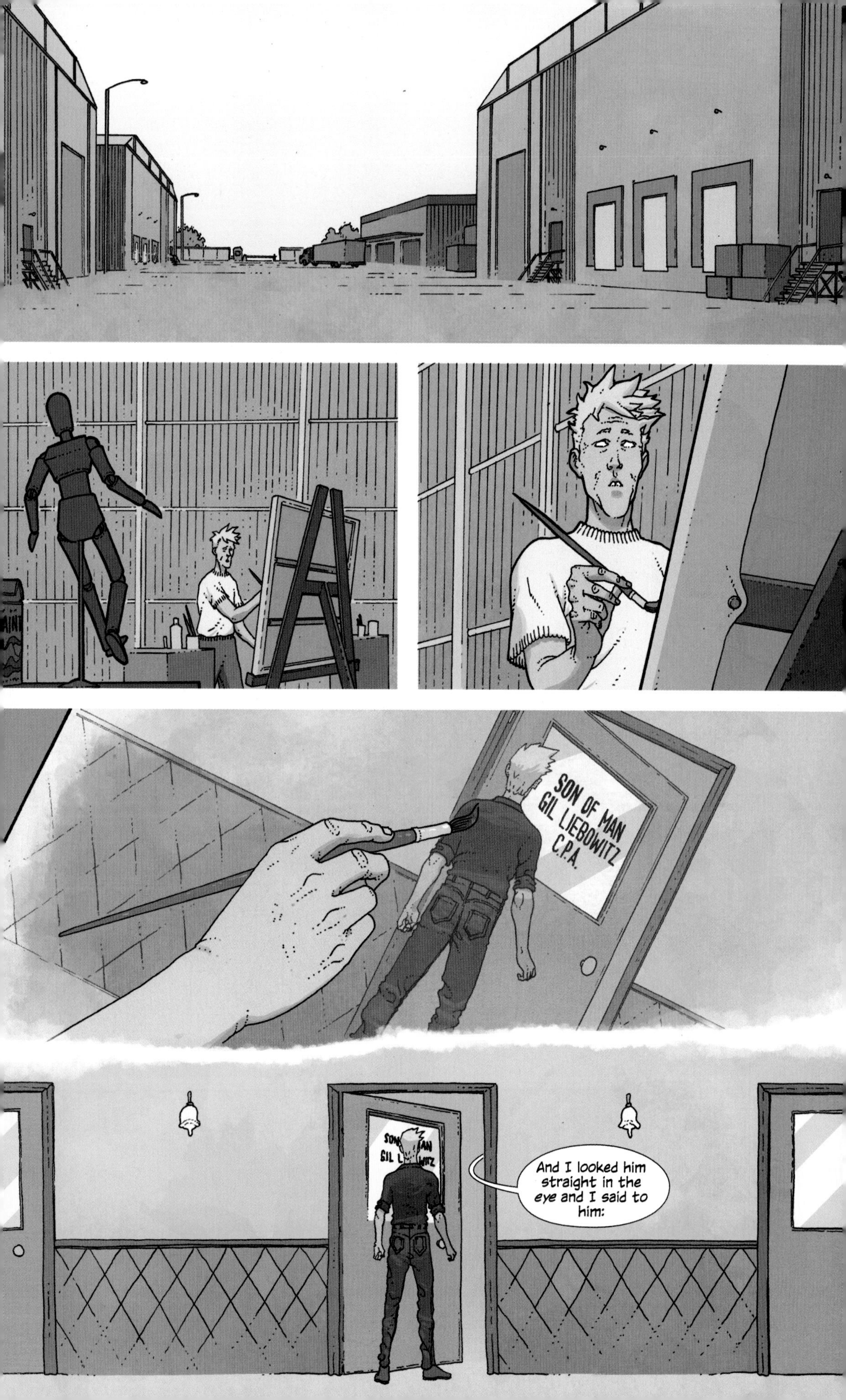
PAINT
SON OF MAN
GIL LIEBOWITZ
C.P.A.
And I looked him straight in the *eye* and I said to him:

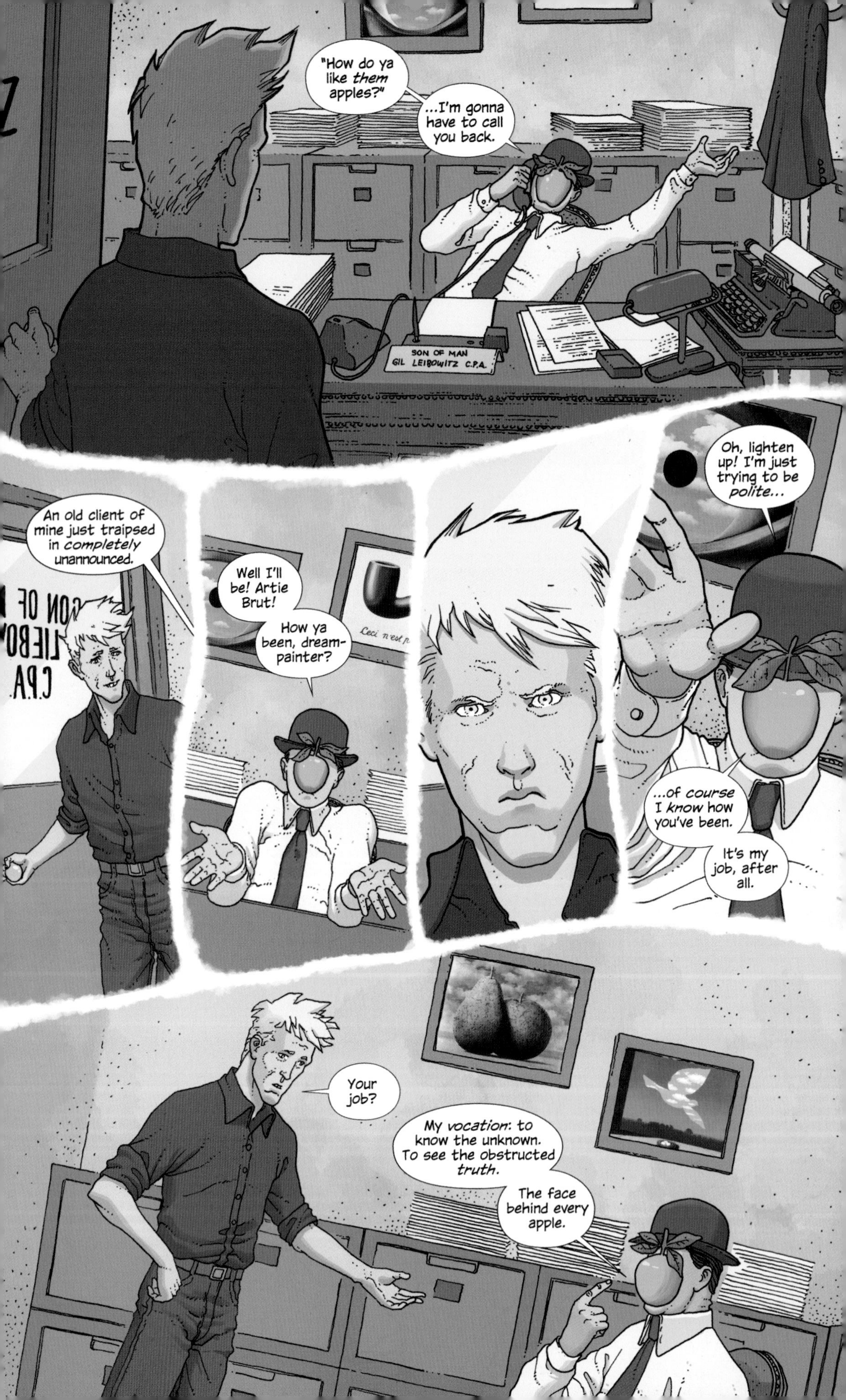
"How do ya like *them* apples?"
...I'm gonna have to call you back.
SON OF MAN
GIL LEIBOWITZ C.P.A.
An old client of mine just traipsed in *completely* unannounced.
Well I'll be! Artie Brut!
How ya been, dream-painter?
Ceci n'est p
Oh, lighten up! I'm just trying to be *polite*...
...of *course* I *know* how you've been.
It's my job, after all.
Your job?
My *vocation*: to know the unknown. To see the obstructed *truth*.
The face behind every apple.

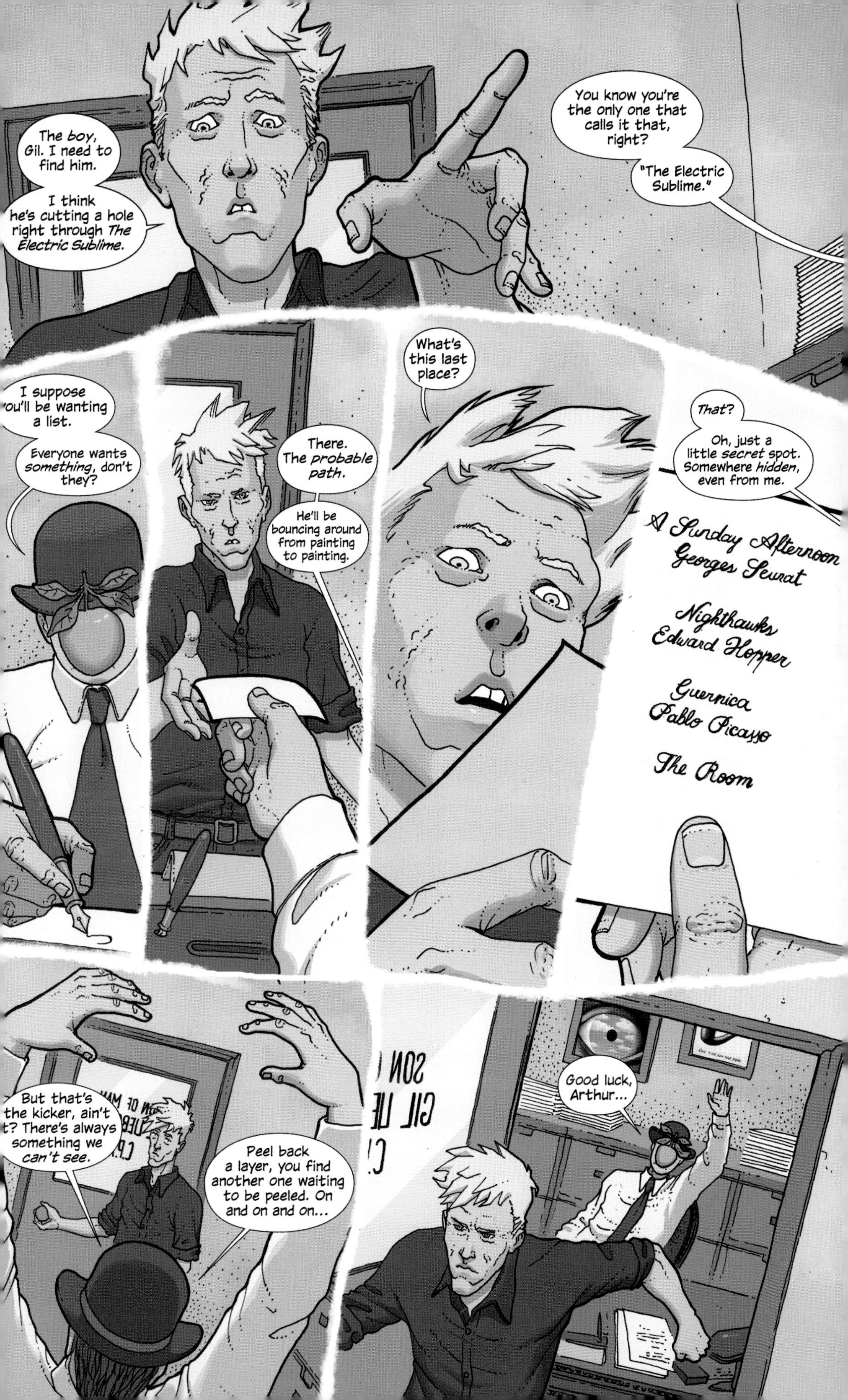
The *boy*, Gil. I need to find him.
I think he's cutting a hole right through *The Electric Sublime*.
You know you're the only one that calls it that, right?
"The Electric Sublime."
I suppose you'll be wanting a list.
Everyone wants *something*, don't they?
There. The *probable path*.
He'll be bouncing around from painting to painting.
What's this last place?
That?
Oh, just a little *secret* spot. Somewhere *hidden*, even from me.
A Sunday Afternoon
Georges Seurat
Nighthawks
Edward Hopper
Guernica
Pablo Picasso
The Room
But that's the kicker, ain't it? There's always something we *can't see*.
Peel back a layer, you find another one waiting to be peeled. On and on and on...
Good luck, Arthur...

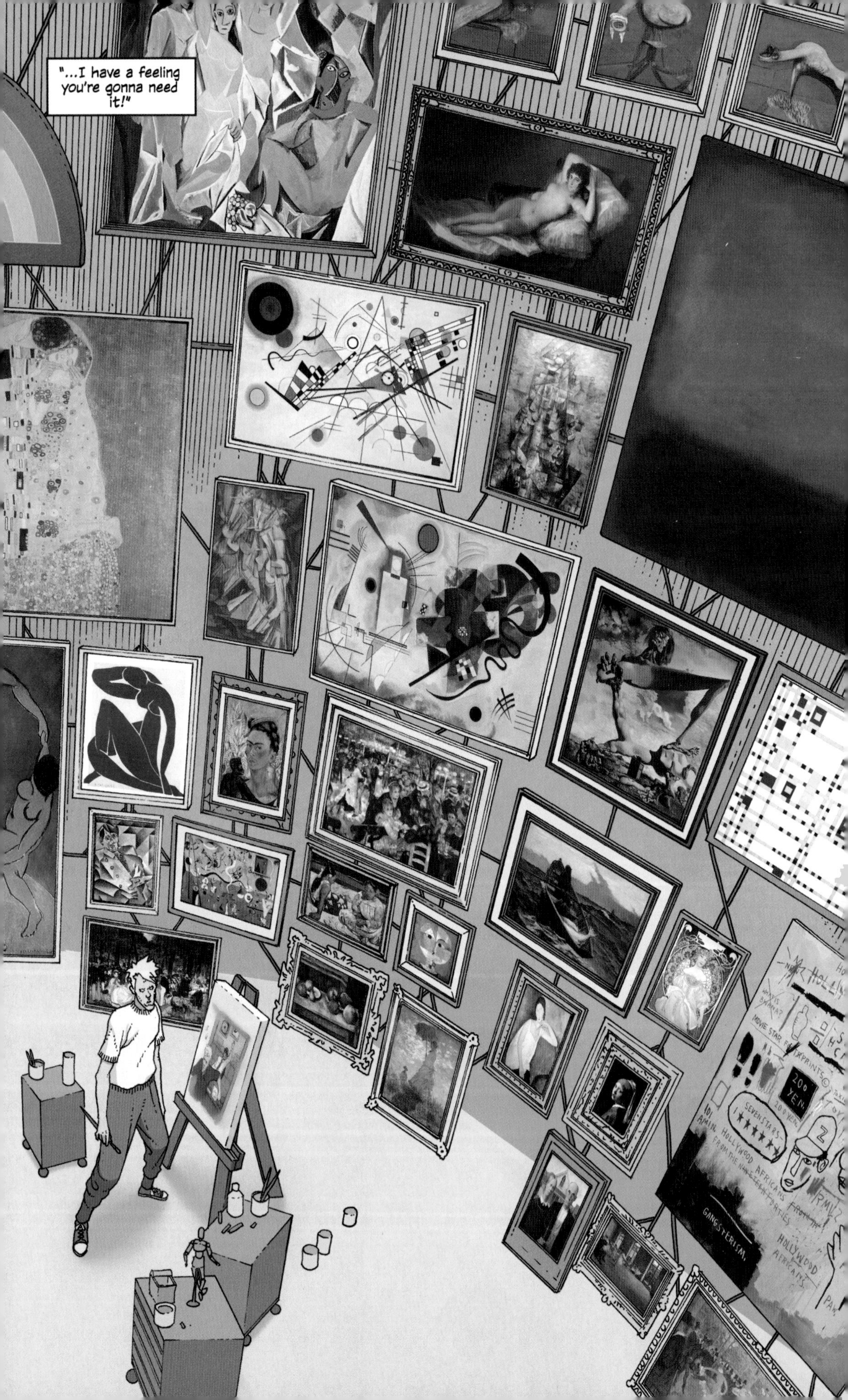
"...I have a feeling you're gonna need it!"

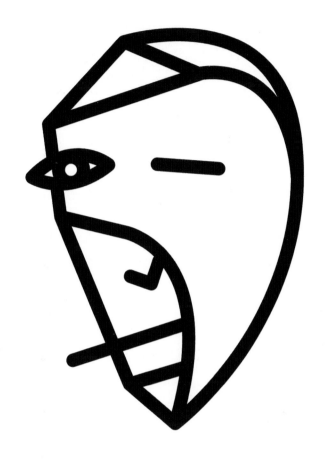

THE UNKNOWN KNOWNS

•

Chapter 4

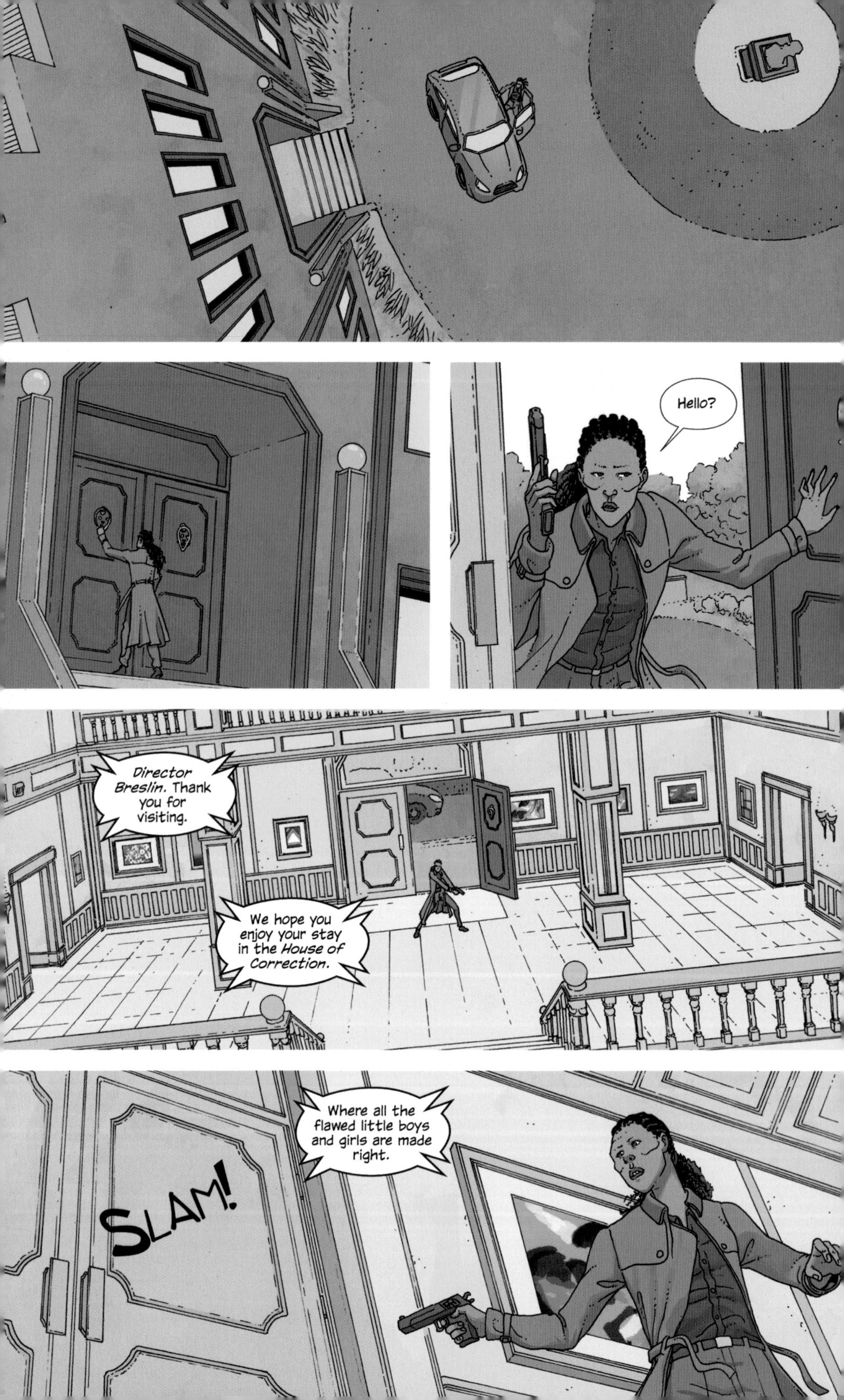
Hello?
Director Breslin. Thank you for visiting.
We hope you enjoy your stay in the *House of Correction*.
Where all the flawed little boys and girls are made right.
SLAM!

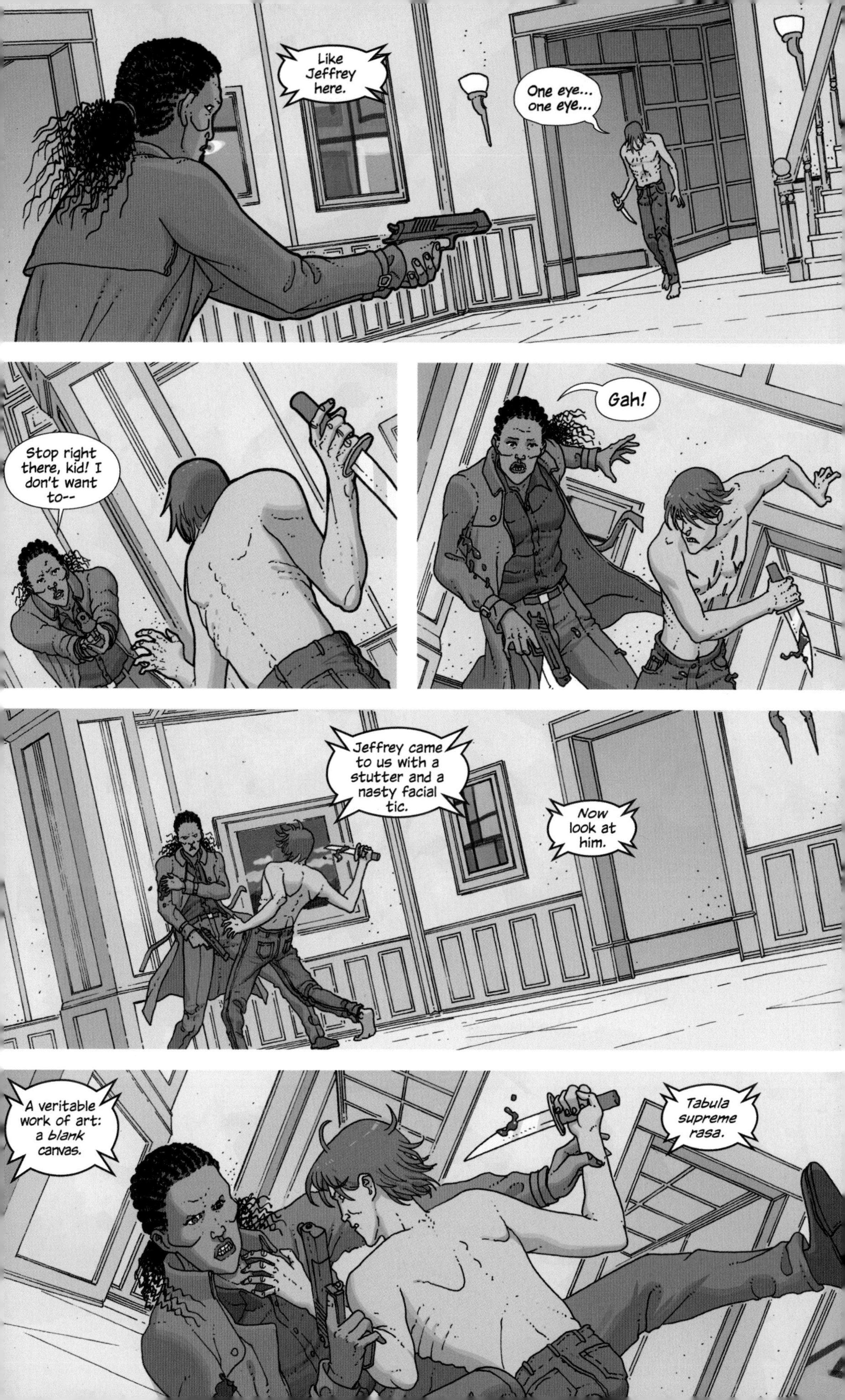
Like Jeffrey here.
One eye... one eye...
Stop right there, kid! I don't want to--
Gah!
Jeffrey came to us with a stutter and a nasty facial tic.
Now look at him.
A veritable work of art: a *blank* canvas.
Tabula supreme rasa.

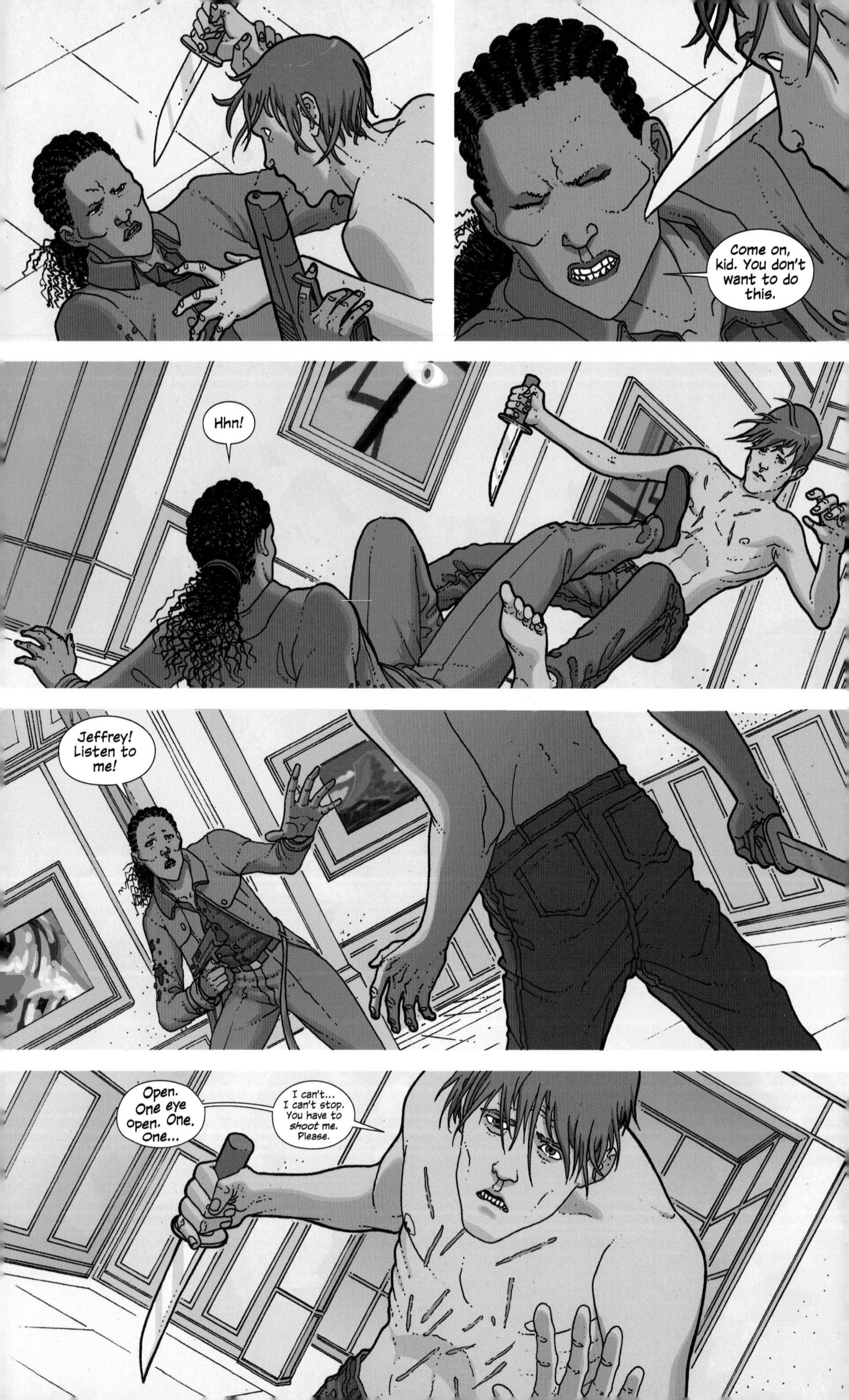
Come on, kid. You don't want to do this.
Hhn!
Jeffrey! Listen to me!
Open. One eye open. One. One...
I can't... I can't stop. You have to *shoot* me. Please.

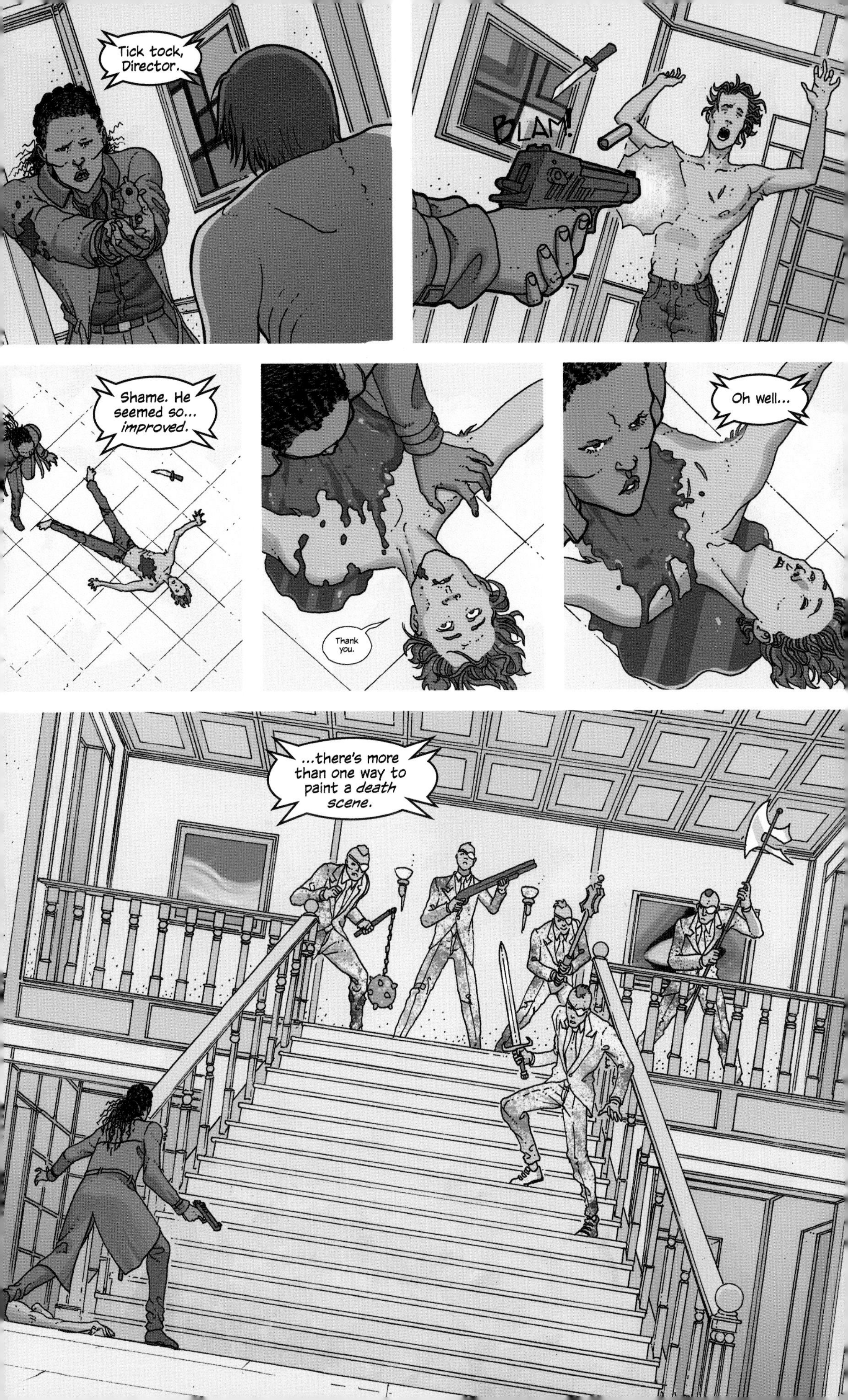
Tick tock, Director.
BLAM!
Shame. He seemed so... *improved*.
Thank you.
Oh well...
...there's more than one way to paint a *death* scene.

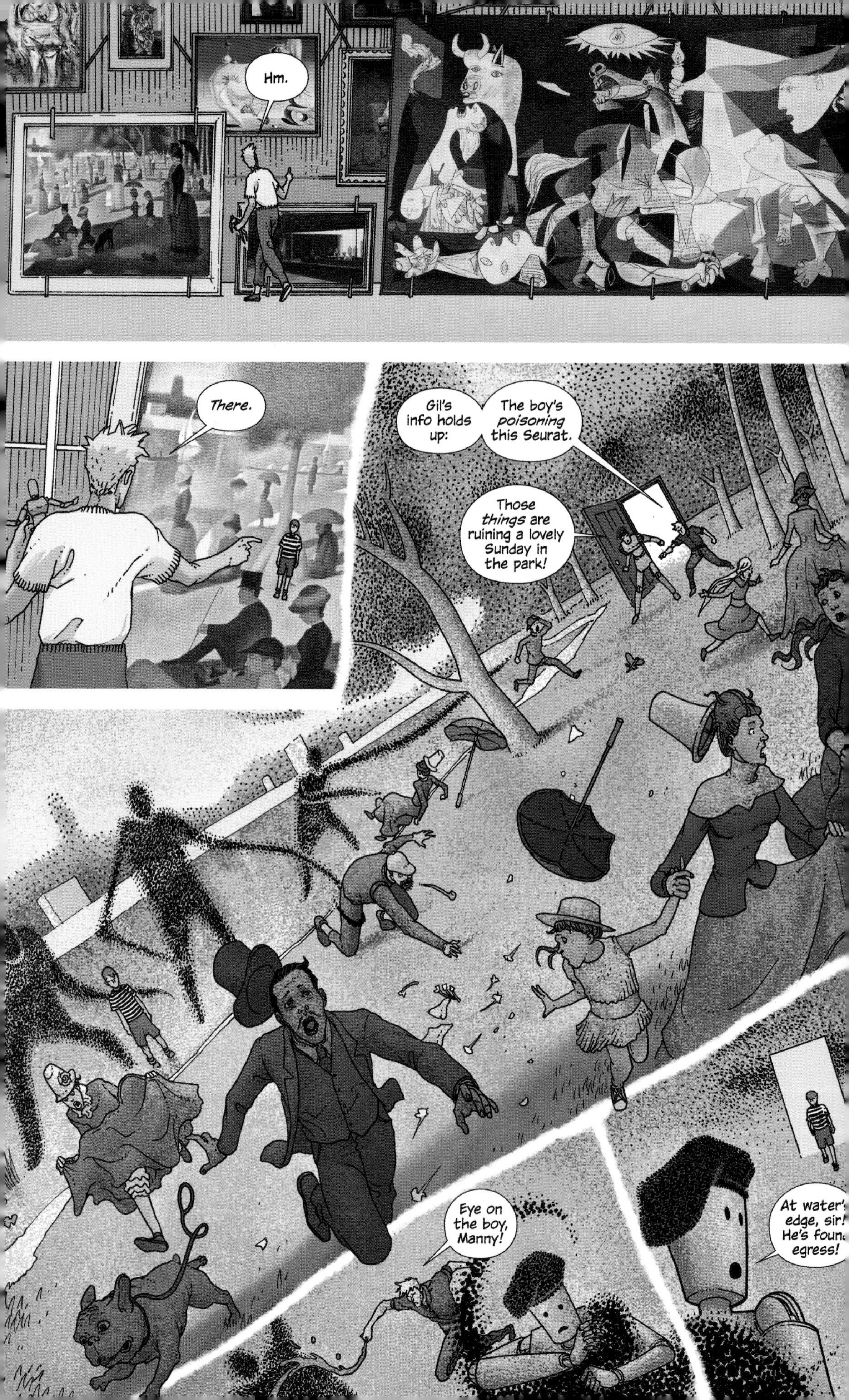
Hm.
There.
Gil's info holds up:
The boy's *poisoning* this Seurat.
Those *things* are ruining a lovely Sunday in the park!
Eye on the boy, Manny!
At water's edge, sir! He's found egress!

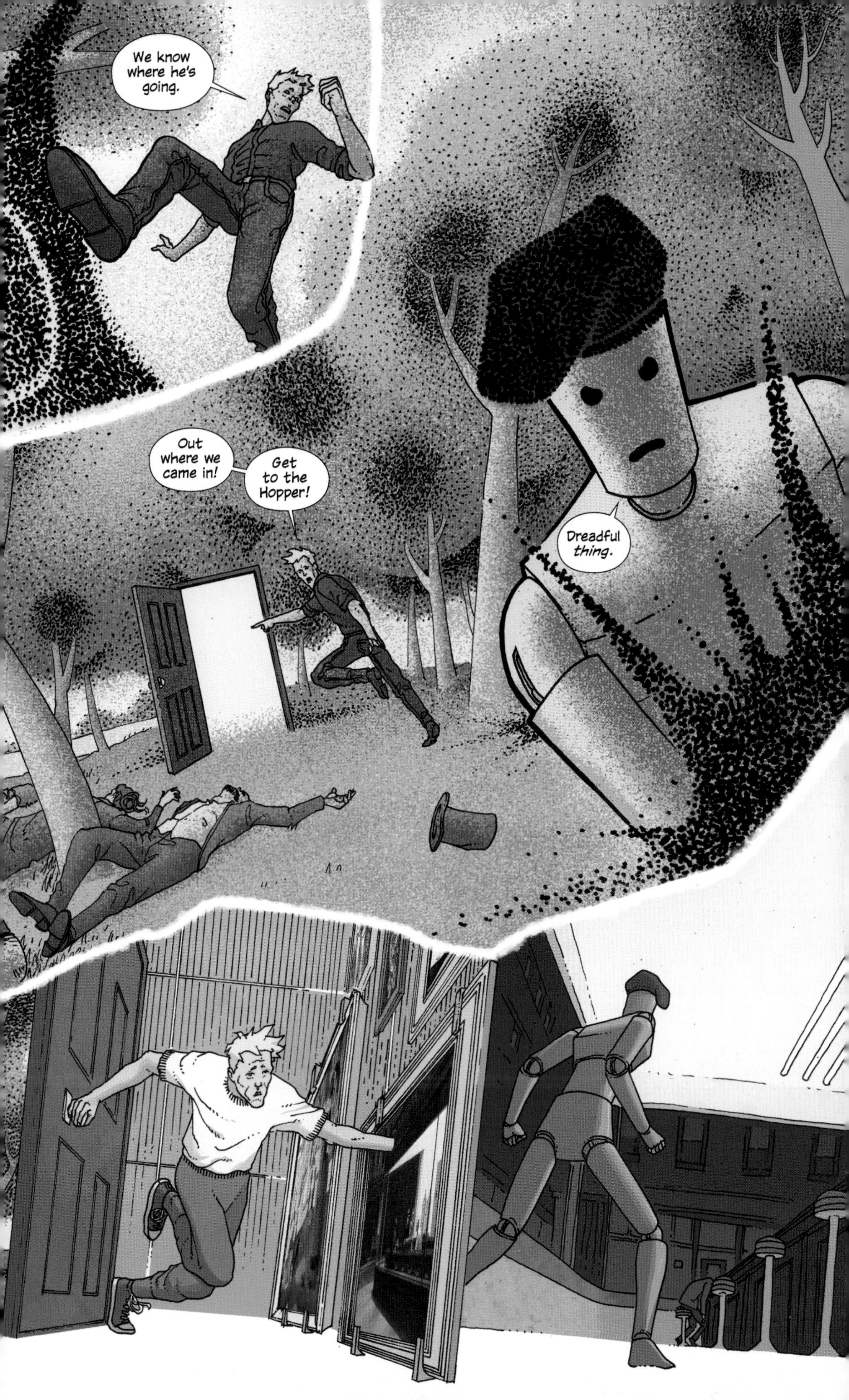
We know where he's going.
Out where we came in!
Get to the Hopper!
Dreadful *thing*.

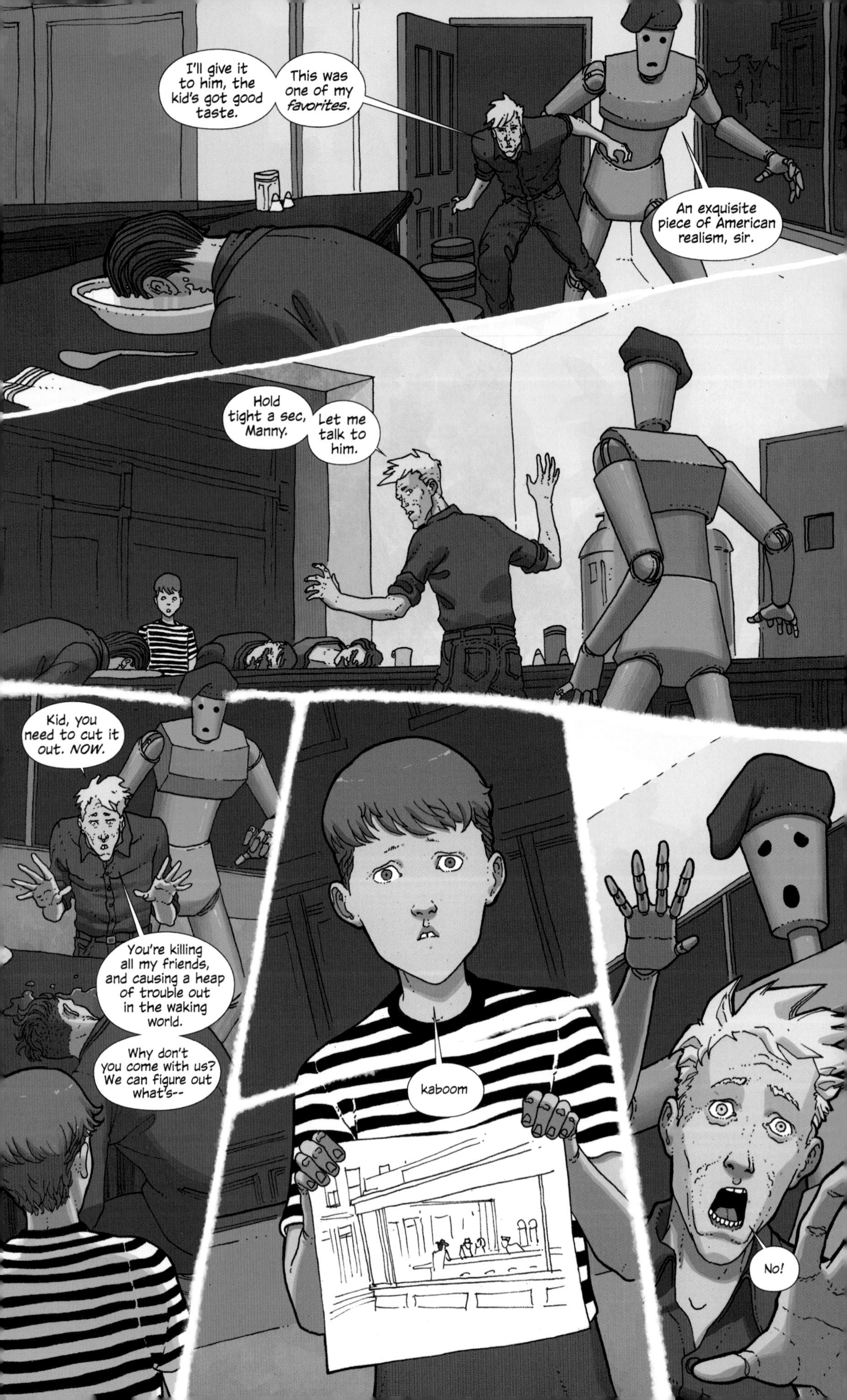
I'll give it to him, the kid's got good taste.
This was one of my *favorites*.
An exquisite piece of American realism, sir.
Hold tight a sec, Manny.
Let me talk to him.
Kid, you need to cut it out. *NOW*.
You're killing all my friends, and causing a heap of trouble out in the waking world.
Why don't you come with us? We can figure out what's--
kaboom
No!

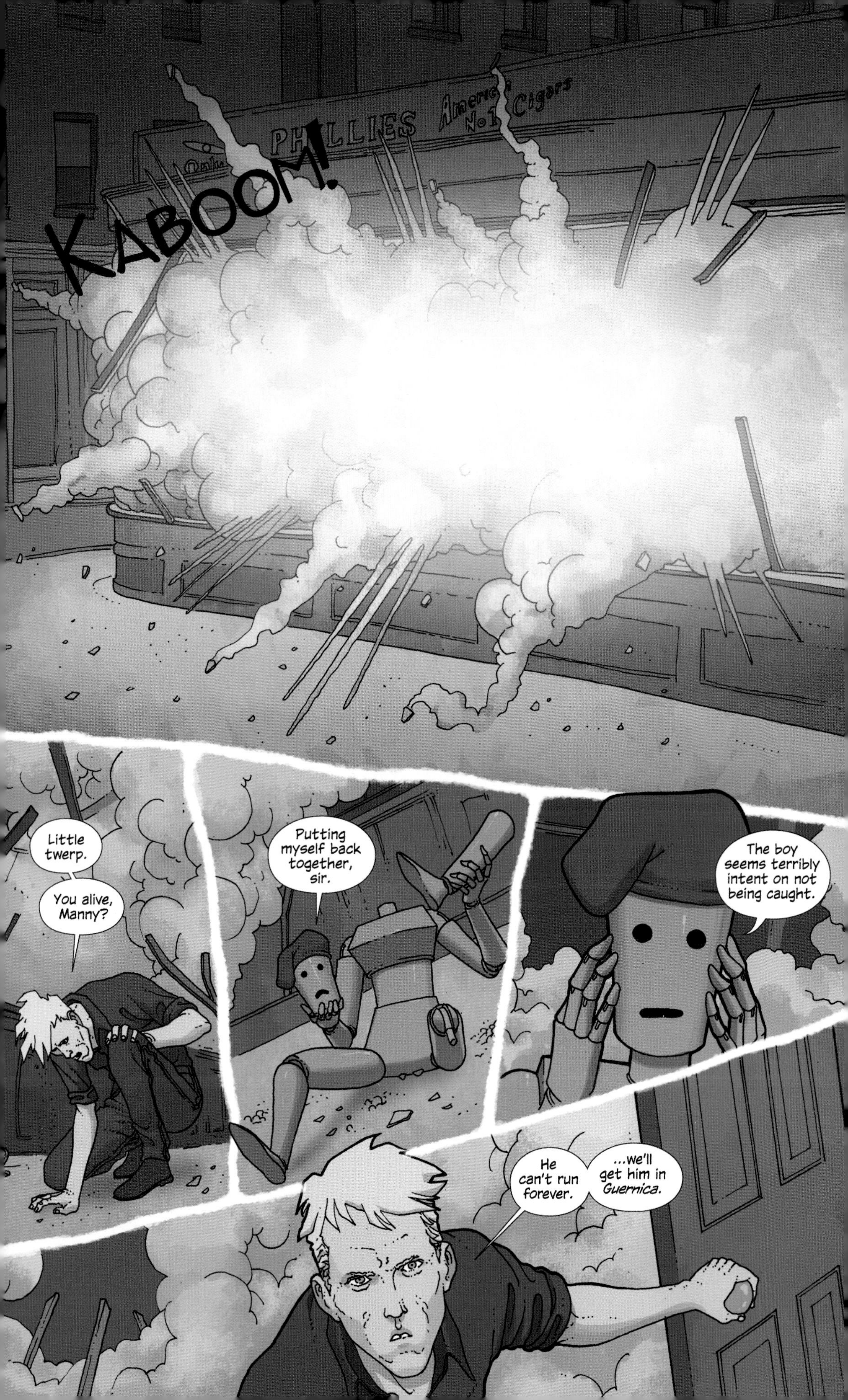
PHILLIES
Cigars
KABOOM!
Little twerp.
You alive, Manny?
Putting myself back together, sir.
The boy seems terribly intent on not being caught.
He can't run forever.
...we'll get him in *Guernica.*

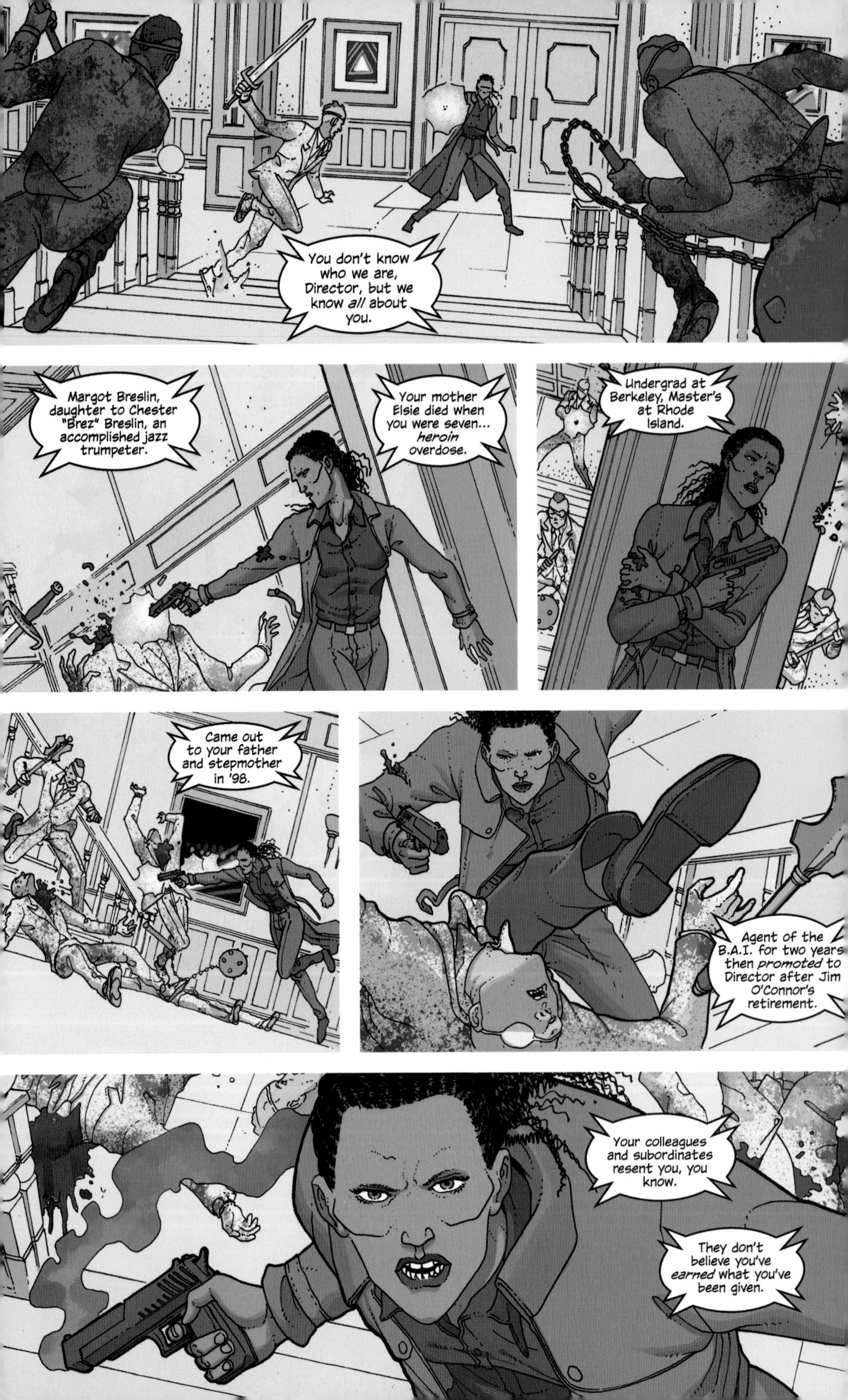
You don't know who we are, Director, but we know *all* about you.
Margot Breslin, daughter to Chester "Brez" Breslin, an accomplished jazz trumpeter.
Your mother Elsie died when you were seven... *heroin* overdose.
Undergrad at Berkeley, Master's at Rhode Island.
Came out to your father and stepmother in '98.
Agent of the B.A.I. for two years then *promoted* to Director after Jim O'Connor's retirement.
Your colleagues and subordinates resent you, you know.
They don't believe you've *earned* what you've been given.

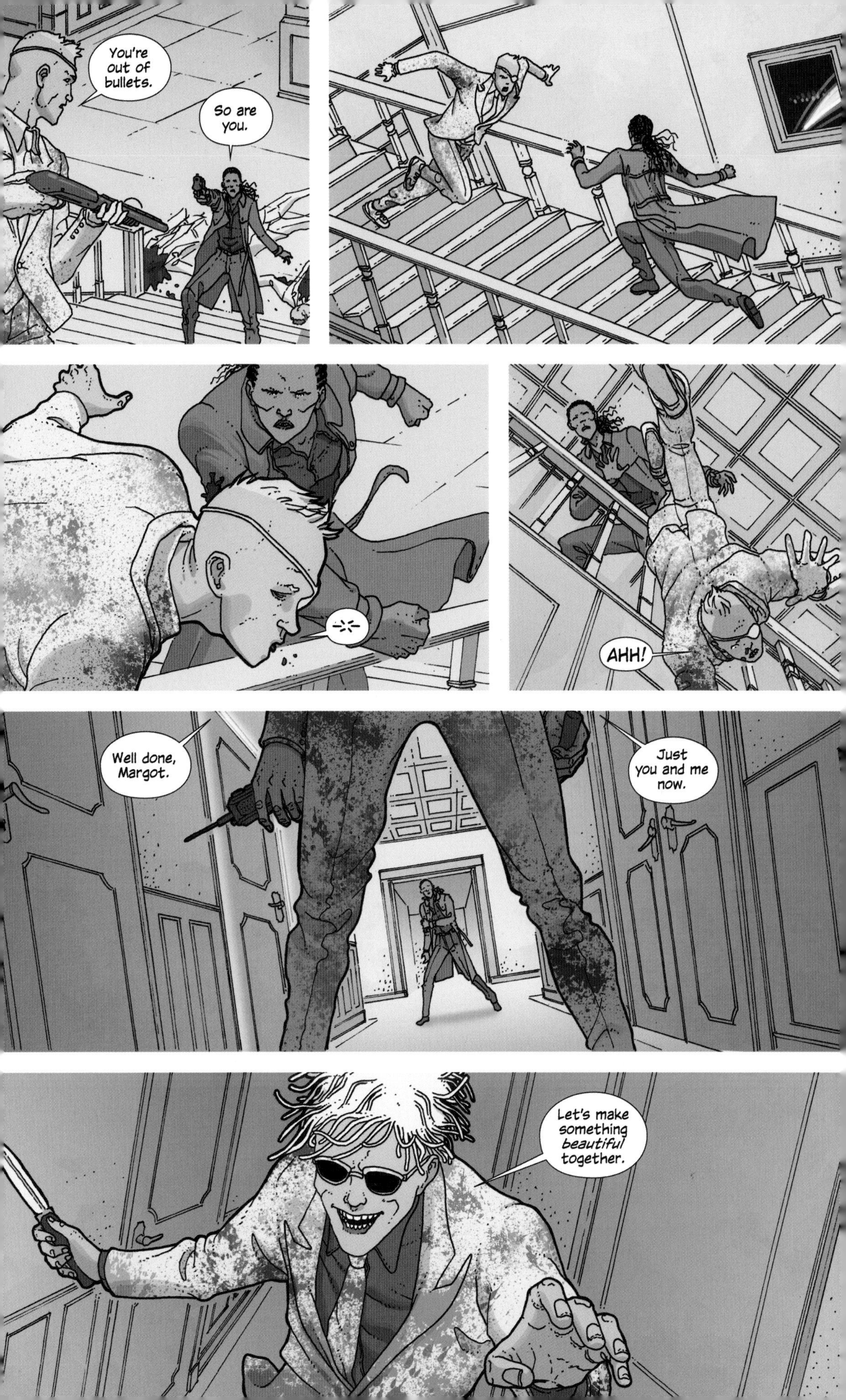
You're out of bullets.
So are you.
AHH!
Well done, Margot.
Just you and me now.
Let's make something *beautiful* together.

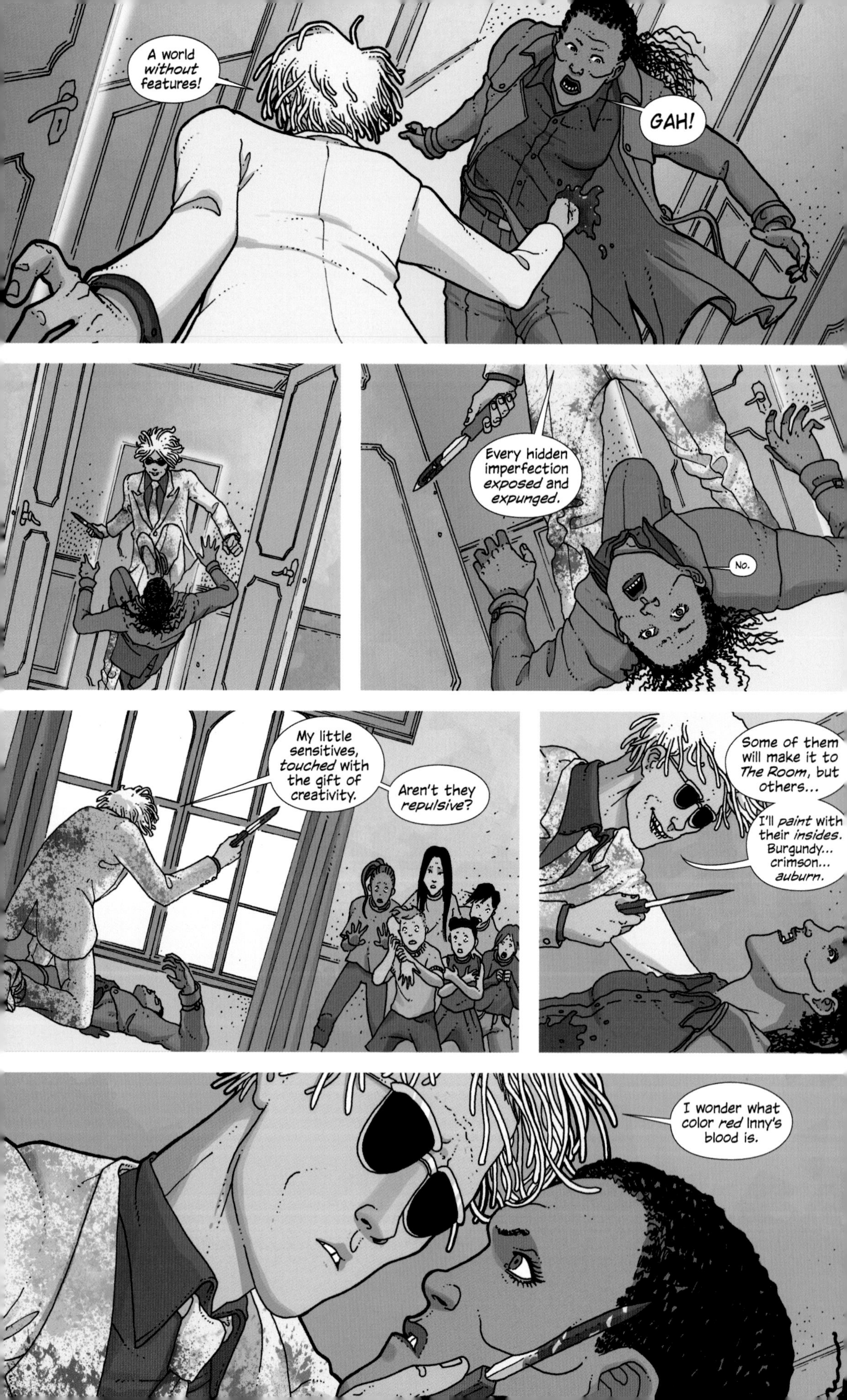
A world without features!
GAH!
Every hidden imperfection exposed and expunged.
No.
My little sensitives, touched with the gift of creativity.
Aren't they repulsive?
Some of them will make it to The Room, but others...
I'll paint with their insides. Burgundy... crimson... auburn.
I wonder what color red Inny's blood is.

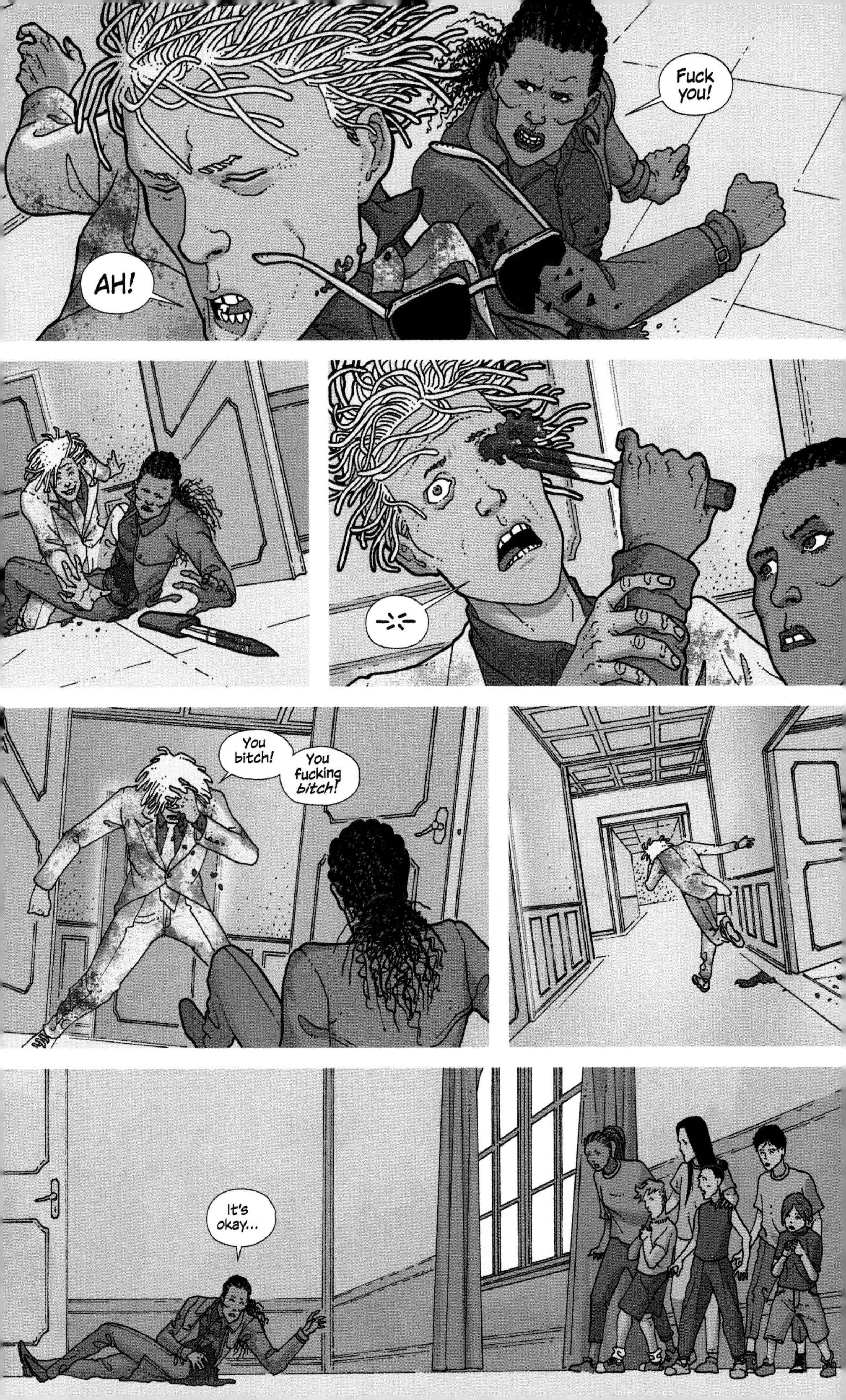
Fuck you!
AH!
-'-
You bitch!
You fucking bitch!
It's okay...

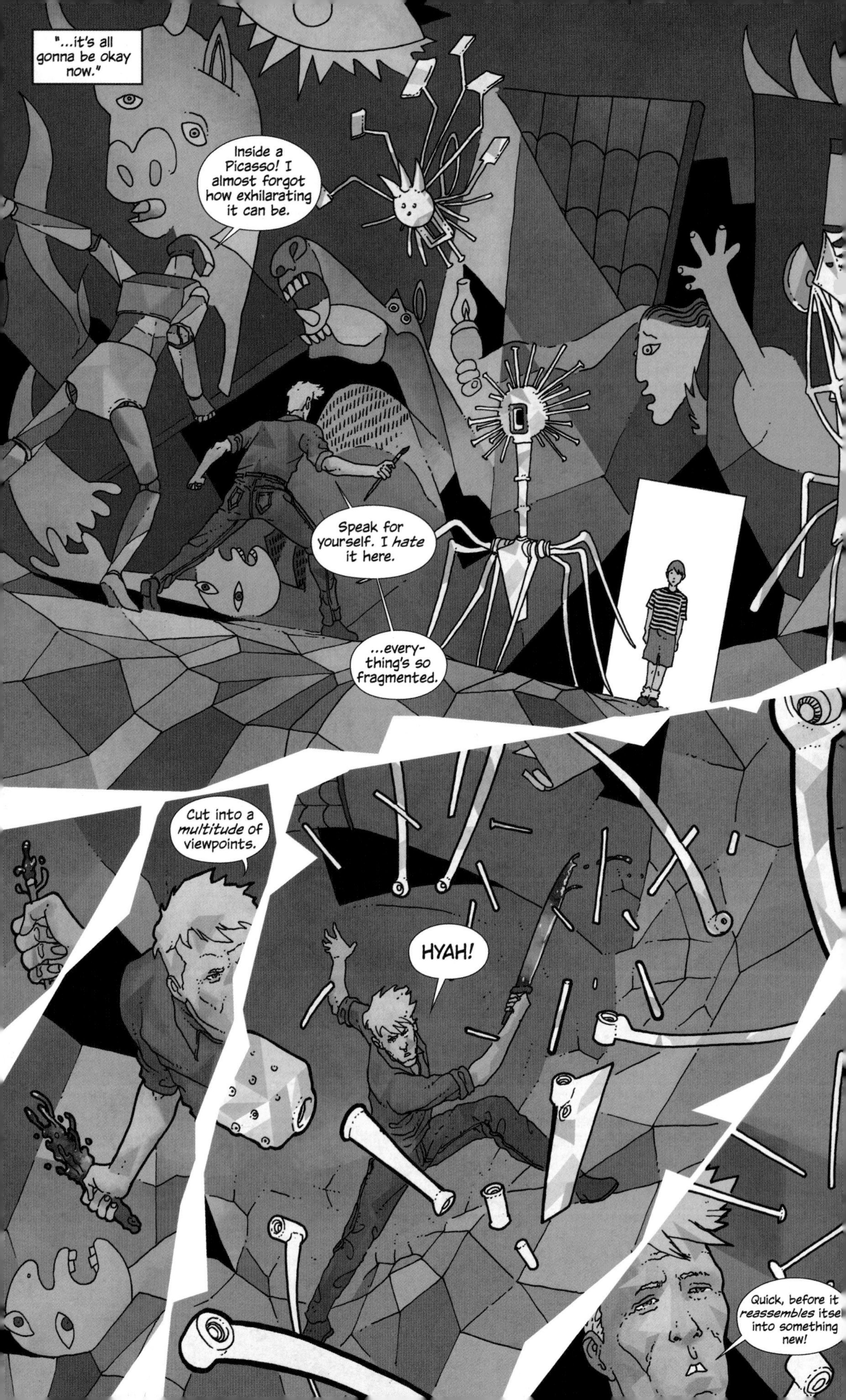
"...it's all gonna be okay now."
Inside a Picasso! I almost forgot how exhilarating it can be.
Speak for yourself. I *hate* it here.
...every-thing's so fragmented.
Cut into a *multitude* of viewpoints.
HYAH!
Quick, before it *reassembles* itse into something new!

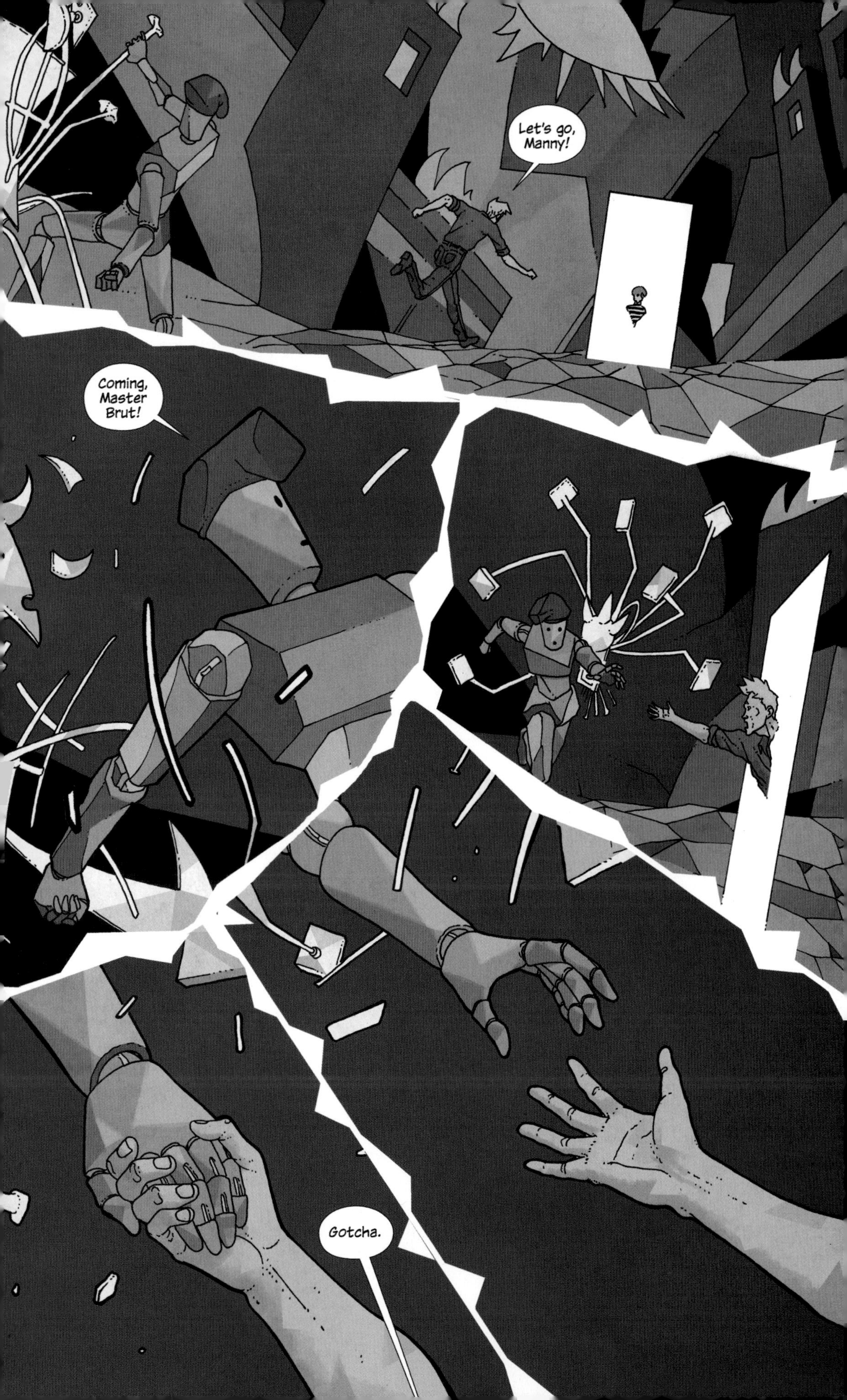
Let's go, Manny!
Coming, Master Brut!
Gotcha.

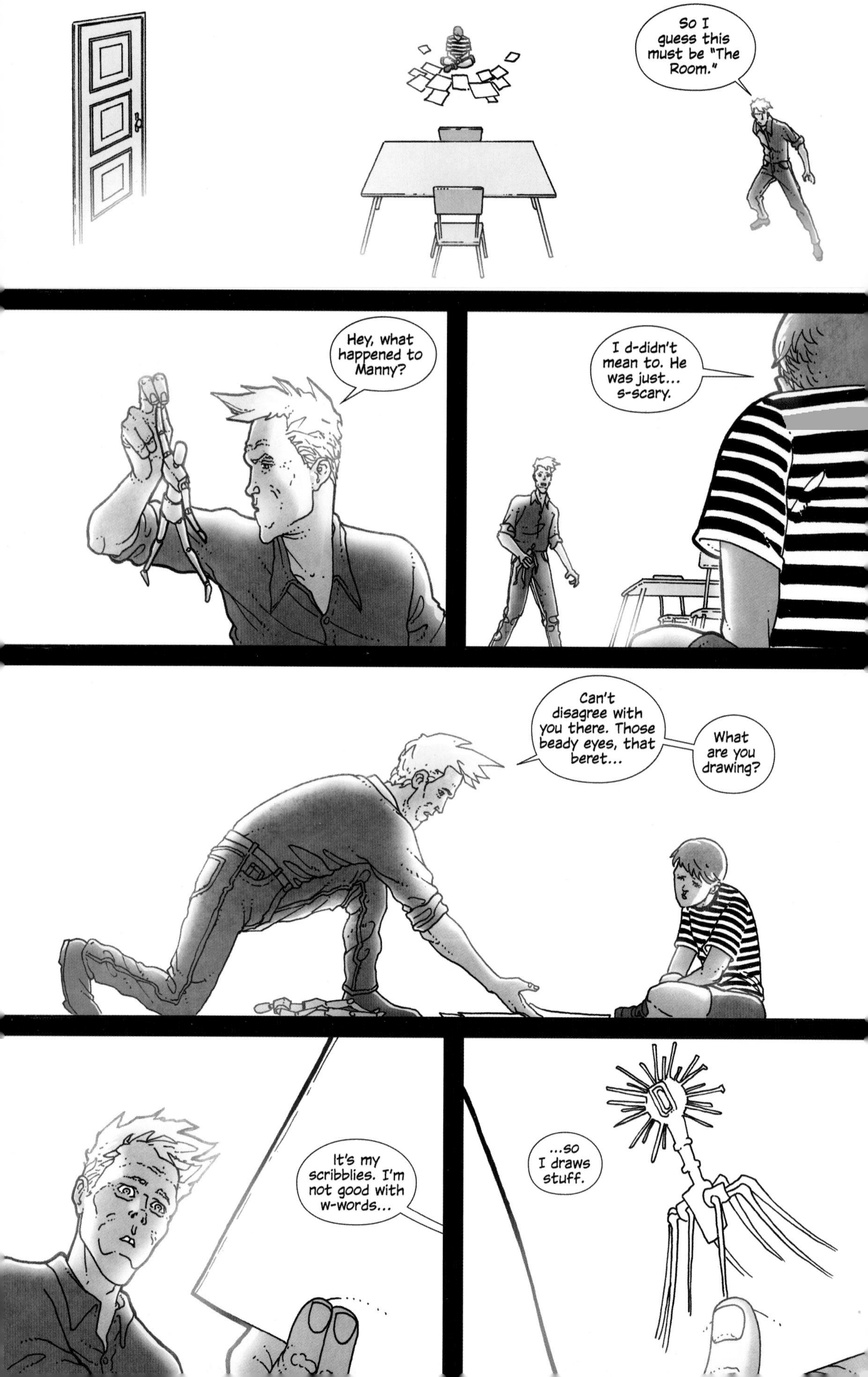
So I guess this must be "The Room."
Hey, what happened to Manny?
I d-didn't mean to. He was just... s-scary.
Can't disagree with you there. Those beady eyes, that beret...
What are you drawing?
It's my scribblies. I'm not good with w-words...
...so I draws stuff.

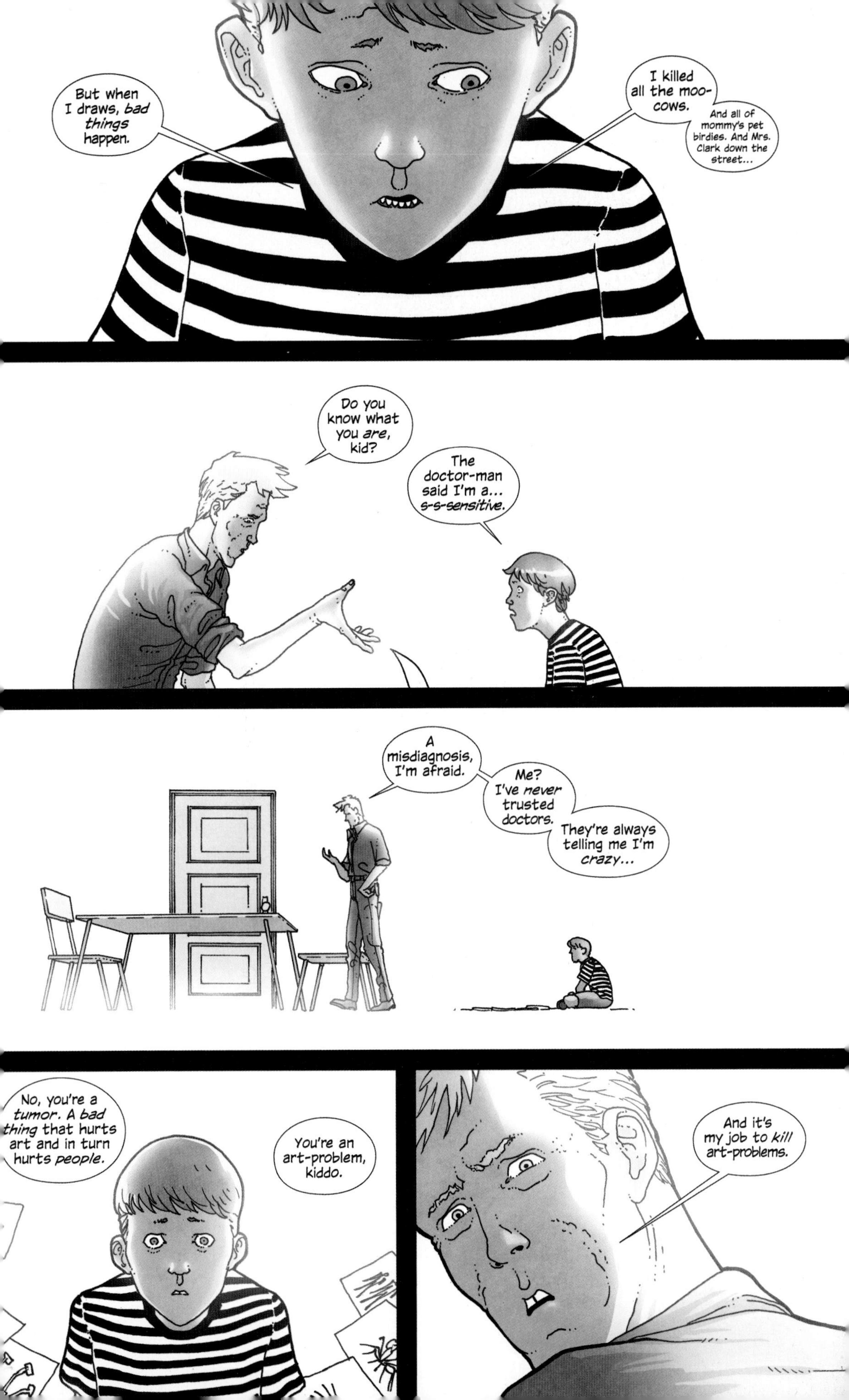
But when I draws, *bad things* happen.
I killed all the moo-cows.
And all of mommy's pet birdies. And Mrs. Clark down the street...
Do you know what you *are*, kid?
The doctor-man said I'm a... *s-s-sensitive*.
A misdiagnosis, I'm afraid.
Me? I've *never* trusted doctors.
They're always telling me I'm *crazy*...
No, you're a *tumor*. A *bad thing* that hurts art and in turn hurts *people*.
You're an art-problem, kiddo.
And it's my job to *kill* art-problems.

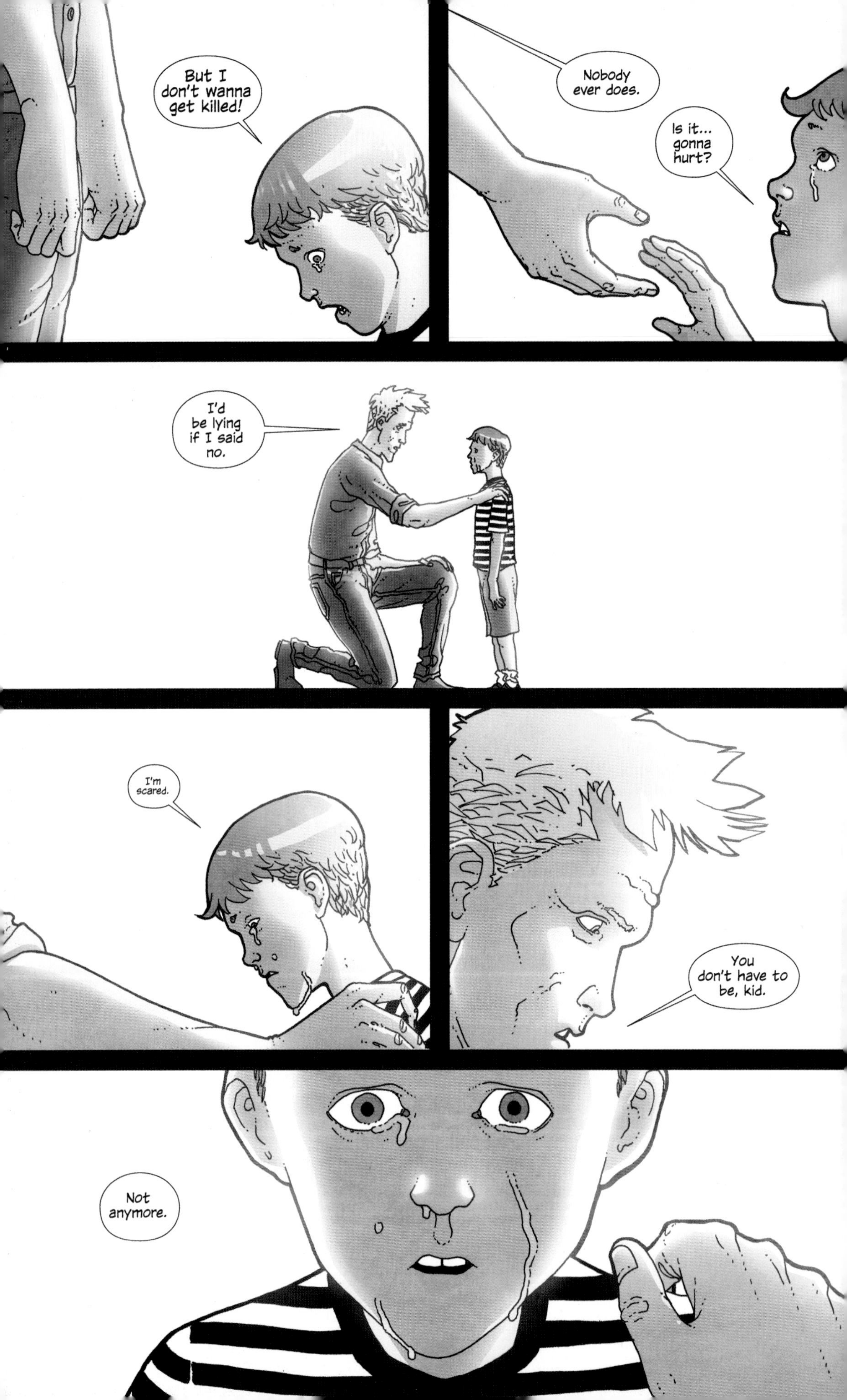
But I don't wanna get killed!
Nobody ever does.
Is it... gonna hurt?
I'd be lying if I said no.
I'm scared.
You don't have to be, kid.
Not anymore.

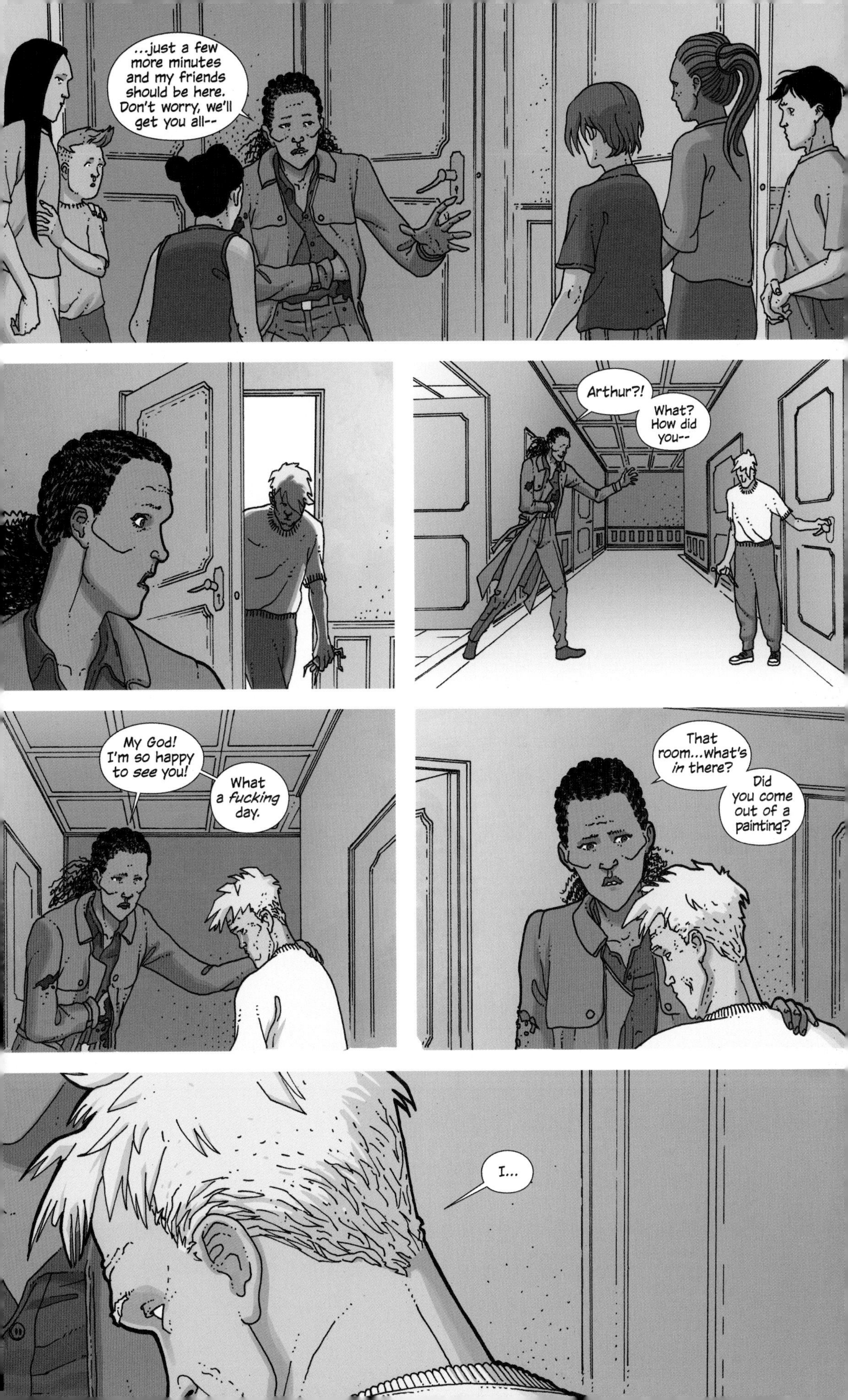
...just a few more minutes and my friends should be here. Don't worry, we'll get you all--
Arthur?!
What? How did you--
My God! I'm so happy to see you!
What a *fucking* day.
That room...what's *in* there?
Did you come out of a painting?
I...

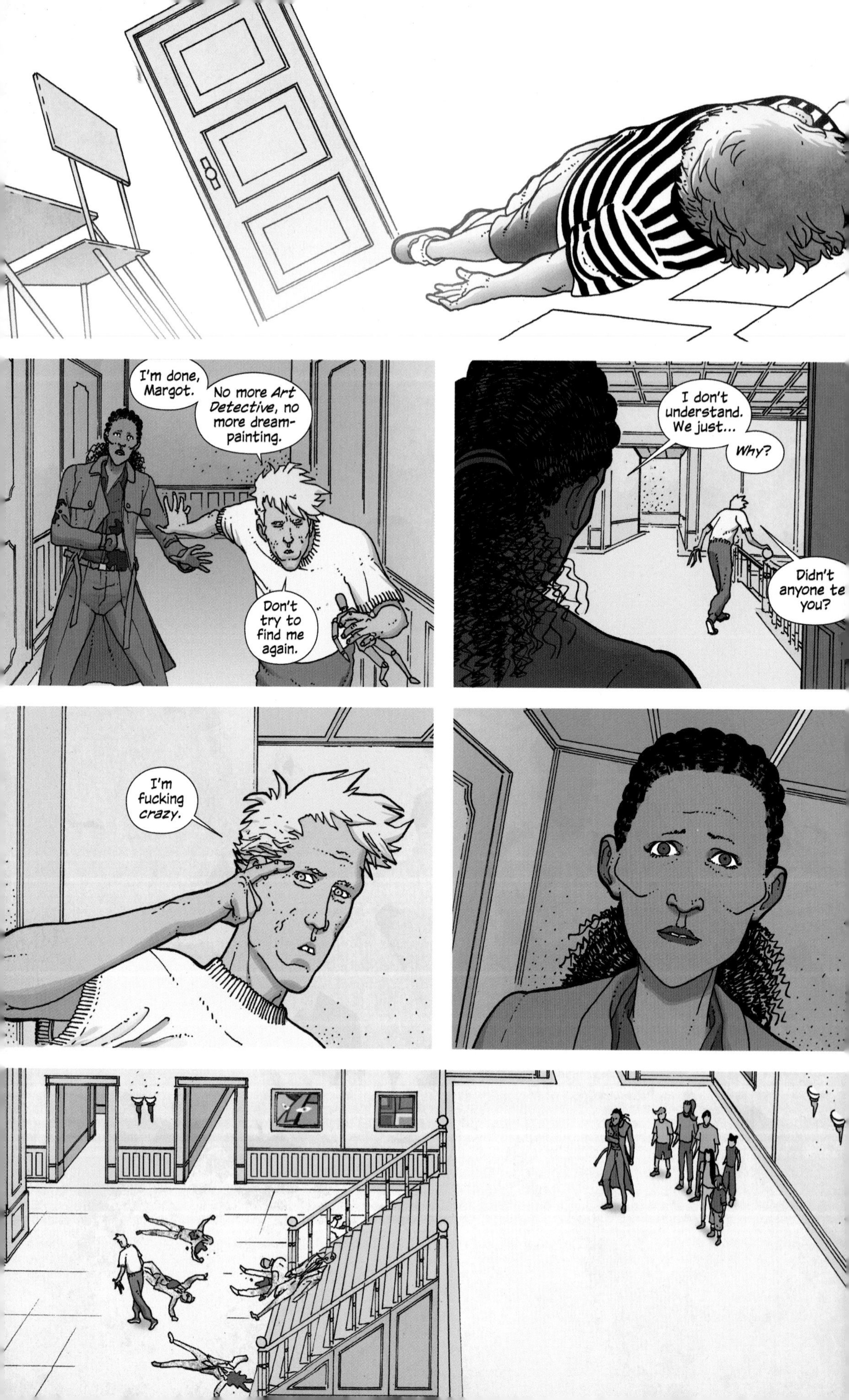
I'm done, Margot.
No more *Art Detective*, no more dream-painting.
Don't try to find me again.
I don't understand. We just...
Why?
Didn't anyone te you?
I'm fucking *crazy*.

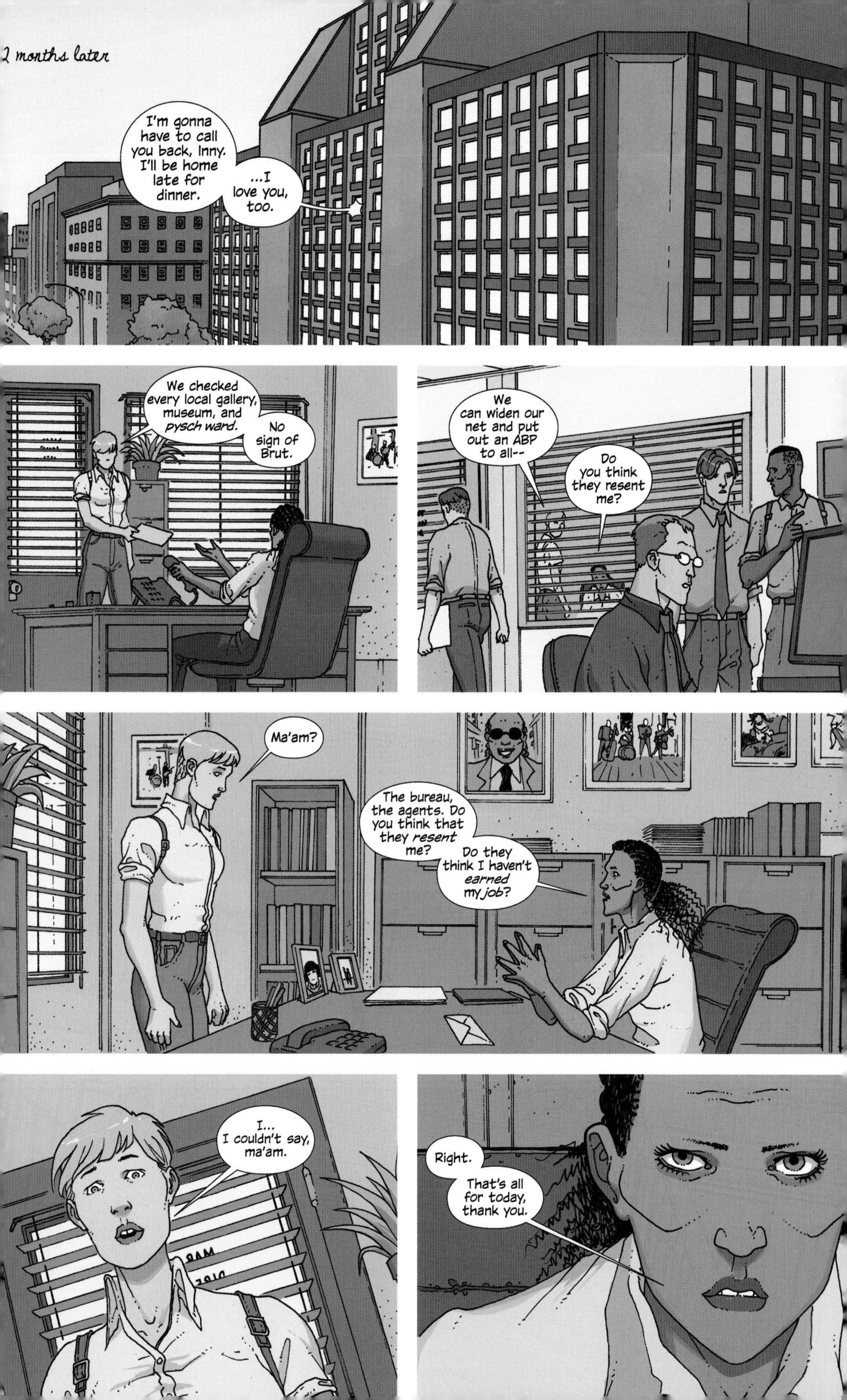
2 months later
I'm gonna have to call you back, Inny. I'll be home late for dinner.
...I love you, too.
We checked every local gallery, museum, and *pysch ward.*
No sign of Brut.
We can widen our net and put out an ABP to all--
Do you think they resent me?
Ma'am?
The bureau, the agents. Do you think that they *resent* me?
Do they think I haven't *earned* my *job?*
I... I couldn't say, ma'am.
Right.
That's all for today, thank you.

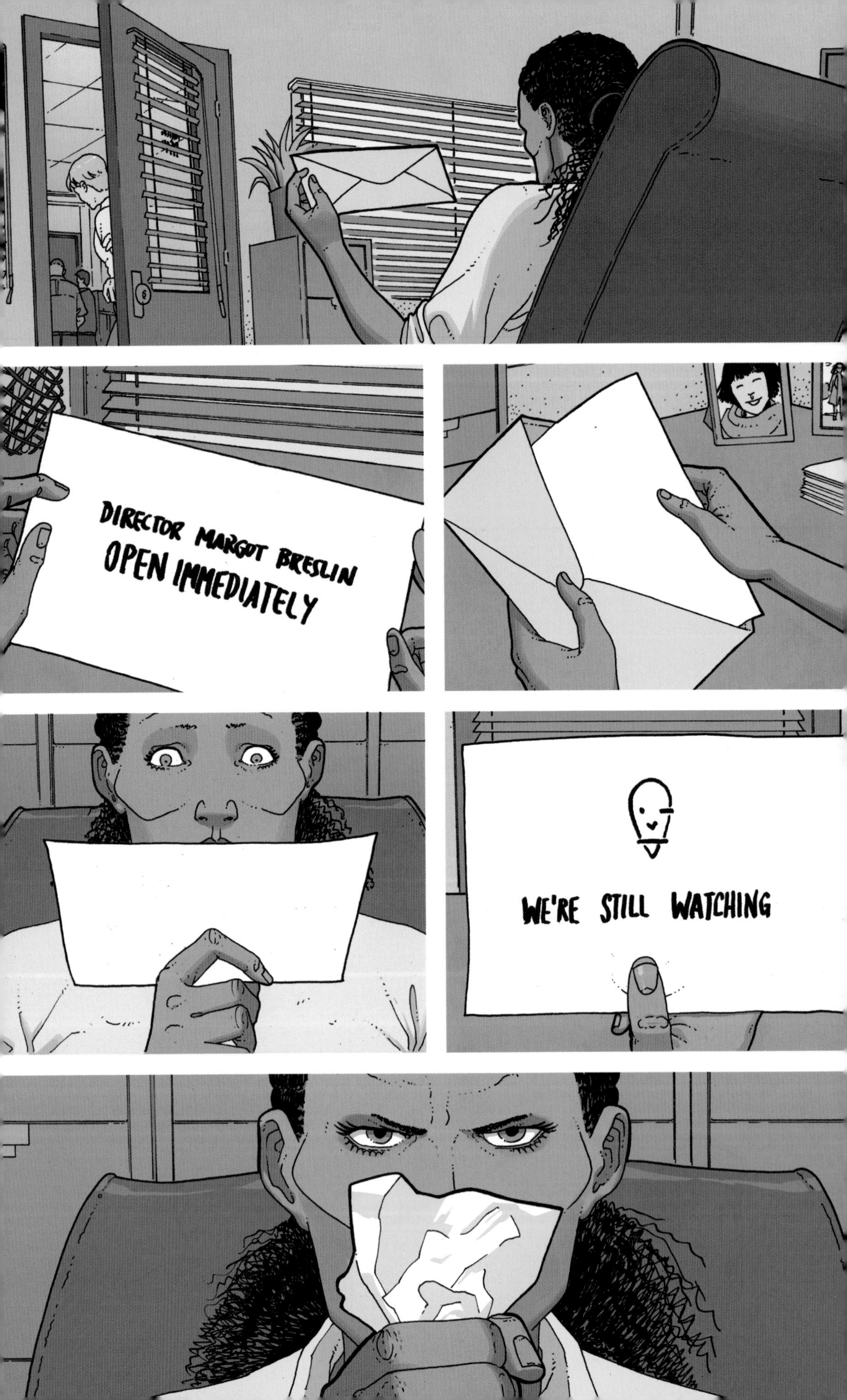
DIRECTOR MARGOT BRESLIN
OPEN IMMEDIATELY
WE'RE STILL WATCHING

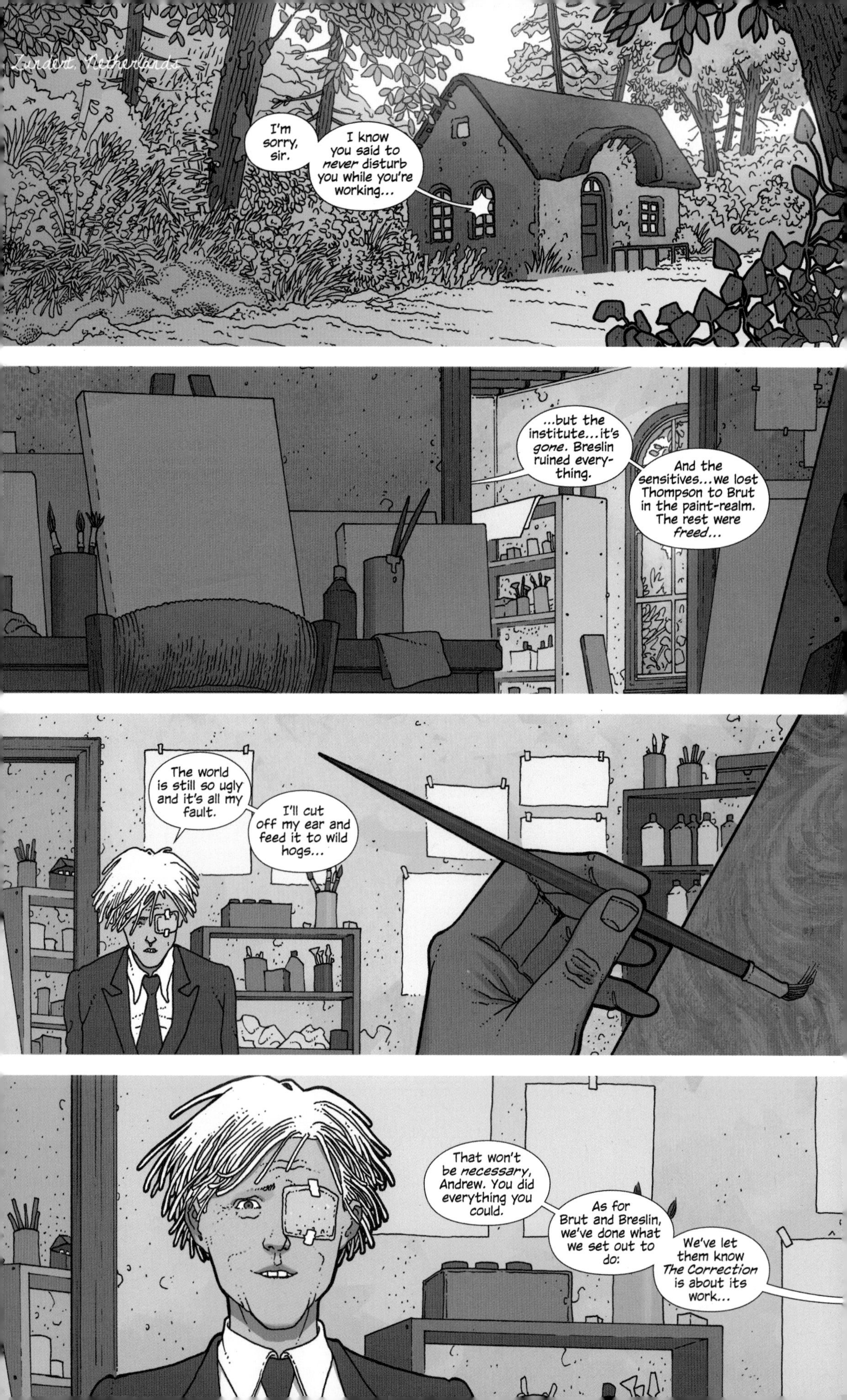
Zundert, Netherlands
I'm sorry, sir.
I know you said to *never* disturb you while you're working...
...but the institute...it's *gone*. Breslin ruined everything.
And the sensitives...we lost Thompson to Brut in the paint-realm. The rest were *freed*...
The world is still so ugly and it's all my fault.
I'll cut off my ear and feed it to wild hogs...
That won't be *necessary*, Andrew. You did everything you could.
As for Brut and Breslin, we've done what we set out to do:
We've let them know *The Correction* is about its work...

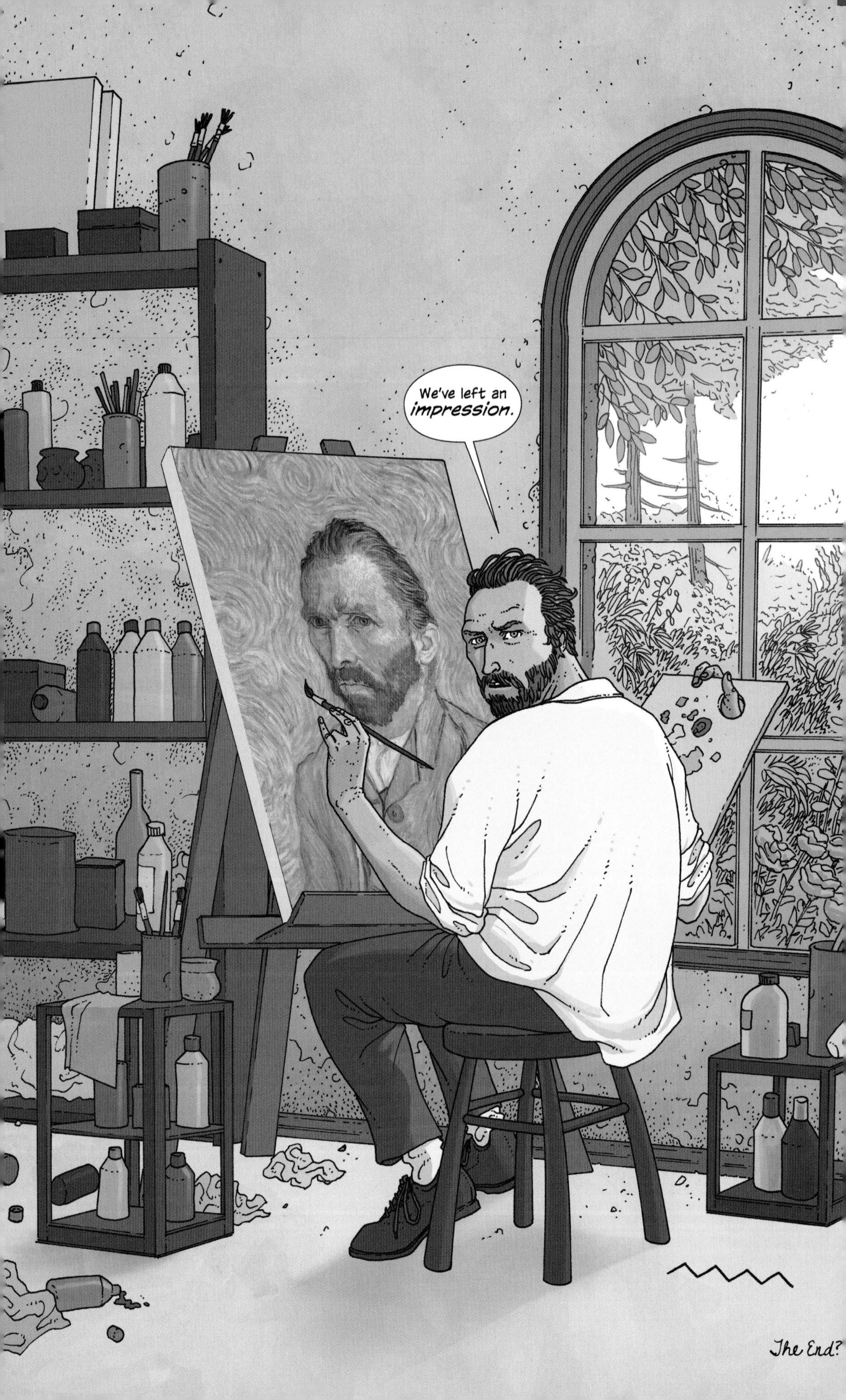
We've left an *impression*.
The End?

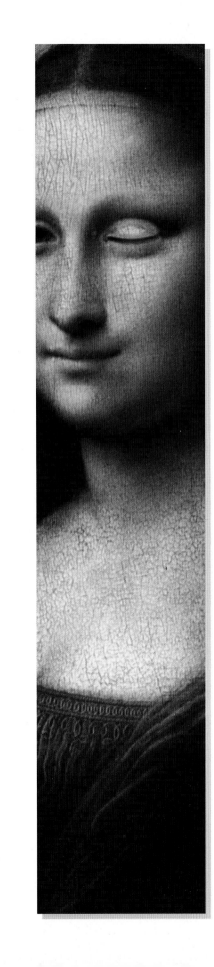

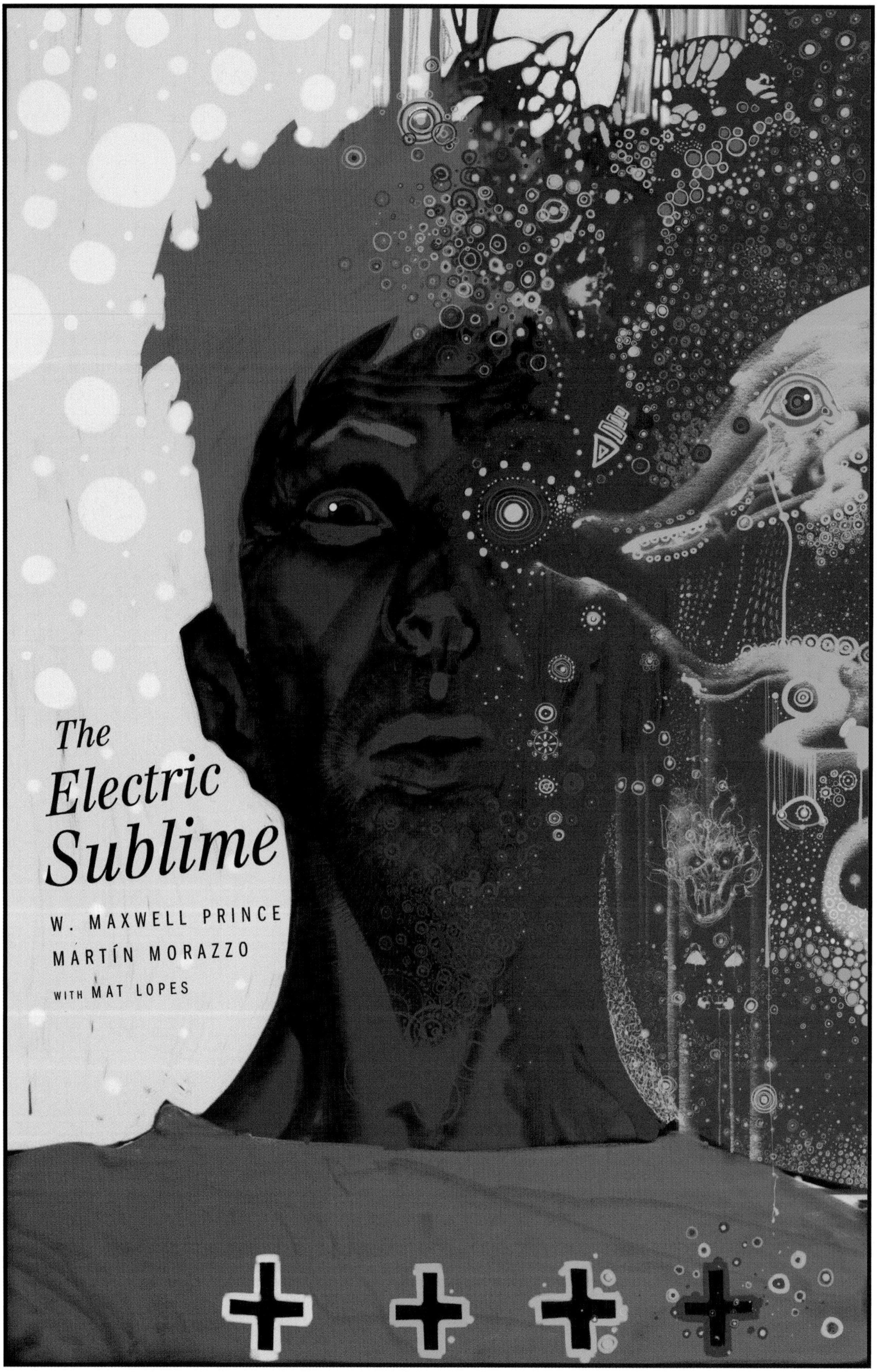
The Electric Sublime
W. MAXWELL PRINCE
MARTÍN MORAZZO
WITH MAT LOPES

COVER ART BY Frazer Irving

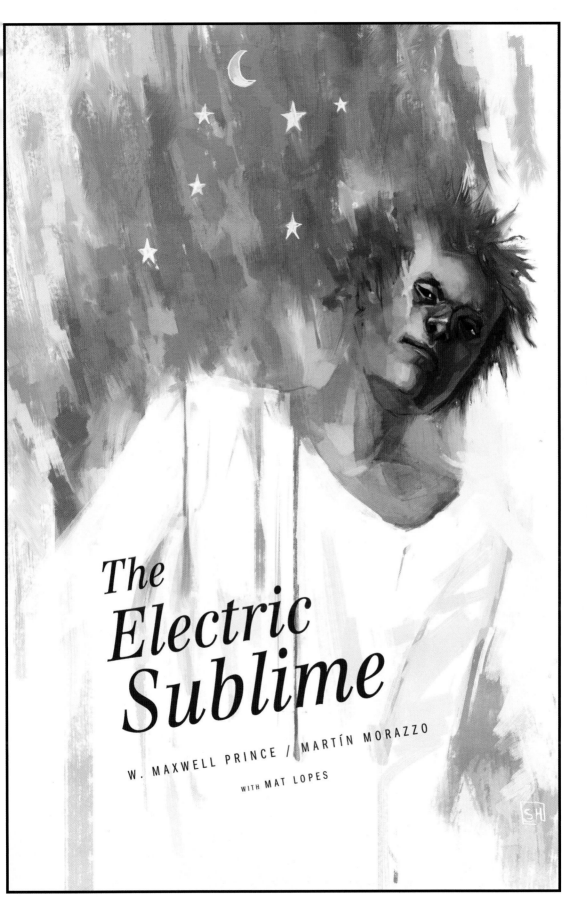

The Electric Sublime

W. MAXWELL PRINCE / MARTÍN MORAZZO

with MAT LOPES

COVER ART BY *Stephanie Hans*

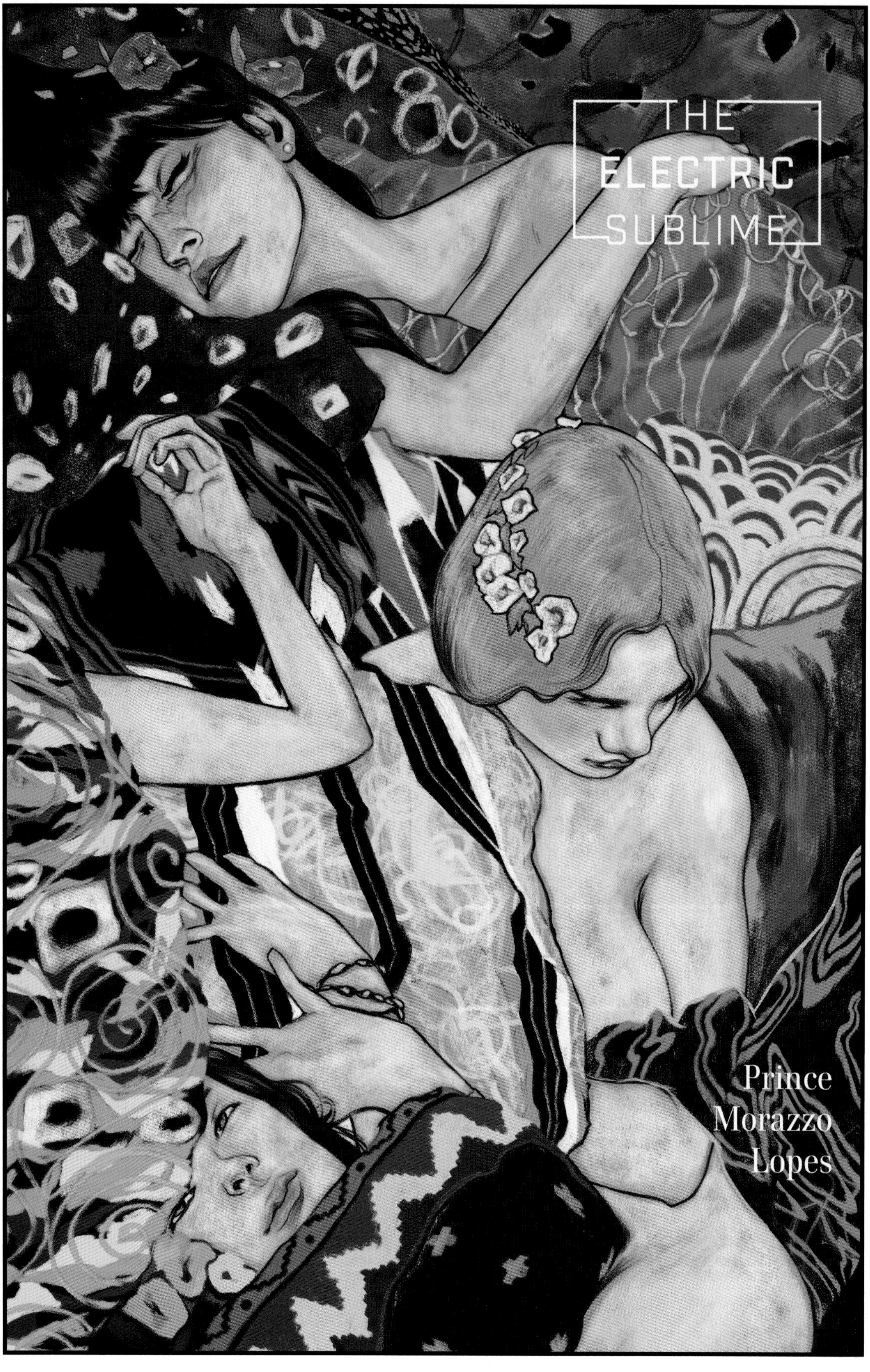
THE ELECTRIC SUBLIME
Prince
Morazzo
Lopes

COVER ART BY Nimit Malavia

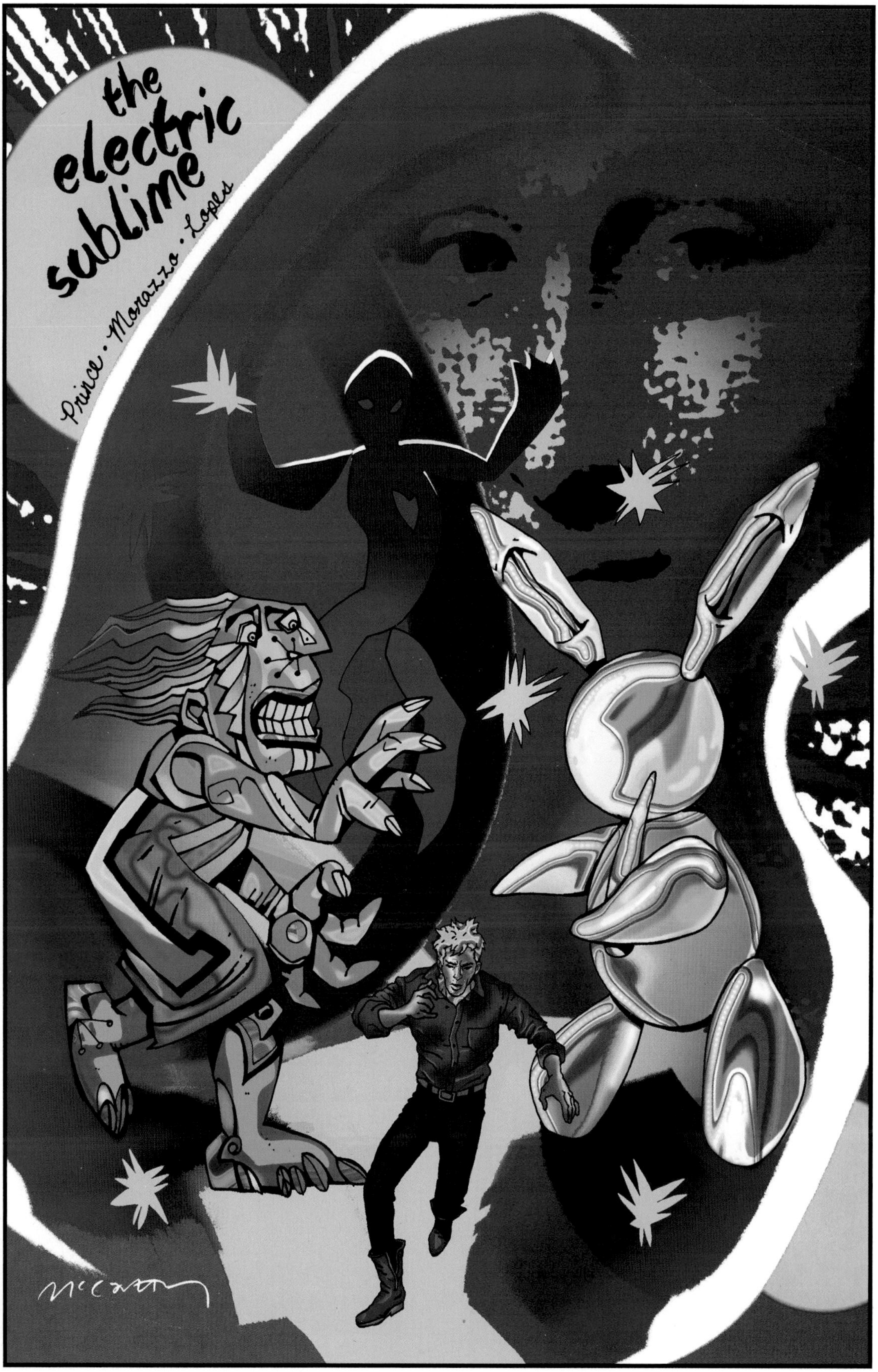
the electric sublime
Prince · Morazzo · Lopes
McCarthy

COVER ART BY Brendan McCarthy

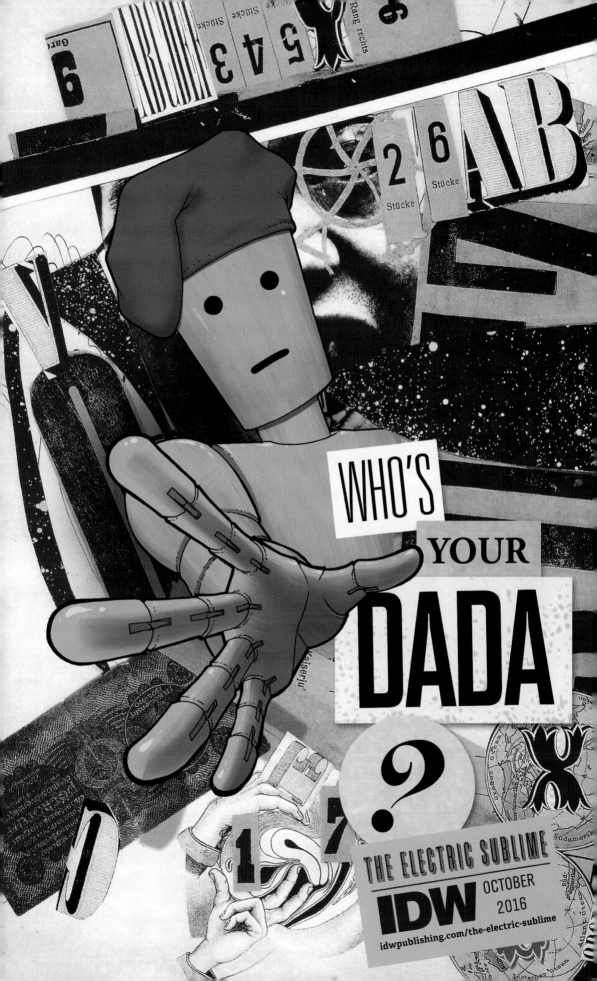

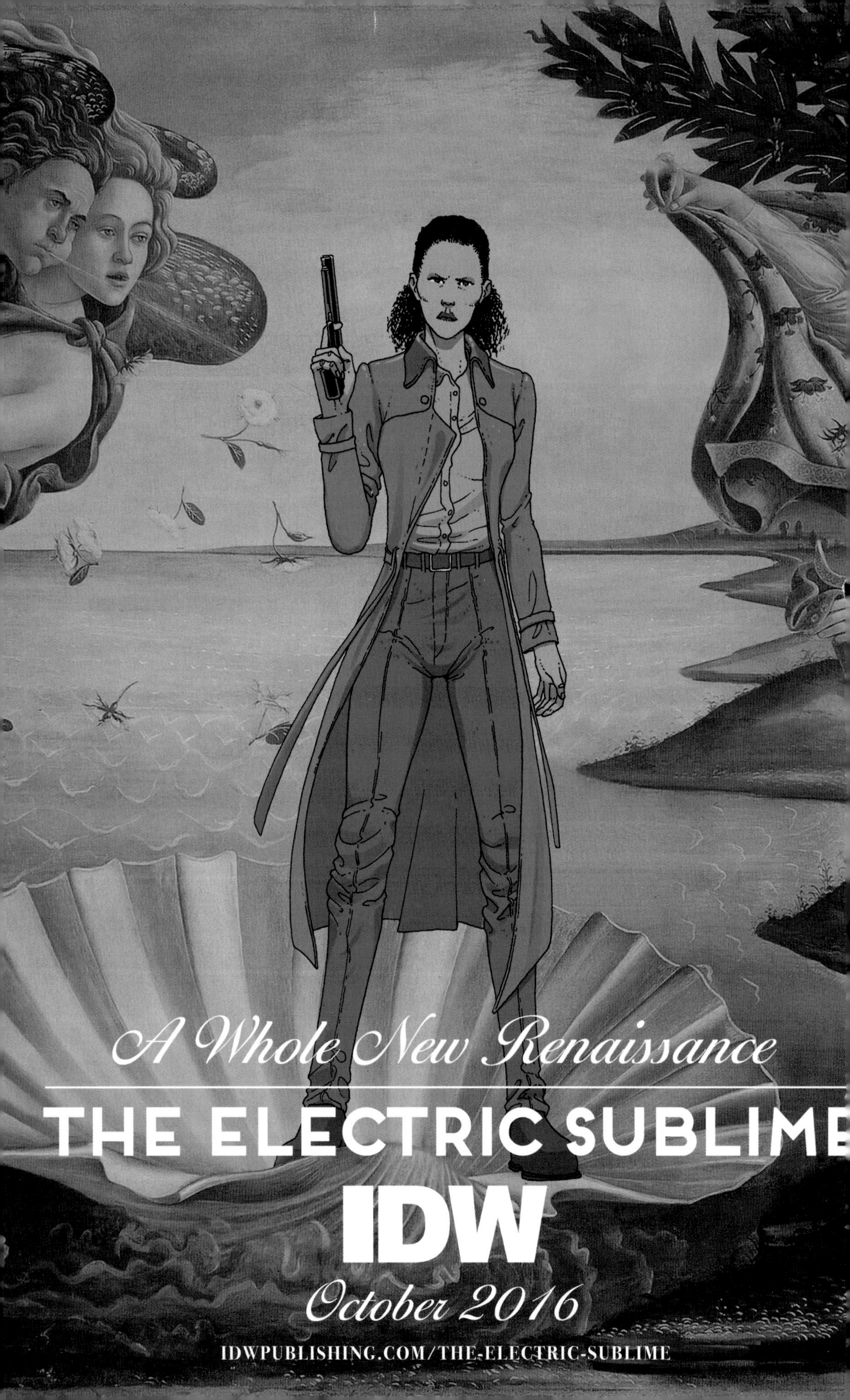
A Whole New Renaissance
THE ELECTRIC SUBLIME
IDW
October 2016
IDWPUBLISHING.COM/THE-ELECTRIC-SUBLIME